"A novel that explores what happens when what you think you want collides with what you really need. Catherine McKenzie's *Arranged* is a rare book: smart, funny, honest, and absorbing."

—Therese Walsh, author of *The Last Will of Moira Leahy*

"Just when you think you've got *Arranged* figured out, time and again, Catherine McKenzie delivers the flawless, unexpected twist that keeps you glued to the book."

—Cathy Marie Buchanan, *The Day the Falls Stood Still*

"McKenzie has crafted a plausible and entertaining story about the complexities of relationships and what makes a marriage work."

—*Winnipeg Free Press*

"Both *Spin* and *Arranged* are entertaining, fast-paced reads, in the vein of Emily Giffin and Jennifer Weiner."

—*Waterloo Region Record*

# ARRANGED

**Also by Catherine McKenzie**

*Spin*
*Forgotten*

# ARRANGED

## CATHERINE McKENZIE

HarperWeekend

*Arranged*
Copyright © 2011 by Catherine McKenzie.
All rights reserved.

Published by Harper Weekend, an imprint of HarperCollins Publishers Ltd

First published in Canada by HarperCollins Publishers Ltd in an
original trade paperback edition: 2011
This Harper Weekend trade paperback edition: 2012

HarperCollins books may be purchased for educational, business,
or sales promotional use through our Special Markets Department.

HarperCollins Publishers Ltd
2 Bloor Street East, 20th Floor
Toronto, Ontario, Canada
M4W 1A8

*www.harpercollins.ca*

Library and Archives Canada Cataloguing in Publication
McKenzie, Catherine
Arranged / Catherine McKenzie.

ISBN 978-1-55468-761-9

I. Title.
PS8625.K4395A78 2012    C813'.6    C2012-900839-7

Printed and bound in the United States

RRD 9 8 7 6 5 4 3 2 1

*For David.*

*And in memory of the nicest Anne I've known,*
*Anne Fish, who always wanted to know what I was reading,*
*and who always suggested the best books.*

# ARRANGED

# PART ONE

PART ONE

# Chapter 1
# Enough Is Enough

"I read your emails," I tell Stuart.

His head snaps up from his copy of *Maxim*. His sock-covered feet are resting on the glass coffee table that sits in front of the leather couch we bought six months ago. An innocent pose, though he's guilty as hell.

"You what?"

"You heard me."

The planes of his angular face harden. "I'd better not be hearing you."

I feel a moment of guilt. Then I remember what I read.

"I read your emails. All of them." He opens his mouth to speak, but I cut him off. "How could I violate your privacy? Is that what you were going to say? Don't you talk to me about violations, Stuart. Don't you even dare."

He shuts his mouth so quickly his teeth click. His wheels are spinning. I can almost see the movement behind his eyes, which can be so warm, so sexy, so everything, but at this moment are so cold, so hard, and so damn blue.

"What do you think you read, Anne?" he says eventually, his voice tightly controlled, a blank slate.

"Are you really going to make me say it out loud?"

He stays silent. The light from the reading lamp glints off his straight black hair. A clock ticks on the mantel above the fireplace, measuring out the seconds I have left here.

I take a deep breath. "I know you slept with Christy. I know you've been sleeping with her for a while."

There. I said it. And even though I knew it, even though I read it, actually saying it brings it to life in a way I hadn't anticipated. It's so much larger now that it's in the room. So much worse. As if Christy is here with us. As if she's repeating the words she wrote to him, in the soft, sultry voice I heard once on the answering machine. Words I can't erase.

The clock keeps ticking. I feel caught, waiting for him to do or say something.

Say something, goddammit. Say something!

He stands up as if he heard me. The magazine slaps to the polished wood floor.

"Well, bravo, Anne, you caught me! What're you going to do about it?"

Jesus Christ. Wouldn't it be great if you could videotape people during a breakup? Wouldn't it be great if you could have access to that videotape at the *beginning* of a relationship? Look how this guy's going to be treating you in six, eight, ten months. Look how he treated the girl he spent three years with! Run away, run away!

My breath rattles in my throat, but I get the words out. "I'm leaving."

"You're leaving," he repeats, maybe a statement, maybe a question. Like something he can't quite bring himself to believe.

"Do you really expect me to stay? After what you've done? Is that what you even want?"

His eyes shift away from mine, the first sign of weakness. "I don't know."

"Oh, Stuart, please. This is exactly what you want. You just don't want to be the bad guy. So instead, you've made sure I'll be the one who ends it. And I've been too stupid to figure that out until now."

"You think you're so smart, don't you?"

"I've just finished telling you I've been stupid. But yes, today I think I'm being smart."

"Well, I'm not leaving the apartment, if that's what you think is going to happen."

"God, you really don't know me at all, do you? After all this time."

He scoffs. "Oh, I know you, Anne. Don't you worry about that."

I consider him: his beauty, his anger, this man I thought I'd marry.

"So, I guess this is it," I say, because this is what people always seem to say in these kinds of situations. At least that's what they say in the movies, and right now my life feels like an invented life.

He doesn't answer me. He watches me walk to the hall closet and reach for the duffel bag I stashed there earlier with everything I need for the immediate future packed inside.

I turn to face him. I look into his eyes, searching for something, I don't know what.

"Goodbye, Stuart."

"Goodbye, Anne."

I hesitate, waiting for him to say something more, to beg me to stay, to tell me I love you, it's all a mistake, I'm a complete asshole, I can't live without you, please, darling, please. But he isn't going to give me that. Not now that I'm finally letting him have what he wants. Because he *is* an asshole, and I'm an idiot for wanting anything from him, no matter how small.

So before he can call me on it, or ask me why I'm still here, I hoist the bag over my shoulder and walk out.

Outside, I get into the waiting cab and direct it to my new apartment.

I don't notice the twenty minutes it takes to travel from my old life to the new. The city streets are blurred streaks of light against the black night sky.

The driver raps on the grimy glass between us to get my attention. I exit the cab and stare up at my new building. Four stories, redbrick, high ceilings, wood floors, shops nearby. The listing seemed too good to be true when I saw it online yesterday. The rent is more than I can afford, but I needed a new place to live, pronto. And while, in the past, I might have stayed at a friend's or, God forbid, my parents', thirty-three seems too old for that. Too old for a lot of things.

I walk up the thick concrete stairs to the front door. The panel next to my buzzer is blank, ready for me to fill it in. My apartment's blank too. There's nothing on the pale cream walls but the dusty outline of the posters that used to hang there. The air smells different, alien. My eyes rest on the nook beneath the curved bay window. It's the perfect place for the writing desk I left across town. I have that itchy feeling I get when I need to write. Only I don't know if I can write about today. Not yet, anyway.

Through the walls (upstairs? downstairs? I haven't figured out the sounds here yet), I hear a woman's voice calling her man to dinner in a loving voice, and it cuts the legs out from under me. In an instant, I'm on my knees, strangled cries in my throat.

Oh my God, how did this happen to me? How did it take so long for me to see through him? How did I put myself, my *heart*, in the hands of a man who would betray me? Again?

My cell rings next to me. A glance at the screen tells me it's Stuart. He's too late. There's nothing he can say that will erase what I read, what he did.

I throw the phone as hard as I can. It hits the doorframe, a loud sound in this quiet, empty place. A chip of paint flies off the wood, and the ringing stops. I hug my knees to my chest and stare at the silenced instrument.

Time passes. Eventually, I start to breathe. The hardwood floor makes its presence known.

My cell phone rings again. The force of my anger wasn't enough to silence it permanently. This time the caller is a lifeline. My best friend, Sarah.

"Hey, it's me," she says, concerned, apprehensive. "We still on for that drink?"

My voice is stronger than I thought it would be. "Are we ever. I'll be there in ten."

I wash my face and grab a thin trench coat from my duffel bag. My new neighborhood waits outside. The brick buildings end where the sidewalks begin—seamless—and the only trees stand in the small parks that dot every other block. Their changing leaves rustle in the fall breeze. The air is thick with car exhaust and the mix of smells issuing from the restaurants. The streets feel alive and claustrophobic at the same time.

I liked the silence of my old neighborhood, where the noise of the city was just a whisper in the background. But I like the energy I'm getting from the noise around me now, the people, and the sensation that something could happen at any moment.

A block from the bar, something on the ground catches my eye. Is that my last name? I bend to pick it up, and sure enough, it's a business card that reads:

Blythe & Company
Arrangements Made
♀♂
4300 Cunningham Street
20th floor
(555) 458-4239

Something about seeing my name on the card gives me a thrill. Without really thinking about it, I put it in the front pocket of my jeans and keep walking.

I enter the bar and scan the dark room for Sarah. The White Lion is halfway toward trendy, with red leather stools tucked under a worn mahogany bar. Tiny white lights frame the wall of mirrors behind it. A Taylor Swift song is audible above the murmur of the Tuesday-night crowd.

Sarah's sitting in one of the dark upholstered booths, typing furiously on her BlackBerry. She's wearing a navy business suit, and her curly blond hair is bunched at the base of her neck. Her pale skin seems almost translucent under the muted lighting.

She smiles at me as I sit across from her. Her teeth are small and even. "So?"

"I did it," I say, waving over the waitress.

"Thank *God*."

"Do you really hate him that much?"

"I really do."

I order a gin and tonic. "And the reason you never said anything is?"

Her cobalt eyes are full of disbelief. "What are you talking about? First of all, I did say something. And second, I figured it would be better for me to hang around and make sure you were okay, rather than have us get into a big fight and never see you again."

Sarah's a lawyer, and she's always making lists. It's the way she thinks—organized. She's been this way as long as I've known her, i.e., since nursery school.

"Thanks for that."

"No worries. I just wish I hadn't dragged you to that party."

I met Stuart at a party three years ago. I was about to turn thirty and was still getting over being dumped by the then love of my life, John. Sarah convinced me it would be good to "get back out there." I wasn't so sure, but Sarah isn't someone you say no to.

I spotted Stuart shortly after we arrived. Straight black hair, clear blue eyes, over six feet tall, slim—he was exactly the kind of man I always fall for, ever since my first crush on a boy. He had a circle of girls around him, vying for his attention. But the girls didn't daunt me. I was used to the girls. You had to be when your weakness was very good-looking men.

I was working on how to get him to notice me when Sarah did it for me by accidentally spilling her red wine down the front of my white sweater. I seized the moment and overreacted, making a dramatic fuss. It had the desired effect, as all eyes, including Stuart's, traveled toward us. I made eye contact with him, held his gaze briefly, and looked away.

When Sarah and I got back from cleaning me up in the bathroom, we found a spot on a couch. I positioned myself so I couldn't look in Stuart's direction. I could tell, though, that he was watching me.

Later, when the boys gathered to do triple shots of Jack Daniel's, I saw my opportunity and muscled my way into the group. A few of them protested that I wasn't strong enough to handle it. I tied my long red hair into a ponytail and told them I could take care of myself, just pour it. We clinked glasses and opened our throats. Only a few of them managed to get it down in one shot, but I turned my glass over with a flourish and brought it down hard on the tray Stuart was holding. I looked up at him, flushed, seeing the interest in his eyes.

"What finally made you leave?" Sarah asks.

"Have you ever noticed how no story that begins 'I read his emails' ever finishes with 'I was completely wrong; he wasn't cheating on me'?"

She wrinkles her small nose. "So he *was* cheating on you?"

"Of course he was. Just like you said."

"Yes, well. It didn't give me any pleasure to tell you that." She fiddles with the lime on the rim of her glass.

"I know, Sarah."

"Good. I have to say, you're taking this awfully well."

Of course, she didn't see me sobbing on the floor. "Am I fooling you too?"

"Almost."

"It's amazing what extreme anger gives you the strength to do."

She smiles. "If someone figured out a way to bottle woman-been-wronged, they'd make a fortune."

"What I really need is a product that can cure a broken heart."

"I think it's called alcohol."

I try to smile but end up crying. Quiet, salty tears.

Sarah slips her hand over mine. "It'll get easier, Anne. In time."

"I know. It always does." I wipe my tears away with the

back of my hand and force myself to smile. "Enough. We're supposed to be celebrating my new life."

I raise my glass. Sarah clicks hers to mine. "To Anne Blythe's new life!"

"That reminds me. Look what I found on the street." I dig the card out of my pocket and hand it to her.

"Why did you pick this up?"

"Because my name was on it, I guess. I wonder what they do?"

"'Arrangements Made,' and the symbols for male and female . . . it must be some kind of dating service."

"Good point. Maybe if I get really desperate, I'll call and find out."

Sarah blushes. "You don't have to be desperate to use a dating service."

"Have you . . . used one?"

"No, but I was thinking about it before I met Mike." Sarah smiles the way she always does whenever she speaks about him. He's a stockbroker who works in her building. They met six months ago at a cocktail party. So far, he's disproving my theory that men who are still single at thirty-five are single for a reason.

As for me: newly single at thirty-three? I've got all kinds of theories.

"You're lucky to have him," I tell her.

"I am. And you'll be lucky too, Anne."

"Yeah, maybe. But for now, I think I'm going to be alone for a while and see how that feels."

I try to sound like I mean it, even though being alone has

never been my strong suit. Not the old Anne's, anyway. But the Anne who was strong enough to walk away from Stuart today *is* going to be on her own for a while. At least she's going to try to be.

We finish our drinks, pay up, and head out into the night. Fall's settling in, and it's cooler than it was a few hours ago. I stick my suddenly cold hands in my pockets, hugging my coat around me. Sarah hails a cab and climbs in.

She rolls down the window. "You'll be fine, Anne. Just believe it and it'll come true."

As her cab disappears into traffic, I wonder if she's right. Can I really make myself better if I wish it hard enough?

I close my eyes and slowly click my heels together three times. I will be okay. I will be okay. I will be okay. I open my eyes and look up to the North Star shining brightly above me, the only star visible in this city sky. Feeling silly, I seal my wish on it and head home.

Back in my new apartment, I walk around the empty, echoey rooms, trying to decide where I should sleep. The guy whose lease I took over left his couch and his bed. I'm not sure which would be less creepy to sleep on. I pick the couch and go to the bathroom to brush my teeth. I clean the loose change out of my pockets, along with the Blythe & Company card. I brush my fingers over the raised lettering and feel a prick of curiosity. "Arrangements Made." It seems so formal, old-fashioned.

Should I call and find out what they do? If it's a dating service, should I use it? No, that's silly. Didn't I just decide I needed to be alone? That's right, I did. So, I'll be alone. And then I'll find a new man, the right man, on my own.

I throw the card in the direction of the wastebasket in my old bathroom. It hits the tile with a sharp *click*. I pick it up and read it again. I feel the same thrill I did earlier. Something about the card feels lucky, like the fortune cookie I once got that said, "You were born to write," which is now hanging, framed, in my cubicle at *Twist* magazine.

I need something lucky right now.

I tuck the card into the black rim of the mirror above the white pedestal sink.

It couldn't hurt to keep it for a while.

# Chapter 2
## Just a Little Bit of History Repeating Itself

I call Blythe & Company two months and seventeen days after I find their card on the street.

Why oh why do I do this?

Well . . . remember all that wishing and hoping I did on the North Star? Turns out it did change my luck. For the worse.

It all started when I ran into my ex-boyfriend, Tadd.

It was about six weeks after the breakup. Through a supreme act of will, I hadn't spoken to Stuart since I left. I'd worked my way through the first three stages of breakup grief—Good Riddance; I Did the Right Thing, Right?; and Maybe I Should Call Him to See if He's Okay?—and settled on I Should and Will Be Alone Forever.

I spent the weekend revising the book I'm writing, after receiving a bunch of comments from my literary agent. I was having trouble making the changes she wanted, and by Sunday, I was feeling down on myself and disconnected. The cold, steady rain—and the fact that I'd spent the entire weekend in pajamas—wasn't helping. When the weatherman said it might snow, I decided to go shopping for a new winter coat. My old one seemed to have gone missing in the move. Hopefully, this was the last time I'd have to send two burly men to pack my stuff in absentia.

Strike that. I will *never* have to do that again. You got that, Anne? Good. Continue.

Anyway, I was walking through Banana Republic when I smacked right into Tadd. Winded, I looked up into his blue, blue eyes. I took in his features, the way the gray crewneck he was wearing hugged his straight shoulders, and I felt my stomach whoosh. Then I realized who it was. Or, to be honest, I realized who it was when Tadd said, "Anne, hi!"

How did this beautiful man know my name? I looked closer. "Oh. Hi, Tadd."

"It's been a long time."

It had been. We'd met when I was twenty-four. I was working at a small weekly paper. The owners hired Tadd as their lawyer when a large company offered to buy him out. Tadd spent a couple of days at the paper to learn the business, and I was assigned to show him around. He was the best-looking thing I'd seen since I graduated from college, and I made sure he knew I was interested and available. We dated for over a year, and then I broke up with him, though the precise reason why was fuzzy to me at that moment.

"Yeah, it has."

"Yeah."

"So," I said after an awkward pause, "what have you been up to?"

"Life . . . work . . . working out . . ."

As Tadd droned on, I remembered why I'd broken up with him. He's the most boring man on earth. In fact, if I'm being totally truthful, the only interesting thing about Tadd is how good-looking he is.

Oh my God, how did I go out with him for over a year? Was there really nothing that connected us except his looks? What the hell was wrong with me?

Through the haze of his boringness, I heard him say, "And I got married last year."

"What was that?"

"I said, I got married last year. My wife's trying on clothes back there." He motioned toward the fitting rooms.

"You're married?" I felt funny, like I'd been winded again.

"Are you all right?"

I tried to seem calm. "I'm fine."

"You look pale."

I guess I failed. "Just store disease, I guess. I hate shopping malls."

"You do?"

Crap. Tadd loves to shop, and in the first flush of love, we spent many weekends in stores like this one, trying on clothes and smiling when the shopgirls said how good we looked together. Tadd looks even better in a store mirror than in real life, and I loved looking at him in that slightly distorted way.

But there was no point explaining this to him. I can't even explain it to myself.

"I do when I'm tired. It's been a long week."

"Oh, sure."

"So, how did you meet your wife?"

His face lit up. "She's a lawyer in my office . . ."

I tried to look interested, but all I could think was that the King of Boring was married and I was still single. Well, maybe she was into his money. Oh, right, she was a lawyer too, she had plenty of money of her own. Well, maybe she was equally boring and didn't know any better. Yeah, that had to be it!

Not wanting to find out, I said goodbye to Tadd and left the store in a daze, forgetting all about my new winter coat.

I still felt unsettled later that night when I met my friend and editor, William, for a drink at a divey bar downtown. He lives a few sketchy blocks away from the bar in an ultramodern condo built in an old meatpacking plant. He keeps insisting his neighborhood is about to change for the better. Since it hasn't yet, I made sure the cab dropped me at the bar's front door. I tried to ignore the slouching teenagers in oversize sweatshirts and droopy pants as they scanned the street for the Five-O.

Inside, the bar was dark and slightly honky-tonk. A Steve Earle song was playing on the fifties-style jukebox, and the tables were made from rough-hewn pieces of wood. A beefy man in his fifties with a full sleeve of blurry tattoos was tending bar. There were a few half-empty bottles of hard alcohol on the ledge behind him. The air smelled like peanuts and stale beer.

Next time, I was meeting William in my neighborhood.

I ordered a pint of Harp and carried it to William's table by the jukebox. He was wearing a navy sweatshirt with white lettering across the front. As usual, his bright yellow hair was sticking straight up.

"Yo, A.B., what up?"

"Are you still allowed to talk like that at your age?"

He rolled his kelly-green eyes. "Geez, thanks for making me feel all good about turning thirty-six."

"Shit, was it your birthday?"

"Pretty sure I saw you eating two pieces of cake at my office party two days ago."

I smiled. "It was three pieces, actually."

"The girls must hate you."

"Sometimes." I took a long drink and wiped the foam off my upper lip. I stared into the amber liquid, watching the reflected ceiling lights float gently on its surface.

"What's up, Anne? You seem . . . gloomy."

"I guess I'm feeling my own age these days."

"Because of the Cheater?"

That's his name for Stuart since the breakup.

"That, and . . . I don't know . . . do you ever feel like you're going to be single forever?"

William sighed. "I know I'm going to regret this, but . . . what's really going on?"

I thought about the disoriented, winded feeling I had when

Tadd told me he was married. How I'd felt that feeling before. How maybe it was the reason I'd stayed with Stuart longer than I should have.

"I guess I feel like I'm never going to meet the person I'm supposed to be with. I keep thinking I've met him, but it never seems to work out."

"How many times have you thought that?"

"Four."

"That seems like a lot."

"I know, right?"

William dug a handful of peanuts out of the bowl in front of him. "Can you explain something to me? Why do women always think there's one particular person they're supposed to be with?"

"Men don't think that?"

"Um, no."

"Huh."

"So," he asked again, "are you going to enlighten me?"

I shrugged. "I don't know what anyone else's excuse is, but I blame my mother."

He laughed. "Of course you do."

"She *is* the one who named me after the main character in *Anne of Green Gables*."

"So?"

"So . . . being named after a character in a made-to-be love story is a recipe for thinking that life should imitate art, particularly when you look just like her."

I said this in a mocking tone, but sad to say, it's pretty much the truth. I do look just like Anne of Green Gables (red hair, green eyes, pale skin, a smattering of freckles across my nose), and I did grow up thinking the perfect man for me is out there, that it's only a matter of time until I meet him.

"It's a book, Anne," William said practically.

"I know, but . . . don't you think those kinds of things happen in real life sometimes?"

"You're hopeless, you know that?"

"Don't remind me."

Despite my best intentions, I never quite managed to shake the feeling that my life isn't what it's supposed to be. And it got worse when I ran into John, the guy I'd been trying to get over when I met Stuart.

John and I met when I started working at *Twist* magazine six years ago. *Twist* is a monthly city-based magazine. John was the hotshot features writer. I was happy to have my own desk. I noticed him on my second day, when we crossed paths in the fax/copy room. He looked so much like the potential James Bond actor on that month's cover that my heart skipped a beat. A few weeks later, I did some research for him on an article about the mayoral candidates. We hit it off, falling into an easy, flirty banter, and started dating soon after.

He broke it off two years later. On my birthday. Apparently, commitment wasn't his thing. In fact, he never dated anyone for longer than two years, his "best-before date," as he so charmingly called it.

It was a messy breakup, one of those heaving "But whyyyy???? I donnn't underrrrstaannd!!!" moments. He didn't have any answers other than "I told you I wasn't into long-term relationships." "Buuttt you saiidd you loovveeddd meee!!!," etc., etc., until he convinced me he wasn't going to change his mind, and I moved out and onto Sarah's couch. Not long after, he got offered a column at the *Daily Chronicle*. I hadn't seen him since.

It was a few weeks after the Tadd sighting, and I was behind on a deadline. I got my own column a year ago, covering consumer products. The article was about the latest in ebook readers. I was having trouble finding an angle. Truth be told, I'm still waiting for life to look like it did on *The Jetsons*.

I ran into John outside the coffee shop on my corner. I was wearing beat-up jeans, an oversize wool sweater (an old one of Tadd's, I think), and a baseball hat. This time I was the one who did the recognizing.

"John! Hi!"

He took a moment to connect the dots. "Anne . . . I almost didn't recognize you."

Why oh why did I have to run into him looking like this? Of course, he looked perfect in his camel-colored hunter's jacket.

I adjusted my baseball hat nervously. "Oh, I just popped out for a coffee. I'm in the middle of writing. Anyway, how are you?"

"I'm good . . ." He raised his left hand to run it through his hair. He has great hair, black and thick. I followed the path of his hand through it. It was then that I noticed a glint of platinum.

"You're married!?"

"Sure. Aren't you?"

"No, I'm not married."

"Oh, sorry. I thought I heard you were."

He heard I was married! Maybe he heard that, and it broke his heart, and he married the first girl who came along, out of misery and spite, and—

"Earth to Anne." He waved his wedding-ringed hand in front of my eyes.

"Sorry, I spaced for a moment. How long have you been married?"

"Three years."

"Three years!?"

Several people on the street turned around at the sharp tone of my voice.

"Anne, calm down."

"You're fucking kidding me, right?" I said, just as loudly as before.

His powder-blue eyes clouded with annoyance. "What's your problem?"

"*What's my problem?* Mister I-Break-Up-with-People-on-Their-Birthday is asking me what my problem is?" My voice rose with each beat of my heart.

"Will you keep it down?"

"Jesus Christ."

He looked ashamed. "Look, Anne, I'm sorry if I hurt you,

and I've had regrets about the birthday thing, but it wasn't right between us. Not like it is with Sasha. I'm sorry to be so blunt, but it's true."

I knew immediately what he meant. I didn't know Sasha or anything about their relationship, but we weren't right together. Not past the surface. Which is my problem. Those damn handsome surfaces that make my heart race and my brain turn off.

"So you met the right woman, and you were suddenly ready to settle down?"

"Yeah."

"It was that simple?"

"Love doesn't have to be complicated, Anne," he said, trying to look worldly and sage.

Hell, maybe he *was* worldly and sage. Or maybe he was full of shit. But his wedding band was real. He was really married.

"There's someone out there for you, Anne."

"Sure. Right."

His cell phone rang. He pulled it from his pocket and looked at the number. And then he smiled this devastating, happy smile. I actually felt my stomach flutter, even though the smile was clearly not for me.

He signaled that he'd be a minute. "Hi, baby."

My heart froze. He used to call me "baby" in that exact same tone of voice.

"Yeah, I'll be there in a few minutes. I ran into Anne, and we're catching up."

*I ran into Anne?* No explanation of who I was, and no hiding it either. How totally annoying. Couldn't I at least be a secret he had to keep?

John closed his phone. "I've got to go, but it was great to see you again."

"Really?"

"Sure. I've often wondered what became of you."

"That sounds so formal."

"Sorry. You know what I mean."

I didn't really, but I let it pass.

"Well, I'm doing the consumer products column now, and I got a literary agent for my book. You know, the one I started writing when . . ."

God, I sounded like a moron!

"That's great, Anne."

"And I've had boyfriends since you . . ."

Amendment. I sounded like a desperate, pathetic *idiot.*

"Of course you have."

"What I mean is, I haven't been sitting around pining for you."

"Good. I was a jerk."

"You were."

He smiled. "You see, we can agree on some things."

"I guess."

"So, are we good here?" He shuffled his feet, eager to go.

I met his oh-so-blue eyes, and I felt my anger melting away. Maybe it was a cop-out, but why not forgive him? It wasn't really his fault we didn't work out. He'd told me early on about his best-before date. I was the one who was stupid enough to think it wouldn't apply to me.

"Sure, we're good."

He looked relieved. "I'm glad. Take care of yourself."

He gave me a brief hug, and I watched him walk down the street until the crowd swallowed him up. Then I went straight to Sarah's office. I just managed to hold in my breakdown until she closed her door.

"He dddin't want to marry meeee," I wailed quietly. "What's wrong with meeee?"

"There's nothing wrong with you, Anne."

I blew my nose. "So why do I keep ending up alone?"

"Maybe a better question is, why do you keep choosing the wrong man?"

"Okay, counselor, why do I keep choosing the wrong man?"

She made a face. "I don't know why, but you do see that you're doing it, right?"

"It's kind of hard not to, given that I seem to be caught in some kind of *It's a Wonderful Life* loop."

"I never did see the appeal of that movie."

"Tell me about it."

"What are you going to do about it?" Sarah asked, ever practical.

"Try not to leap the next time a black-haired, blue-eyed man smiles at me?"

She laughed. "That might be a good start."

• • •

So now, a few weeks later, I'm at work writing an article comparing a new crop of cell phones that are apparently going to revolutionize communications. My beige fabric cubicle is littered with notes and discarded drafts. I've already had three cups of extremely strong coffee, and my left leg is jittering up and down. The air is full of the usual office sounds of phones ringing, keyboards clacking, and the jumble of my coworkers' voices, a white noise I usually manage to tune out.

My phone rings loudly, sending my frayed nerves over the edge. "Yello."

All I hear is gibberish.

"Sarah, is that you?"

More gibberish.

"Sarah, are you okay? I can't understand a word you're saying."

"I *said*, Mike and I are engaged. Mike and I are engaged!"

I've never heard Sarah this hyper without the influence of a lot of alcohol. A lot.

"Wow!" I say, sounding thrilled but feeling that same old queasy feeling.

"I know! Isn't it totally exciting?"

"It's *so* exciting. Tell me all about it. I want to hear all the details."

"Well . . ."

I try to concentrate, but as she tells me about the most romantic moment of her life, my queasiness grows. I can't help but wonder if I'll ever be calling Sarah and speaking incomprehensibly about the most romantic moment in my life.

God, why do I care so much? Why do I need to be with someone, to be married? I have a career and great friends. Why isn't that enough? But is it so unreasonable to want more from life? To want what so many other people have? I want a permanent connection with someone who loves me. I want to have kids. And not alone, in the sperm-bank-supermom way. I want by-products of me and the one I love. To see his elbow or the slope of his shoulder in miniature, whoever he is. If there ever is a he.

When Sarah and I get off the phone, I walk to the staff room in a daze, searching for a strong cup of something. Steaming mug in hand, I lean against the cold glass wall and stare at the high-rises that surround me. The weak November sun glints off the metal and glass. A few dead leaves swirl past the window.

My best friend is getting married! I should be smiling and happy and planning a big celebration for her, but instead, *instead*, I go back to my desk and dial the number I've memorized from looking at it each night as I wash my face.

A woman with a crisp, mid-Atlantic accent answers the phone. "Blythe and Company."

I lower my voice so the nosy fashion columnist (who's been nicknamed the Fashion Nazi because of her judgy fashionista ways) can't hear me. "Oh, um, right, I was calling for an appointment."

"You're interested in an arrangement?"

"Yes, I think so."

The lyrics to an old song start running through my mind. *I wanna man, I wanna man, I wanna mansion in the sky.*

"We have an opening tomorrow afternoon at two. Would that suit you?"

"Does it take a long time?"

"The first meeting takes about an hour."

I check my schedule. "That should be okay."

"I'll book you in, then."

"Great, thanks." I start to hang up the phone, but I hear her talking to me through the receiver. "Sorry, I didn't catch that."

"I said, please give me your name."

"Right, sorry. My name's Anne Blythe."

There's a slight pause. "Blythe?"

Do people give fake names to dating services? And if I did give a fake name, would I be stupid enough to use the same name as the company I was calling?

"Yes, that's right."

"Fine, Ms. *Blythe,* you're booked for tomorrow at two."

I add the appointment to my calendar and hang up the phone, feeling nervous but excited. I spin my chair in circles until I feel dizzy, like I used to do when I was little.

*I wanna man, I wanna man, I wanna mansion in the sky.*

# Chapter 3
## Through the Looking Glass

The next day at two, I ride the sleek glass elevator of the Telephone Tower to the twentieth floor. The doors slide open, and I follow the signs for Blythe & Company along a thickly carpeted hall. I pause at the glass front doors and look inside. The waiting room is empty except for a receptionist working on a large silver computer. She has smooth dark brown hair and is wearing a tailored navy suit. She fits well into the plush surroundings. I'm glad I took the trouble to wear my best black skirt and a green dress shirt that matches my eyes.

I take a deep breath and push through the doors. "Hello, I'm Anne Blythe. I have an appointment."

She looks at me with a bland gaze of unconcern. "Of course, Ms. Blythe. You'll be meeting with Ms. Cooper. She'll be with you in a minute. Please take a seat over there." She motions to the waiting area.

I sit down on a gray leather chair. The teak coffee table holds a stack of glossy magazines. I pick up an *Atlantic* and thumb through it. After a moment or two I hear a small cough and look up. A woman in her mid-forties is standing in front of me. She's about my height and thin, almost emaciated, with white-blond hair pulled back into a tight knot. She has pale blue eyes and a sharp nose.

"Ms. Blythe?" She reaches out her hand. "I'm Samantha Cooper. Pleased to meet you."

I stand up and shake her hand. It's dry and cold. "Nice to meet you too."

"Will you follow me?"

We walk through a door in the taupe wall behind the receptionist and down a long hall to a corner office. The walls are all glass, and the blinds are up to show off a spectacular view of the downtown core and a slice of gray-blue river behind it. I sit in the visitor's chair as Ms. Cooper settles herself behind her spare mahogany desk. It's immaculate and almost empty, holding only a phone and a large desk blotter.

"What can I do for you, Ms. Blythe?" Her accent is hard to place. It's cultured and has a hint of something underneath. British? French? Southern? I can't tell.

"Um, well, I guess you can find me a man I can marry," I say in a joking tone.

"Of course. That's what we do. How did you hear of us?"

"A funny story, really . . ."

I tell her how I found the Blythe & Company card on the street and why I picked it up.

"So Blythe *is* your real name?"

"Yes. Do people really give fake names?"

"You'd be surprised what people do, Ms. Blythe."

I guess she must see a lot of weirdos in her business. I hope they weed them out.

"Sure, I understand."

"Normally, past clients refer new clients to us. Your situation is quite . . . unusual. In fact, I can't remember the last time we accepted someone who wasn't referred to us."

"Oh, um, right, well . . . if you need a reference or something . . ."

What am I saying? Why would I need a reference to use a dating service?

"Thank you for your offer. We'll let you know if that's necessary."

"I tried looking you up on the Internet—"

"And you didn't find anything? Yes, we're very discreet. It's one of our policies, and if you're going to use our services, we'll ask for your discretion as well."

"Of course. So how does this work, anyway?"

"I apologize. Usually, our clients are familiar with our methods before we meet. We begin with an extensive romantic history and psychological testing. This forms the basis of our evaluation of whether you'll be a suitable subject for our services. If you are cleared to continue, we use our expertise to create the match."

Evaluation of whether I'll be suitable? "You turn people down?"

"Every day, Ms. Blythe."

How odd. "I didn't realize you were so exclusive."

"We've found it's the only way we can operate successfully."

"And are you very successful?"

"We have a ninety-five percent success rate," she says matter-of-factly, as though she's telling me the sky is blue.

"Wow."

"Indeed. You can understand, then, why we're so particular about whom we accept."

Yeah. Or maybe you only accept people who'll take whatever's thrown at them.

"I guess, but psychological testing? That seems a little extreme."

"The psychological assessment is an important part of our process, I assure you. It ensures that both persons are committed and ready, and that they can deal with the pressures that come with using our services. It also weeds out the wackos." She smiles as she says this last part, a joke I assume she's used before.

I smile back. "It all sounds very serious."

"Do you think finding a husband isn't a serious task, Ms. Blythe?"

I know there's a right answer to this question, but I feel like everything I've said since I came in has been wrong. I try to change the subject. "So, what's the next step?"

"Once the matter of our fee is resolved, we can set up an appointment for the tests."

"And what's your fee?"

"I apologize again. I'm entrenched in my habits. The fee is ten thousand dollars."

I draw in my breath sharply. "Ten thousand? Isn't that pretty steep for a dating service?"

"Dating service? Oh no, Ms. Blythe, we aren't a dating service. We're an arranged marriage service."

Thirty minutes later, I'm outside on the sidewalk, tugging at the collar on my shirt, trying to breathe. The air is full of the sounds of honking cars and grinding truck gears, and I'm having trouble remembering what I agreed to in Ms. Cooper's office. All I know is, I'm clutching a pamphlet full of facts and figures, and I have an appointment tomorrow for my psychological evaluation. Just the thought of it makes my brain go into overdrive. An arranged marriage. An *arranged marriage*? There's just no fucking way. No. Fucking. Way.

I need a strong drink and a cigarette, but it's no longer acceptable for journalists to drink or smoke on the job. I'm pretty sure productivity has gone down 50 percent since that policy was implemented, but I guess that's not the point.

I spend the rest of the afternoon trying to do research on environmentally friendly cleaning products. But I end up Googling "arranged marriages" and reading through the long list of hits instead. In North America, arranged marriages seem limited to bad reality television featuring sexy singles in their twenties, but in many other countries, it's an accepted practice. And not only in countries where women aren't allowed to vote. Educated Indian women, for instance, participate in arranged marriages in large numbers. If divorce rates are a measure, these marriages are successful.

As I scan through the pages of entries—separating the facts

from the crazy fiction—snippets of what Ms. Cooper said keep coming back to me.

She explained that the cost of the service was so high because of the all-inclusive vacation that came with it. After a lot of experimentation (I couldn't bring myself to ask what that meant), they'd discovered that the best policy was secrecy. Apparently, it's more acceptable in our love-obsessed society to spontaneously marry a complete stranger while on vacation than to deliberately marry one. Hence the all-inclusive cover story.

She also said something about having to go into therapy, that it was part of the program. One year of couples therapy was the bare minimum. It helped new husbands and wives deal with the "transition" and taught them about the "friendship philosophy" of marriage. It was one of the reasons they were so successful.

And then she said I wouldn't be able to see a picture of him, whoever "he" was, before I met him.

"No picture?"

"No," she said firmly.

"Why not?"

"Because our romantic expectations are often based on our idea of what makes a member of the opposite sex attractive. If you see a picture of the man we pick for you and he doesn't look like you think he should, you'll never fully open yourself to the process, and you'll be more likely to fail. We believe a marriage based on the tenets of friendship—shared goals and experiences—is what works in the long term."

"Aren't I going to see what he looks like before we get married? And won't I know after, anyway? If looks are my problem, what's going to change once we're married?"

"You're going to change," she said with assurance.

"I'm going to change?"

"Yes."

"How do you know that?"

"The fact that you're here means you're changing already. That process continues through the therapy sessions you have before and after the marriage."

I didn't point out that I hadn't come for a husband; I'd been looking for a date. But now, as I think it over in the calmer confines of my cubicle, something she said clicks with me. Maybe I *can* change. I know I need to.

Could it work? Could they really have a 95 percent success rate? Is love just a front, a distraction? Is expecting the love of my life to show up what's been keeping me from acquiring what I really want?

I brush these thoughts aside. An arranged marriage is not going to happen. Because it costs ten grand. Because it's a crazy idea. Because I'm not going to marry a complete stranger. Because marriage is about love.

Isn't it?

I meet Sarah after work at an Indian restaurant located in the lobby of a hotel. It's equidistant from her office and mine, and we eat there about once a month. It's a bit kitschy—the walls are terra-cotta red and saffron yellow and covered with blown-up photographs of the Taj Mahal—but the lamb saag is the best in the city.

She's there before me, as usual, sitting at a table that's illuminated by an enormous fish tank built into the wall. I catch her admiring the way her engagement ring reflects the watery blue light.

"Okay, okay, so I *am* a girl," she says, laughing at herself.

"I never doubted it. Now let me see it properly." She holds out her hand shyly. It's a beautiful square-cut diamond on a platinum band. Very Sarah. "It's beautiful. Perfect."

She looks at it again before putting her hand in her lap. "It really is."

"So, tell me the story."

"I already told you the story."

I know, but I wasn't listening, because I was wondering why no one wanted to marry me.

"Tell me in person. Tell me everything."

"Well . . . remember our first date was at that Portuguese restaurant on Elm Street?"

"Of course."

"He took me back there and re-created it. He remembered every little detail: the appetizers we ordered, the wine, where we were sitting . . . About halfway through dinner, he started acting really weird, knocking over his water and then his wine, and coughing every few minutes, like he had something caught in his throat. I actually started thinking he was going to break up with me."

"Sarah, you did *not* think he was going to break up with you!"

She nods. "I did, I really did. I was sitting there trying to decide how I was going to handle it. Should I be calm, or should I have a hissy fit right there in the restaurant?"

"Which way were you leaning?"

"Being calm."

"Figures."

She sticks out her tongue at me.

"Anyway . . ." I prompt.

"Right, anyway, so there I am, freaking out, when suddenly he's down on one knee, taking my hand, and telling me that he can't imagine life without me. And then he said, 'Please be my wife.'"

Sarah starts to tear up, and I can feel my own throat closing.

"Go on."

"He took out the ring, and I actually started *crying*. All I could do was nod as he put the ring on my finger. And then everyone in the restaurant started clapping."

Sarah's cheeks are tinged with pink. She's a fairly private person. I'm surprised Mike proposed in a public place.

"Uh-oh."

"No, it was okay. I was surprised. I thought I'd hate a public proposal, but I didn't. I really didn't." She looks wistful as she turns the ring on her finger.

"That's great, Sarah. I'm really happy for you."

"Thanks. Anyway, enough about me. What's up with you?"

I get a flash of my conversation with Ms. Cooper, but there's no way I can tell Sarah about that. She'd just draw up a list of reasons why I shouldn't do it, and I can do that on my own.

"Oh, nothing much."

"What's going on with your book? Did you get those changes done?"

"Yeah, finally."

"So, what now?"

"Now I wait to hear back from the publishers Nadia is sending my book to."

Nadia is my literary agent. She agreed to represent my book, *Home*, about six months ago. It's this interweaving story of a group of friends in high school and what happens when they return home for their tenth reunion. At its core is the love story of Lauren and Ben—high school sweethearts who've drifted apart and might drift together again.

She looks sympathetic. "That must be hard. Just waiting."

"I'm trying not to think about it."

"How's that going for you?"

I smile. "About how you'd expect. Constant email and voice-mail checking."

"Well, I know it's going to sell. It's great."

Sometimes I believe her when she tells me this—on the days when I think my book might be good. On the days when I want to put it through the shredder, I think she's being kind.

I catch Sarah looking at her ring again.

"Happy?"

"Surprisingly happy."

I reach across the table and give her hand a squeeze. "I love you, Anne."

"I love you too."

Suddenly, I think maybe friendship *is* enough.


When I get home from dinner, my hair smells like cumin, and my stomach feels tight from eating too much. I collapse on the creepy left-behind couch. I've covered it with a moss-colored cover from Pottery Barn, and it's almost comfortable. When I save up some money, it's the first thing out the door.

I sort through the pile of mail that's accumulated over the last couple of days. It's mostly bills and junk mail, but there's also a bright red envelope containing a Christmas card from my friend Janey. She's a friend from college with whom I've fallen out of contact recently. It's something I've noticed a lot since the breakup: the dwindling of my friends. When Stuart and I started dating, my life wasn't much different than it was in college. We spent the week working and the weekend playing. It felt like it would be that way forever. But somewhere between the triple shot of Jack Daniel's that got Stuart's attention and the day I read his emails, it all changed. Janey and Nan and Susan got married and started having kids. And despite their twentysomething bluster that they'd never live anywhere you couldn't get a drink past eleven, none of them live in the city any longer. Janey had a baby not long ago, a little boy named Tanner. His round, perfect face smiles out at me from the tasteful card. *Happy*

*Holidays from the Jenners!* it reads. *Look what I've been up to while you've been wasting your time with a no-good cheater!* it screams.

Tanner Jenner. The poor kid.

I toss the card on the coffee table and wrap myself in a fleece blanket. I start reading Andre Agassi's autobiography, *Open*. Half an hour later, I'm totally lost in it the way I never seem to be these days.

I'm startled when the phone rings. "Yello."

"Can't you answer the phone like a normal person?"

"Hi, Mom. Are you watching *CSI* again?"

"How did you know?"

Because it's blaring in the background, as usual.

"Lucky guess. Why are you calling during your program?"

"I've seen it already."

"Then why are you watching it?"

"Nothing better to do."

"What's up?"

"Can't I call my daughter to chat?"

I feel annoyed for no particular reason. I often react to my mother this way.

"Of course you can. It's just that you don't normally do that."

"Well . . . I spoke to your brother tonight."

"What's new with Gil?"

Yes, that's right. My mother not only named me Anne Shirley Blythe, she named my older brother Gilbert, after Anne of Green Gables' love interest. It's a miracle that I haven't needed massive amounts of therapy. Yet.

"Cathy's pregnant!"

Of course she is. My brother got married at twenty-eight, had his first kid a year later, and has had two more since then. I now have three nieces, and this fourth pregnancy is right on schedule. The whole family kind of makes me want to puke, probably from jealousy, but I pretend otherwise.

"Surprise, surprise."

"There's no need to be sarcastic. You could do with being more like your brother, you know."

"I know you think that."

"What's that supposed to mean?"

"It means that not everyone has to get married and have kids, Mother."

Even though this is exactly what I want, I can never admit it to her. I'm not sure why, but it's always been like that between us.

She sighs. "Do you want to be alone forever?"

"Of course not."

"Well?"

"What am I supposed to do about it? It's not like I've chosen to be alone."

"Haven't you?"

"What's *that* supposed to mean?"

"You're not married, are you? You're not even dating anyone."

"And that's my fault?"

"I never could see anything wrong with your boyfriends. You're too picky."

I know on a rational level that it's my fault she thinks this, since I've never filled her in on the gory details, but still, this is going too far.

I try to keep my voice calm, though I'm feeling anything but. "That's so completely unfair. Just because I don't tell you why my relationships end doesn't mean there isn't a good reason. Why do you assume it's because of me?"

"What about Stuart?"

I grip the phone cord tightly. "What about him?"

"There didn't seem to be anything wrong with him."

"Stuart was a lying, cheating bastard."

She sucks in her breath loudly. "There's no need to use that kind of language, Anne."

"Sorry."

"Humph. Well, how was I supposed to know that? You never tell us anything."

Yeah, I wonder why? "I don't tell you things because I don't want to be judged all the time."

"That's not fair. You know we've always been supportive of you." She sounds hurt, like maybe she's on the verge of tears.

Ah, crap. "Look, don't get upset, okay?"

She sniffles. "I don't want you to be alone, Anne. I want you to be happy."

"I know, Mom. I want that too."

"You want to get married?"

"Yes."

"And have kids?"

"Of course. Maybe not as many as Gil, but at least two."

"If you have a boy and a girl, you can call them Diana and James."

Those are the names of two of Anne of Green Gables' kids. My mother is *obsessed*.

"I can name them whatever I want, Mother."

"Of course you can, dear. I'm only making a suggestion."

"Okay."

"Are you going to call Gil to congratulate him?"

"Yes."

"You *are* happy for them, aren't you?"

"Yes."

"All right. Well, I should go."

"Enjoy your show."

I hang up the phone more aggressively than I should. I contemplate calling Gil but decide to put it off until tomorrow. I want to muster the appropriate amount of enthusiasm, and I'm so not up for that right now.

I read a few more chapters and climb into bed. Normally, I go right to sleep, but tonight my mind won't settle. I can't help wondering if maybe Blythe & Company has the answers I've been looking for all this time, as crazy as that sounds. Does even thinking this *make* me crazy?

But maybe that's what finding the card meant all along. Maybe someone, something, is trying to show me the way. Giving me a sign.

Only . . . I don't believe in signs.

I could read the pamphlet Ms. Cooper gave me. She said it might answer some of my questions. I retrieve it from my purse and climb back into my warm bed. The front section describes the "friendship philosophy" of marriage. Next come the testimonials from Blythe & Company couples explaining how the therapy sessions helped them connect and put aside the superficial ways in which they used to decide who to be with. I stare at the happy faces smiling out from photos taken at a beach resort, and follow their progress over five, then ten, years of marriage. Through the having of babies, the purchasing of homes, the living a happy life together, wondering the whole time if this could be me.

When I close the pamphlet and turn out the light, I feel calmer. Maybe I *can* do this. Maybe I can finally find the right person, someone I can be happy with. Anyway, it can't hurt to stick it out through the psychological evaluation. And maybe it'll work.

Maybe, maybe, baby.

# Chapter 4
## Me, Myself, and I

The next day, I'm back in one of the gray leather visitor's chairs facing Ms. Cooper. Her hair is pulled into a French twist, every white-blond strand in place with a neatness I can never achieve. There's something about this woman that intimidates me, but I can't quite put my finger on it.

"So, um, what do these tests involve again?" I say, applying pressure to a small piece of gauze in the crook of my elbow. A uniformed nurse has just finished taking a blood sample. She tucks the small tubes of my thick red blood into a small carrying case and leaves us alone.

"The blood samples are to test for STDs and to do some basic genetic testing. Next you'll be answering a series of questions about your background, family history, and romantic history, so we can assess whether you're ready for the process. Then you'll be doing a thorough psychological evaluation to determine your personality type. We use these last two tests to find you a husband."

"How do you know if I'm ready for the process?" I resist an urge to place air quotes around the word "process."

"As I told you yesterday, one of the prerequisites is having six failed relationships. We've determined that people aren't ready to give up their attachment to the concept of romantic love if they've had any fewer than six."

Did I tell her yesterday I'd had six relationships? I must have, but I don't even remember talking about it. Oh, the mind-numbing power of extreme shock.

"Oh, yes, of course," I say, hoping this sounds like a suitable answer.

"You'll learn more about all of this in therapy."

"Right."

"Shall we get started?"

"Sure."

She coughs politely. "Ms. Blythe, you may recall that we require the first payment before we can proceed."

The first payment? Shit. How much is that supposed to be? I don't have ten thousand dollars, and even if I did, I certainly wouldn't give it to Miss Perfect Hair. Besides, what if I don't pass the test or they can't find me a match? Do they provide a refund if the man they find is no bloody good?

Easy, Tiger.

"I can't remember how much I'm supposed to pay today," I say, feeling lame.

"The first payment is five hundred. If you pass the psychological evaluation, the second payment will be twenty-five hundred. The balance is due once we find you a match."

I reach into my purse for my checkbook. "Do you take personal checks?"

"Of course."

I rest the checkbook on her desk and write out a check. I look at it for a moment before handing it to her. Five hundred bucks to find out if I'm sane enough to do the craziest thing I've ever heard of. Is that supposed to be a bargain?

"Thank you. Now, if you're ready?"

She leads me out of her office, down the hall, and into a room with a small glass desk in the middle. On the desk is a questionnaire. It looks thick, as if the questions will be hard. I feel like I'm about to take the SATs again. Love is to marriage as . . . I never was any good at those kinds of questions.

I sit down and look up at Ms. Cooper. I feel small and nervous. "Is there a time limit?"

"No, Ms. Blythe. Take all the time you like. You can use that button to call me if you need assistance." She points to a yellow button on the wall. "Please follow the instructions carefully."

She leaves the room, closing the door gently behind her. I open the exam booklet and begin to fill it in.

Full name: *Anne Shirley Blythe*
Age: *33*
Birthday: *October 29*
Height: *5'7"*
Hair: *Auburn*
Length of Hair (short, medium, long): *Long*
Eyes: *Green*
Weight: *125 lbs.*

Occupation: *Journalist/writer*

Employer: Twist *magazine*

Years of employment with this employer: *6*

Highest level of education and major: *B.A. in English*

Ever owned a business? *No*

Ever thought of owning a business? *No*

Hobbies: *Reading*

Sports played: *Tennis*

Do you have any siblings? *Yes*

Provide name and age of each: *Brother, Gilbert, 35*

Occupation of sibling(s): *Lawyer*

Parents still married? *Yes*

Age at which parents married: *27 (mother), 28 (father)*

Age of parents when had first child: *28 (mother), 29 (father)*

Occupation of mother: *Housewife*

Occupation of father: *Insurance salesman*

The questions seem to go on forever and in no particular order. What kind of house did I grow up in? What kind of street? How many elementary and high schools did I attend? Did I have lots of friends growing up? On and on until the final series of questions, which are all about my sexual preferences, and now the room feels hot and close, and I'm wondering if I can skip ahead . . . I mean, it's an arranged *marriage,* so obviously, that's part of it, but . . . shit. Will you relax already? You're acting like you're Sandra Dee in a white nightgown and there's a big bad man in the other room, waiting for you with a predatory look on his face.

Right. So. I take a deep breath, willing myself to calm down. It works, after a fashion, and I make it through the blush-inducing questions. The hard part over, I read the next question.

*Describe each of your adult romantic relationships and why they failed. Be as objective as possible. Describe the person physically. Explain how you met, how long you were together, whether you lived together, whether you were engaged or married, etc., etc., etc.*

Damn. Ms. Cooper said I needed six relationships to qualify. Is that a firm rule? How can it be? How can it matter whether I've had only five or four or none? Love isn't a science. And this isn't about love, anyway. I'm supposed to be forgetting about love. But she said I needed six. Crap! I'm going to fail out . . . Wait a minute, hold on. I make things up all the time. I can do this.

I write out the details of my real ex-boyfriends, and in between I invent two relationships, one with "Brian" and one with "Seth." The physical description is easy, and I vary the other details by picking and choosing moments from my real relationships. As I get into it, I find it kind of fun, like writing a short story. I start imagining what it was like to be with these fictional men and what I felt when we broke up. I decide that I broke up with Brian (he didn't want kids), but Seth broke up with me by leaving all my stuff on the curb with no note. Damn that Seth. I get a little choked up as I write about it.

Okay, Anne, now you're taking it too far.

My hand starts to cramp, like it did in college when I tried to cram a semester's worth of knowledge into a lined exam booklet. I finish up with Stuart and flip back through the pages, reading what I've written. This is the sum of my knowledge about love. I wonder what it says about me that I didn't ask for a second booklet.

I turn to the second part of the questionnaire, the psychological profile. I read the instructions: *Answer these questions honestly. There are no right or wrong answers. Answer the questions instinctively and do not change your answer. Answer "yes" or "no" to each question. You must answer each question. If you find a question difficult to answer, go with the answer that first comes to mind.*

The test is filled with questions like "Generally, are you more concerned with current events than the future?" (yes) and, "Do you find it difficult to express your feelings?" (no). Some of the questions seem so banal, and others are important life questions like "Are you concerned about the future of humanity?" (I have to say yes, right? Who isn't concerned about the future of humanity?) Others are middle-of-the-road personality stuff: "Are you an outgoing person?" (yes); "Are you a spontaneous person?" (no); "Do you enjoy experimentation?" (no). Crap. Is this answer alone going to disqualify me? Fuck it. I press on.

The next question makes me laugh out loud: "Do you get emotionally involved in the stories in romantic comedies?" (Embarrassing answer: yes.) What the hell? What possible relevance could this have?

Then a question that makes me think: "Do you rely on your instincts?" *No* is what I finally write down. The real answer is: *I shouldn't.* Sigh.

And then the last question. The reason I'm here: "Can you commit to one person?" (yes). I underline this answer, though it'll probably make whoever reads this think I'm making up the answer, or not answering instinctively, or whatever it was they told me to do at the beginning.

Reaching the end of the test gets my nerves going again. Is this really all they're going to use to find me a husband? A background story and the yes-or-no answers to fifty questions about my likes and dislikes and whether I have a lot of friends? It doesn't seem like enough.

Is the person they match me with someone who has the same profile or the opposite or partly the same? And who does the analysis—a human, a computer? I wish I'd paid more attention to Ms. Cooper yesterday.

Here is what I do remember her saying: 95 percent success rate.

I close the booklet and run my hand over the edge to flatten it. I press the button on the wall. A few moments later, Ms. Cooper opens the door.

"Yes?"

"I'm finished."

"Already? Are you sure you answered everything?"

I look at my watch. It's taken me an hour and a half. "How long do people usually take?"

"Generally over two hours."

"I always finished tests first in school," I say, feeling foolish.

"That's fine, Ms. Blythe. Would you like to come with me?"

Back in her office, I ask Ms. Cooper what the next step is.

"It will take a few weeks to analyze your answers. If we believe you're ready for the process, we'll let you know. Once you've paid your next installment, we'll begin looking for your match."

"How long does that usually take?"

"It can take up to six months."

"Six months!"

She frowns. "Husbands don't grow on trees. We aren't trying to find you a date. This will be a real match with whom you can build a life."

"Okay, right."

"Many of our clients feel the way you do, Ms. Blythe. However, the time we take is necessary, I assure you."

"Who does the analysis or matching or whatever?"

"Our staff psychologists. They analyze the data with the aid of a sophisticated computer modeling program we've developed."

"What happens if you don't find anyone?"

"Then you don't have to pay the next installment."

"What if you do find someone but it doesn't work out in the long term? Do I get my money back?"

"No. We don't guarantee the final outcome. If you choose to go ahead with the process, you're ultimately responsible for the success or failure of your marriage. Of course, we have tools to help you succeed."

"Such as?"

"We'll go into that in more detail if you're cleared to continue. Right now I have another client waiting for me."

She stands up to show me out.

"Can I ask one last question?"

She hides her frustration well. "Of course."

"How long have you been in business, and how many matches have you made?"

"That's two questions, Ms. Blythe, but I will answer them. We've been in business for fifteen years, and we've matched approximately twenty-five hundred couples." She stands a little taller as she says this, as if she's personally responsible for each and every one of those matches.

"And ninety-five percent of them are still together?"

"Yes."

"Wow."

"Indeed. Now, if you'll excuse me . . ."

"Yes, thank you."

"We'll be in touch."

I stand and walk toward the door.

"Ms. Blythe." I turn to face her. She's looking at me intently. "I wanted to remind you that you've agreed to keep this confidential."

"I understand the rules."

As though anyone would believe me if I told them.

# Chapter 5
## Try This on for Size

I'm sitting at my desk a few days later, working on an article for the next issue. It's a year-end summary of the latest trends in home electronics called "Anne Sees the Future." The irony of this title is not lost on me.

"Hey, A.B.," William says, popping around the edge of my cubicle. He takes great pleasure in trying to scare the living crap out of me a couple of times a week. Clearly, he's fighting every one of his thirty-six years as hard as he can.

"Will. I. Am. What's the haps?" I crumple my latest page full of scribbles and throw it toward the wastebasket I've positioned far enough away to make it a challenge. "And the crowd goes wild as Blythe scores her third basket of the quarter!"

William looks sympathetic. "That kind of morning?"

"You said it."

He dumps a pile of magazines off my ugly beige visitor's chair, sits down, and runs his hands through his already sticking-up hair. He's wearing a light gray sweater and black pants that suit his tall, almost gangly frame.

I put another piece of paper on my desk and smooth it flat

to start over. As I bite the end of my pen, I notice that William is giving me a bemused look.

"You know what this thing on your desk is for, right?" He taps his fingers on the top of my computer screen.

"For keeping up with celebrities and their lifestyles?"

"Seriously, A.B. Why are you still writing things out longhand?"

I think about it. "I guess it's because my dad was an old-movie freak, and I grew up watching *All the President's Men* and *The China Syndrome* and *Bringing Up Baby . . .*"

"Good films."

"Awesome films. Anyway, all the journalists in those movies typed on typewriters that went *clackety-clack, ding!* at the end of each line, and when their stories didn't work, they crumpled up the paper—"

"And threw it in the wastebasket."

"Exactly."

He shakes his head. "You became a journalist so you could play scrapped-story basketball?"

"No, but it's definitely a perk."

"Why not get a typewriter, then?"

"Have you ever tried using one of those things? The littlest mistake, and you have to start over. Besides, there's no spell-check, and you know what a crap speller I am."

"Why did I hire you again?"

"My winning smile?"

He slaps his hand to the side of his head. "Oh, yes, of course, that's it!"

"Did you come here for some specific reason or just to make fun of me?"

"Both, actually."

"Can you get to it? I've got a deadline, and my editor's a real stickler."

His green eyes glow. "You heard Larry left?"

Larry was the features columnist who replaced dumped-me-on-my-birthday John.

"Of course."

"Right, well, he took off without completing his column, which leaves me with a gaping hole in the next issue."

I feel a flutter of excitement. "Are you asking me to fill that hole?"

"For this issue. The job gets posted tomorrow."

The features column! Writing about real human beings instead of just the things humans buy. And the money, shit, the money is so much better. Not that I write for money, but still.

"You don't need to post that job."

"What's that?"

"Come on, William. Let me do it."

He looks uncertain. "I don't know—"

"I'm ready. I know I am."

"It's a lot more work—"

"I know exactly what it is. Please, William? Don't make me beg."

The side of his mouth curls up. "Now, that might be fun to see."

"Fucker."

"Nice."

"So?"

"How about this: If you deliver on this column, you'll get the gig."

I feel a burst of happiness and fight off the urge to hug him. He's not so down with the hugging. Plus, it might give the Fashion Nazi ideas I'm pretty sure she already has.

"Thank you so much. That's amazing!"

He grins. "Just don't say I never do anything for you."

"Never again. What should I write about?"

"It's not enough that I give you the slot, I have to come up with an idea for you too? You really want me to baby you like that?"

"Oh, shit."

"What?"

"I forgot to call my brother and congratulate him on being pregnant again."

"What's this, baby number ten?"

"Just four, I think."

"Maybe you should interview him."

"Yeah, right."

He leaves, and I swirl my chair around in excitement. When it stops spinning, I check my email for the thousandth time, searching for signs of life from my agent. When I find nothing, I resist the near-constant urge to email her—*Well? Well? Well?*— and call my brother. He works a hundred hours a week in a big law factory, pumping out debenture agreements and share certificates. Or at least that's what I think he does. I've never paid much attention.

"Gilbert Blythe."

"Wow, you actually answered your own phone. I didn't know you could do that anymore."

"What's up, Cordelia?"

That's the name Anne of Green Gables wished she was called as a child. Gilbert's been torturing me with it my whole life.

"Knock it off."

"What?" he asks innocently.

"I told you never to call me that again."

He chuckles. "I assume Mom gave you our news."

"You should get yourself fixed."

"What's wrong with having a big family?"

"Nothing. I'm happy for you."

"Lots of people are having big families these days. You should try it."

"Ha ha."

"There's probably even a dating service out there for people who want to have big families. Like that family on TV with nineteen children and counting. eHarmony, the supersized edition."

My heart leaps into my throat. Christ, that's hitting a little too close to the bone.

Wait a second, maybe I can use this. Maybe there's a way I can find out more about arranged marriages *and* advance my career.

"Is that your not too subtle way of telling me I should be Internet dating?"

"Are you saying you *haven't* been Internet dating? I just assumed that's where you met Stuart."

"You're a humor machine today, aren't you?"

Maybe I could write an article about modern women who have arranged marriages. Not about Blythe and Company, but what if I tracked down some of those women I read about on the Internet . . .

"I do what I can," Gilbert says. "Do you want to come over for dinner next week? The girls have been asking for you."

"Yeah, that sounds great. Look, Gil, I've got to go. I've got a deadline."

"Sure. Call Cathy to set up dinner."

"Will do."


Two days later, I've got a binder full of research and three appointments: one with a marriage broker and two with real, live arranged-marriage couples.

The marriage broker's office is located in a small storefront on a street full of Indian restaurants and fragrant grocery stores. I've been here before—the street is within walking distance of the apartment I shared with Stuart (his apartment still, I assume). The Indian restaurant we always used to order from is just down the block. The street smells like memories, and I feel stressed and furtive as I ring the bell, even though it's the middle of the business day and Stuart will be far away, at work.

A buzzer sounds and the door unlatches. An extremely short woman with crinkled chocolate skin is standing behind a standard-issue Office Depot desk. Her long black hair is streaked with gray and pulled back from a high forehead into a schoolteacher's bun. She's wearing a navy blazer and has a saffron-colored scarf tied loosely around her neck.

"Mrs. Gupta?"

She smiles broadly. "You must be Mrs. Blythe."

"*Ms.* Blythe. Yes."

"Ah, yes. Ms. Such a silly term, don't you think?"

"Um, I guess."

She makes a sweeping gesture. "Will you sit?"

I sit in one of the black office chairs facing her desk. I pull out my notepad and pen and rest them on my knees.

"So," Mrs. Gupta says, "you are interested in writing about our service?"

"Yes, that's right . . ." I trail off as I catch sight of the credenza behind her. It has three Mac computers on it, and their giant screens contain a grid of smaller screens filled with live video of women wearing headsets.

What the fuck?

Mrs. Gupta follows my gaze and glances over her shoulder. "Oh, yes, those are my little marriage bees."

"Pardon?"

"They work in my call center—in Bangladesh. Doing customer service."

You mean in case someone's marriage is broken?

"You don't arrange the marriages personally?"

She smiles. "I used to do all the matches personally. But now, with the Internet, we can help so many more people."

"So arranged marriage is big business?"

"Big business? Yes, I suppose it is. Though we prefer to call them planned marriages."

"Is that a marketing thing?"

"You might say that. Our young people today, they are so influenced by your culture. An arranged marriage seems old-fashioned to some, something their parents did, and their parents before them."

"And is it their choice? To use your services?"

"Of course, Ms. Blythe. The young men and women, they want this, as you will see for yourself."

"Yes, thanks for setting that up."

"I'm happy to oblige. But tell me, what angle are you taking on this story?"

"What do you mean?"

She lays her hands flat on her desk. A burnished gold band digs into the flesh of her wedding-ring finger. "You are not the first journalist to call me, *Ms.* Blythe. Every couple of years, this idea for an article comes into fashion again, and a woman—always a woman—calls and says she wants to learn about what I do. And always these articles, they are the same."

"How so?"

"Mocking."

My pen feels slippery in my hand. I know exactly what she

means. The articles in my bag are heavy on the mock, many with a side of snark. And until extremely recently, that was exactly how I'd write this article, if I were writing it at all.

"That's not my angle."

"Oh?"

"I promise. I have . . . no interest in making you or your service look bad."

She smiles, but her eyes say, *We'll see about that.*


Next up are Mr. and Mrs. Singh. I know in about fifteen seconds that I'm going to get very little for my article and even less that will dispel the whiff of crazy I've been smelling since my first appointment with Ms. Cooper.

The Singhs own and operate one of the stores down the street from Mrs. Gupta's office, and as I approach it, I'm pretty sure I've eaten here before. If I remember correctly, it has a small eat-in counter where they serve excellent but very spicy curries. Sure enough, my nose starts to itch the minute I push open the door.

A bell above my head tinkles, announcing my presence. The store has four aisles, all too close together and stuffed with colorful foreign packaging. A tall, beefy man in a red turban is standing behind the lunch counter, wearing a serious expression. He has one of those faces that could put him anywhere from thirty-five to fifty-five, and his upper lip is covered by a black mustache. A much younger—twenty-three at the outside—shy-looking woman is tending the cash. Her hair is partially covered by a gauzy white shawl that trails across her shoulders.

"Mrs. Singh?"

"Yes," answers the man in a gruff, unaccented voice.

My gaze lingers on the woman for a moment. She gives me a nervous smile and looks away.

"What do you want?" the man asks.

"Are you Mr. Singh?"

"Yes."

"I'm Anne Blythe. The reporter. Mrs. Gupta sent me?"

His eyes shift back and forth. "Oh. Yes. She called."

"She said that it was okay, that you agreed to be interviewed?"

"Yes."

"Is now a good time?"

He frowns, clearly thinking about saying no, although the store is empty and the street is deserted. Maybe it's just me, but I'd talk to a reporter simply to break the monotony. This store is freaking depressing.

"Are you eating?" he says eventually.

"I'm sorry?"

"Have you had lunch?"

I look at the bubbly pot of goodness behind him. My stomach rumbles. "I could eat."

His eyes narrow, but he nods. I take a seat at the counter, placing my notepad on the worn Formica. He busies himself at the stove, not bothering to ask what I want. I watch him cut a piece of dough and form it into a recognizable shape—naan bread. I sense someone at my elbow. Mrs. Singh has come up behind me on cat feet. She slips onto the chair next to me. She says nothing, just smiles a shy smile.

When the naan has been placed into the oven, Mr. Singh turns to me with his arms folded across his chest. "That bakes quickly. It has to be watched."

I take this as tacit permission to start asking questions right quick. "Yes, okay. So, you and Mrs. Singh, you had a . . . planned marriage?"

Mrs. Singh raises her hand to cover her mouth.

"Yes, that's right," Mr. Singh says.

"And do you mind telling me why you chose to marry this way?"

"I was too busy to look for a wife," he says without even the hint of a smile.

Nice.

"And you, Mrs. Singh?"

She looks surprised that I'm addressing her directly. "I also want husband," she says haltingly. "I ask my parents, and they agreed. It is normal, normal way."

Mr. Singh grunts and turns to the oven. A blast of heat escapes as he opens the door, lifting out the golden naan with a large, flattened wooden spoon. He dips a ladle into the bubbling pot and removes a generous serving into a round copper dish. He sets it down in front of me, and I know immediately that it's going to be hot, spicy hot, too spicy to eat.

"Why are you writing this article?" he asks.

"Oh. Um, well, it's something that's always interested me, the way different cultures treat marriage . . ."

"But you are not married?" Mrs. Singh sighs softly.

I feel like sighing too. "No."

"You going to eat that?" Mr. Singh asks.

"Of course. It looks delicious." I pick up my spoon and swirl it through the reddish-brown sauce. My nose starts to twitch. I'm going to sneeze any minute now, any second now . . .

I bring my hand up too late and let out a full-body sneeze that has enough force to spray what I can now confirm is an extremely hot vindaloo up onto the Plexiglas screen between Mr. Singh and me. I reach for a napkin, gasping, my skin tingling.

"Bless you," Mrs. Singh says as she covers her smile.

I feel so discouraged after meeting the Singhs that I almost don't go to my last appointment. But then I think about the uncertainty in William's eyes when I asked him for this job, and the doors it could open for me, and I suck it up.

Ashi Sharma, speaking to me on condition of anonymity, lives with her husband and two children in a two-bedroom walk-up not far from my apartment. When she opens the door, the first thing that strikes me is her beauty. She has almond-colored skin, light brown eyes, and thick black hair that falls past her shoulders in waves. She's wearing a loose pair of jeans and a T-shirt with a baby handprint on the shoulder. The baby in question is sitting fat and happy on her hip.

We settle onto a toy-filled couch in the sunny living room while her three-year-old runs loud circles from us to the dining room to the kitchen and back again. I ask her a few preliminary questions, and she fills me in on her background. She was born in Mumbai into an upper-middle-class family. When she was twenty-two, she did a master's degree at Oxford in English literature. She even had a serious boyfriend there, a Canadian Ph.D. student. But when it came time to marry, she chose the traditional path her parents encouraged. I ask her why.

"You know, there are days when I ask myself that question," she says in her soft voice, her accent a flawless British. "Even though I grew up with parents whose marriage was arranged, I always thought that was the old way of doing things. But I realized as I grew up that we're too quick to reject the old ways sometimes. We confuse information with wisdom. And were my friends who married for love happier than my parents? It didn't seem like it. It seemed to me that they were often lazy about their relationships. They didn't work at them. And when that heady falling-in-love sensation went away, they were disappointed."

"When did you meet your husband?"

"He was here and I was at home, so we corresponded before we met face-to-face, but I suppose we met two days before the wedding. Maybe three?"

"What was that like?"

She shifts her baby in her arms. "In a word: awkward."

"I can imagine."

"Yes, but you know, that changed very quickly. We had so much in common, you see. That's the real benefit of using a broker like Mrs. Gupta. She ensures that everything is right. Caste, religion, values. It is not just 'Oh, we have a girl for you, Mr. Sharma, very pretty girl.'" She says this last part with the stereotypical accent of a street peddler, hunching over. "A good marriage broker looks at hundreds of possible mates. If it's left to the individual, it depends so much more on chance."

I scratch out some notes. "So it's all about similar backgrounds?"

"No, I don't think so. That's part of it, but . . . from almost the first email I received from my husband, I felt this connection—one I'd never felt before. The same things made us laugh, made us angry. I'd find myself looking forward to his emails, and after a few weeks we were zipping messages back and forth for hours sometimes. He just . . . understood me. Do you know what I mean?"

A chill goes down my spine. Because I don't know what she means, but I want to.

I want to.

# Chapter 6
## You Are Cleared for Takeoff

A week later I'm drafting away furiously. My article is due in two hours. The floor around my desk is littered with crumpled-up papers, and I have a shoulder injury from too many basket tosses. My phone rings.

"Yello."

"Is this Anne Blythe?" The voice is cold and formal.

"It is."

"This is Karen from Blythe and Company."

My lungs constrict. "Yes?"

"Will you please hold for Ms. Cooper?"

I count twenty beats of my heart until she comes on the line.

"Good day, Ms. Blythe. I'm calling to let you know your test results."

"You can tell me the results over the phone? Isn't that a breach of protocol or something?"

"We aren't a doctor's office, Ms. Blythe."

The Fashion Nazi pops her curious, overly made-up face above the fabric wall that divides us. I turn my back to her and cup my hand over the phone. "Oh, right, sure . . . so, can I, I mean, am I . . ."

"Your results were positive. You can go on to the next step, if you wish."

My results were positive? Oh, right, that's a good thing in this instance. I think. Yikes. I feel like my chest is going to explode.

"Great. So, um, what happens next?"

"I have an opening tomorrow to discuss that, if you'd like. And, there's the matter of the next payment."

"Yes, of course. That's twenty-five hundred, right?" I almost gulp as I whisper this figure.

"That's correct. Would you be free tomorrow at eleven?"

I agree and we hang up. My hand rests on the phone, immobile.

Oh my God. I passed the test. I'm ready, or I'm not crazy, or at least not crazy enough to get myself disqualified from this crazy process. And if I pay 2,500 more of my hard-earned dollars, I can find out if there's a perfect man out there for me.

"Results for what?" the Fashion Nazi asks in her nasally twang, popping up again. The ever-changing rainbow of her hair has settled this month on Matchbox-car red. "Are you sick?"

I look up at her slowly and give her my innocent face. "Not yet."

Her overplucked eyebrows rise in disappointment. "Oh."

She slides out of view and I resume my internal freak-out.

Because if I want to continue the process, I have one small problem. Scratch that. I have one *big* problem. I pull out my checkbook and take a look at my current balance. That's what I thought. I have a grand total of forty-two hundred dollars. And I need that money for rent and utilities and food. I look down at the final draft I'm working on. If I can do this right, if I get the features column, I might be able to swing the next payment. If I really, really want to.

I know suddenly that I do. But where the hell am I going to come up with the rest? I can charge food and other expenses on my credit card for the next couple of months, but seven thousand more dollars are not going to magically appear in my bank account. I'm also pretty sure—nearly certain, in fact—that bank loans are not available to buy husbands.

Maybe Gil would lend it to me? No, that's a terrible idea. The last time I borrowed money from him, he set up a payment schedule and called me every month to remind me the payment was due. We almost weren't speaking by the end, and I vowed to live on the street before I ever asked him for money again. Besides, if I ask him for it, I'll have to tell him what it's for, and I don't want to do that. I can't.

I catch sight of the time on my computer screen. Shit. If I'm going to have a chance to do any of it, I have to finish this thing right quick.

I pick up my pen and write the last few paragraphs, feeling that flowy feeling I get when all is right in the writing world, as if the words are just there to be discovered. I'm pretty sure the article will pass muster with William. And if that happens, maybe I *will* get the features column. And didn't Ms. Cooper say it could take six months to find a match? So, maybe I can pay the $2,500 now and save up enough to pay for the next part. It's time I learned how to save, anyway.

I stack the pages of my article in front of me and start typing it into the computer. When I get to the end of a line, I mutter to myself, "*Clackety-clack, ding!*"

When I show up for my appointment the next day, Ms. Cooper is as taciturn as ever. It's a bright, sunny day. The sky is immaculate and endless. The cold sun streaming in through the windows makes her office feel harsher and less forgiving than usual, if that's possible.

"So I'm not nuts?"

"No, Ms. Blythe. Did you expect to be?"

I'm not sure why my IQ drops twenty points every time I walk into this office, but it's starting to piss me off.

"Of course not, it's just— "

"You must be a little nuts to be here in the first place?"

"You said it, not me."

"Do you think what you're doing is crazy?"

"You have to admit, it's kind of unusual."

"Well, yes, it is, Ms. Blythe. But sometimes the unusual gets results."

"Right."

"Arranged marriage was the norm for centuries. Romantic love is a modern notion."

"That's what the pamphlet said."

And my article. Mmm. Wonder what she's going to think of that? Oh well, too late now.

Her lips approach a smile. "Have you brought the next payment?"

I take out the check I wrote earlier and hand it to her. She tucks it into a buff-colored file with my name printed on the side. *Blythe, Anne.* Desperately seeking husband. As I watch her hands, I notice she isn't wearing a wedding band. How could I not have noticed that? Isn't being married a prerequisite to work here?

"Are my test results in there?"

"They are."

"May I see them?"

A trace of disdain crosses her face. "Tell me, Ms. Blythe, do you have an advanced degree in psychology?"

There she goes again. By the time she's done with me, my IQ will be down to moron level, and I won't even be able to tie my shoes.

"No."

"Then I see no reason to show you your test results."

"I don't understand. Are you trying to discourage me from moving ahead?"

"Why do you ask?"

"You aren't being very friendly."

"I'm not here to be your friend, Ms. Blythe. I'm here to find you a husband."

"I know that. But you're asking me to take a big leap of faith. I would've thought you'd be more . . . I don't know, advertorial or jingoistic."

Take that, lady. I didn't read the dictionary as a child for nothing!

She isn't impressed. "I'm not here to sell you anything or anyone, Ms. Blythe, or to convince you to do something you don't want to do. You came to us. You asked me to help you find what you couldn't find yourself. If you don't want to use our services, that's your choice. If you do, you've passed the test and can proceed. The decision is yours."

"I want to proceed," I say, surprising myself with the certainty in my voice.

She gives me a tight smile. "Fine. Now, as I explained to you previously, it can take up to six months to find a match. We'll call you when we do. However, your therapy sessions will start now. You can make your first appointment with the receptionist. Do you have any other questions?"

"No, that's fine, thank you." I stand up. "I'll be waiting for your call."

I show up to my first therapy appointment a week later, feeling extremely nervous.

My therapist's office is in the same building as Blythe & Company, one floor down. The atmosphere, though, is entirely different. Where Blythe & Company is all glass and steel and antiseptic, Dr. Szwick's office looks like a family room in a house that's too busy to care about keeping things tidy. That description applies to Dr. Szwick too. His brown hair and overgrown beard are two weeks past a good trim, and his striped shirt looks like it might've been ironed the last time he wore it. But his hazel eyes are kind. They crinkle with intelligence and something more, something I can't quite place.

"Welcome, Ms. Blythe. Can I call you Anne?" He motions for me to sit in the large, squashy armchair facing his. It's covered in chocolate-brown corduroy. I can see the faint impression of his last patient on the seat.

"Sure." I perch on the edge of the armchair and keep my feet planted firmly on the ground. There are heavy curtains pulled over the floor-to-ceiling windows. The room is lit by the soft glow of several floor lamps. I assume it's supposed to make the clients feel at ease, but it isn't working on me. My heart is fluttering like a bird's, and my clothes feel too tight.

"So, you've decided to use Blythe and Company's services?" Dr. Szwick says as he sits down. He opens a black notebook in his lap and writes the date in the left-hand corner with a fountain pen.

"Yes."

"Funny coincidence about the name."

"True."

"Do you think you're ready for an arranged marriage?"

You tell me, buddy.

"I guess so."

He gives me an indulgent look. "Now, Anne, I know this all feels very awkward, but you're going to have to relax."

"What do you mean?"

"Frankly, you're being about as forthcoming as my teenagers when I ask them where they're going and who they're going to be with."

"Sorry. I guess I'm just nervous."

"I understand. Let's try something. I want you to sit back so your feet don't touch the ground. Come on, scooch back." He waves his stubby hand to encourage me.

I reluctantly push myself back until my feet are dangling.

"That's better. How does that make you feel?"

Five. Annoyed.

"I don't know."

"Yes, you do. It's written all over your face. It makes you feel like a child. And you don't like it, because children aren't in control of what happens to them."

Who *is* this guy?

"Yeah, I guess."

"Good, that's how it's supposed to make you feel."

"I thought . . ."

He leans forward. "Yes? Come on, Anne, tell me what you want to say."

"I thought you were supposed to be making me feel comfortable."

"Ah, yes. That's what I implied a minute ago, isn't it? When I asked if I could call you Anne."

I nod.

"And now you're confused?"

I nod again.

"I want you to trust me, Anne, but these sessions aren't about making you comfortable. I want to make you aware of your surroundings and how you react to them so we can break down the patterns that led you to Blythe and Company. All right?"

"I guess so."

"Mmm. We'll have to work on that." He writes something in his notebook. His handwriting is too spiky for me to read upside down. Not that I was trying to. He looks up. "Let's start at the beginning. Why are you here?"

"Um . . . I'm here because I don't know how to pick the right men."

"And why do you think that is?"

I swing my feet like I used to do under the dinner table when I was small. "I don't know. All of my relationships have ended badly, and all the men I've been with have been kind of the same. Physically the same, I mean, and I guess I'm the same with them . . ."

"Go on. How are you the same?"

"I . . . I guess I focus on what they look like rather than what they are like."

"Why do you think you do that?"

Would I be here if I knew the answer to that question?

"I'm not sure."

"Come on, Anne. Tell me what your instinctual answer is, just the first thing that pops into your head."

"Because I'm shallow and superficial."

He frowns. "No, I don't think that's it. I think there's something else operating here."

But that was my instinctual answer.

"I think you do it," he continues, "because you believe love is supposed to be easy."

"I do?"

"Yes. You don't want to *work* to fall in love, you want to *be* in love. Like in a fairy tale."

Seriously, who is this guy?

"How can you possibly know that about me? I only met you a few minutes ago."

"Does it seem inaccurate to you?"

"I don't know. You might be right. But why do you think that?"

He smiles. The edges of his beard creep toward his eyes. "I've been reading all about you, Anne."

"You mean my file? Am I that transparent?"

"Not at all. I've simply been doing this a long time, and it's a pattern I've seen before."

"So I'm the same as everyone else?"

"Would that bother you?"

"Everyone likes to think they're unique, I guess."

"Everyone's path *to* here is unique, Anne. It's what you do *from* here that counts."

"Does that mean I have to conform from now on?"

"No, no. What I meant was, we have to find your own personal barriers to happiness and work together to take them down. Once we do that, you'll be able to open yourself up to the person Blythe and Company matches you with."

"Does that mean they could match me with anyone? The match doesn't matter?"

"It's the two elements together that make it work. A personality match *and* a new perspective." He brings his hands together, palm to palm.

"And my perspective is fairy tales?"

"Isn't it?"

I think about it. About all the times I dreamed I was Anne of Green Gables, about all the other books and television shows and movies I've obsessed over because they were about two people who were meant for each other.

"That kind of makes sense. I mean, I would've said more romances, not fairy tales, but I get it."

"Are you ready to let go of it?"

"You mean to stop expecting a happy ending?"

"To stop expecting that you don't have to work to get one."

"Isn't that why I'm here? So I don't have to work at this anymore?"

He flashes me another smile. His teeth are large and square. "You think I'm not making any sense, right?"

"Pretty much."

"And you're feeling discombobulated and unsure of yourself?"

"Ever since you made me sit like this." I wiggle my feet for emphasis.

"Good. Now we can start getting somewhere."

"Where?"

"We can start getting you to here, Anne. To this very moment."

"I thought I was already here."

"You will be, Anne, you will be."

# Chapter 7
## Waiting and Waiting

It's after work, and I'm taking a commuter train to Gil and Cathy's. They live in the same suburb we grew up in, twenty-four minutes away by train and three decades away in perspective. Every time I go there, it feels like nothing's changed since my braids were caught up in yellow barrettes. I've often wondered what brought Gilbert back here, so close to our parents and the past.

I disembark at the quiet train station a few blocks from their house and walk to their street. The white clapboard houses are all decorated with twinkling Christmas lights. Cathy and Gil's neighbors have taken it to the next level, adding a string of nodding reindeer to their front porch. The faint echo of "Rudolf the Red-Nosed Reindeer" pollutes the otherwise still night.

I stop in front of the long concrete walkway. The house is the mirror image of the neighbors', sans reindeer. Through the front window, I see a large Christmas tree covered in colored lights and tinsel.

I ring the bell. Jane, age six, bright red hair, gap in her front teeth, opens the door. She's wearing a pair of flared jeans with pink flowers embroidered around the bottom and a matching pink sweater. "Aunty Anne, Aunty Anne!"

I stoop down to give her a hug. She smells like Johnson & Johnson's baby shampoo. "Hey, Jane-girl."

She wiggles away from me. "Did you know I'm getting an American Girl doll for Christmas?"

"Oh, you are, are you?"

"Uh-huh."

"How do you know that?"

She gives me a sly look. "Mommy and Daddy said so in the living room last night."

"They were talking about your Christmas present with you in the room?"

"Nah. It was sleep time, but I was thirsty." She pronounces it "tirtsy."

"You shouldn't listen to other people's conversations, Jane-girl."

She clasps her hands behind her back, swinging them back and forth. "I wasn't doing it on purpose."

"I know, cutie. It's okay."

"You won't tell Mommy, right?"

"Don't worry."

I ruffle her hair, and Jane takes my hand, pulling me toward the kitchen at the back of the house. The smell of baking chicken makes me instantly hungry.

Cathy is standing at the stove, stirring a pot of gravy. Elizabeth, four, blond, big blue eyes, a little tubby, is clinging to her knees. Mary, also blond, and two, is in a playpen in the corner.

"Hey, Cath."

She turns toward me, and I notice that pregnancy glow she always seems to get. Her dark blond hair is in a thick braid that hangs halfway down her back, and her clear skin shines like those girls' in the Neutrogena commercials. If she weren't one of the warmest people I've ever met, I'd hate her.

"I'm glad you could make it, Anne. It's been a while."

I pick a cookie off a plate sitting on the counter and pop it into my mouth. It tastes sweet and buttery. "Would you accept 'I've been really busy at work' as an excuse?"

She smiles. The slight gap between her front teeth matches Jane's. "Not a chance."

"I knew I was pushing my luck, you being a mother of almost four and all."

She laughs a deep, happy laugh. Elizabeth looks up at her adoringly. I can see her storing this laugh in her brain for when she's older.

"You think we're certifiable, don't you?" Cathy asks.

"Not the whole couple, just you. You're the one who chose to spend your life with my brother, after all."

I sit in the worn flowered chintz chair they keep in the corner of the kitchen, and Jane climbs into my lap. She puts her silky head against my chest and pops her thumb in her mouth. She looks so much like me at her age that it breaks my heart. Watching her these last six years has been like watching myself grow up all over again.

"He has his good points."

"If you say so."

"Nice article, by the way. How'd you come up with the idea?"

I hide my blush by burying my face in Jane's hair. "I heard of a friend of a friend who was thinking of having an arranged marriage."

"How odd."

"Do you really find it that odd?"

"I'm not sure. I guess some of the things that Oxford girl said made sense, but I'm not sure I could get through all the hard times if love weren't on the line."

"She never said she wasn't in love with him."

"Did she say she was?"

"No, but . . ." I stop myself. Cathy's right. Ashi never used the word "love." I only thought I felt it. "You guys have had hard times?"

"You think we've survived being the parents of three kids without serious arguments?"

"No. I just meant you make it look easy, that's all."

"Love isn't always easy."

"I know."

It's her turn to blush. "I'm sorry, I didn't mean . . . I should've asked how things are going . . ."

"Since I left Stuart? Some days are better than others."

"Are you seeing anyone?"

"No."

"Oh, good, because there's this guy at Gil's work—"

"Oh, no."

"Why not?"

"Because I'm not sure I feel like dating right now."

Jane pops her thumb out of her mouth with a wet plop. "What's dating?"

"It's a silly thing grown-ups do to make themselves unhappy."

"Come on, Anne. He's a great guy who's ready to settle down."

"Translation, he's s-c-r-e-w-e-d every twenty-year-old he could, and now that he's getting older and having less success getting l-a-i-d, he's ready to date a woman near his own age and waste a few months of her time until she realizes he's never going to commit."

"He's not like that, really. He was in a long-term relationship and they broke up."

"Because he cheated on her?"

"No."

"Because she wanted kids and he didn't?"

"Nothing like that, Anne, I promise. It just didn't work out. He's a nice person, and she's a nice person, and they fell out of love. No big drama."

"Where are my girls?" Gilbert calls from the front hall.

Jane jumps off my lap, and Elizabeth untangles herself from Cathy. They both run toward the front door, squealing, "Daaddddyyyyy!" at the top of their voices. And there it is. The knot of jealousy I often feel when I come here, the thing that keeps me from coming as often as I should.

Gil comes into the kitchen holding a girl in each arm.

My brother is six feet two, has hazel eyes and curly brown hair with a glint of red in it. He's starting to go gray at the temples, and he has laugh lines around his eyes. In contrast to my too-white skin, his is golden and tans easily. If it wouldn't tag me as a *Flowers in the Attic* type, I'd describe him as handsome. As it is, he's just my sometimes annoying big brother.

"Heya, Cordelia, glad you could make it."

My jaw tenses. I give him a curt nod. "Gilbert."

He kisses Cathy on the nape of her neck. "Hey, beautiful."

She pushes him away. "Hey, yourself."

"Why so bashful? Anne's seen us kiss hundreds of times."

"I'll close my eyes," I tell her.

"Stop it, both of you," Cathy says.

Gilbert dumps the girls in my lap. Elizabeth promptly goes back to her station at Cathy's feet. Gil loosens his tie and drapes his jacket over the back of a chair tucked under the breakfast bar. "Did Cathy tell you about Richard?"

"Is Richard the dating?" Jane asks.

"That's right, muffin," Gilbert says as he gives me a wicked smile.

By the end of dinner, Gilbert somehow convinces me to go on a date with Richard, a lawyer in his firm, even though I'm not sure I should be dating, given the whole Blythe & Company thing. But in the end I figure, what do I have to lose?

Unfortunately, the answer to that question turns out to be several hours of my life.

The night starts out fine. Richard chooses a good restaurant. It has light wood floors, exposed brick walls, and square, intimate tables with an individual oblong chandelier hovering over each one. The room glows with the right kind of light, feeling cozy and alive at the same time, and I can smell a delicious blend of aromas coming from the kitchen.

I follow a waitress through the restaurant, feeling good in my flirty black skirt and a soft sweater that's the one shade of pink I can wear. I'm even having a good-hair day.

Richard stands when I approach and kisses me hello on both cheeks. I've never liked this quasi-European practice, but I hear Gil's voice in my head telling me to relax, to give this guy a chance, so I smile and take a seat in the chair Richard pulls out.

He's wearing a dark charcoal suit and no tie. His sand-colored hair is cut close, and his dark brown eyes are deep and chocolaty. He's a handsome man, just not my kind of handsome.

I order a gin and tonic.

"Tough day?" Richard says.

"Why do you ask?"

"I just thought because of the drink you ordered . . ."

"I like gin and tonics." I try to keep my voice even, light. I don't quite manage it.

"That wasn't the right thing to say, was it?"

"Probably not."

"What was the right thing to say?"

"That I look great," I say jokingly, flirting a little.

"Sorry. It's been a long time."

"I heard."

His face constricts in pain. Crap.

"Sorry. I guess that wasn't the right thing to say either."

"That's all right," he says, but his tone says otherwise.

He picks up his menu and starts looking through it, and after a moment I do the same. We spend way too much time picking our food. The waitress comes back with my drink. I take a large gulp, choking on the bitter tonic.

"I have an idea," Richard says when the waitress leaves.

"What?"

"Let's pretend I said the right thing and you said the right thing, and we're five minutes into the night and everything's going well."

I smile. "Sounds like a plan."

We clink glasses, and for a few minutes I think this might work out.

I'm not sure what pushes that feeling away, exactly, but the instinct to say the wrong thing to each other keeps coming back. It's nothing big, only a continuous stream of small annoyances. I order fish and he's allergic to fish, but instead of mentioning it as I order, he brings it up when I offer him some and he pushes my fork away. I ask him what Gil's like at work, and he tells me stories about how Gil rode him into the ground when he was a first-year. These are supposed to be funny stories. They're stories I'd tell to tease Gil, and yet hearing them from him makes me defensive about my brother.

But the worst part is that Richard doesn't seem to notice how badly the date's going. His moment of insight, when he could tell we'd started off on the wrong foot, was just that, a moment that passed.

We spend two awkward hours together, and now we've been waiting for the check for at least twenty minutes. Even clueless Richard is beginning to look restless.

"What are you doing next Friday?" he asks.

Uh-oh.

"Um, not sure yet. I have a lot of deadlines around then."

The waitress finally brings the check. She's about to leave again, but I grab her by the arm to keep her at the table. "Hold on a second, we'll pay now."

I reach into my purse, but Richard gives his card to the waitress before I can get mine out.

"You in a hurry or something?" he asks when she's gone.

Is he really going to make me say it out loud?

"Oh, I had a long day. I'm kind of tired."

"Sure, I understand," he says in a disappointed tone.

Thankfully, the waitress comes back quickly, and we get up to leave. Outside on the street, I thank him for dinner.

"My pleasure. We should do this again sometime."

"Um . . ."

"I'm pretty busy this week, but Friday's free."

"You mentioned that in the restaurant."

"Right, right. And you said you might not be available . . ."

"Yeah, sorry."

"That's okay. I'll call you during the week when you have a better idea of your schedule."

I look over his shoulder for a cab and realize too late that he's coming in for a kiss. I stand there, frozen, unable to turn away. His lips touch mine briefly. I'm too stunned, and the kiss is too brief, to tell what kissing him would be like. I see the flash of a cab light approaching, and I throw up my hand to get its attention. "Thanks again for dinner." I jump into the cab before he can say anything else, and the driver pulls away. I look at my watch. Ten-fifteen. I'll risk it.

"Hello," Gil answers in his quiet, this-better-be-important-to-risk-waking-up-my-kids-just-after-I've-gotten-them-to-bed voice.

"You've got to be kidding me."

"Who is this?"

"You know very well who this is."

He chuckles. "Oh, hello, Cordelia."

"Don't 'Oh, hello' me. Did I do something to piss you off that I don't know about?"

"I take it you didn't have a good time?"

"No, I did not have a good time. How could he and I have a good time together?"

"It's Anne," he whispers to Cathy, then to me, "What's wrong with him?"

"He's clueless, insensitive, and doesn't drink coffee."

"Seriously, Anne."

"I *am* being serious. We didn't click at all. I mean *at all.*"

Gil sighs. "I don't get you."

"What's to get?"

"What do you want?"

"Someone I can connect with. Someone who'll treat me right."

"Of course you do, honey." Cathy has picked up one of the other extensions. "And that's what you'll find."

"Thanks, Cath."

"I think you should give him another chance," Gil says.

"Why?"

"Remember Mom and Dad? Remember the rule?"

My parents' rule is that you have to go on three dates with someone before you write him off forever. Why? Because they had two horrible dates, and it was only on the third that they found their rhythm. I'd always assumed Mom kept going on the dates because of Dad's last name (she could marry a man named Blythe, just like Anne of Green Gables!), and Dad kept going because Mom was the hottest girl who had ever gone out with him.

"Well?"

"I'll think about it."

"Will you really?"

"I said I would. Lay off."

"Why don't you see if he calls you again and decide then?" Cathy says practically.

"Maybe. I'll talk to you guys later."

I hang up and watch the car lights flash past the window.

When I get home, I boot up my computer and check my

email. Halfway through a long list of reply-alls from people at *Twist*, there's an email from my agent, Nadia, titled "News!!" I'm having trouble breathing.

I stare at the email, feeling like I did when I got my college acceptance letters. Only then, thin envelopes meant no and fat meant yes. This email looks like all the others.

Yes or no. Yes or no. I won't find out if I never open it.

I click it open. My heart is booming.

Anne, sorry for doing this in an email, but I've misplaced your cell number. Anyway, great news! The editor at Wesson got back to me today. She loves the manuscript, and they've made the following offer . . .

Yes, yes, yes! I'm going to be published. They think my manuscript's in great shape and they want to rush it for a spring launch. They like it so much, they're giving me a two-book deal. And they're offering me an advance of fifteen thousand dollars. Jesus!

I can finally buy a car, or go on a great vacation, or . . .

Get married.

I can get married now.

I can.

# Chapter 8
## Smells Like a Party

"*Hi, this is Sarah. Leave a message.*"

"Sarah! I can't believe you didn't pick up! I have news. Big news! I know I should wait to speak to you in person, but I can't wait. My book's being published! They're giving me an advance and all kinds of shit. Anyway, where are you? Call me!"

"*You know who this is and you know what to do.*"

"William! Where the hell are you? Call me immediately when you get this message! You know who this is too."

"*You've reached Gilbert, Cathy, Jane, Elizabeth, and Mary. Some of us can't answer phones yet, and the rest of us are busy. Leave a message.*"

"Gilbert, Cathy, it's Anne. Where the hell are you guys? We just got off the phone a few minutes ago. By the way, Gil, that message isn't funny. Anyway, I have some news. It's kind of big, give me a call."

"*You've reached the Blythes. Leave a short message, and we'll return your call.*"

"Mom, Dad, it's Anne. Pick up. Mom, turn off the damn *CSI* and pick up the phone! All right, I guess you're not there. Call me when you get this message."

I can't believe no one's answering the phone. The biggest moment of my life, and I can't reach anyone to celebrate with at ten-thirty on a Friday night.

I so need a husband.

No one calls me back that night. The return calls trickle in over the weekend in predictable order. Sarah first, my mother last. Everyone's extremely happy for me. My father's oddly concerned with the financial details. My mother wants to know to whom I'll be dedicating the book. This is the most interest she's ever expressed in my book. She's never even asked to read it, and to pay her back, I haven't asked her to. To be fair, I'm sure she'd want to read it if I told her what it's about, but that's not really the point, is it?

Sarah and I decide we're going to have a joint "getting published and getting married" party. We spend half an hour going through the details, giggling like we're organizing our sweet sixteens. She offers to ditch her plans with Mike and come over, but I won't hear of it.

When we get off the phone, I feel restless. I should leave the apartment, but it's raining in a heavy, dark way that discourages going outside unless it's absolutely necessary. I flip through the channels on TV, but all that's on is paid programming for weight-loss programs. I try to read, but I can't concentrate. Ditto for writing. I briefly consider going to my parents' house, but I know I'd regret it within minutes of arriving.

In the end, I decide to rearrange the furniture in my apartment. There's always been something about furniture in a new position that comforts me.

I start with the bedroom. I move my bed under the window so I can read by the morning light on weekends when I wake up early. I find eleven hair elastics and several large dust balls. Next I take the drawers out of my dresser so I can drag it to the opposite wall. I sort through my clothes and start a bag to give away to charity. Then I dust all the surfaces in the room, sneezing mightily as I go.

When I'm done, I stand in the doorway admiring the things that belong only to me. It's stopped raining, and the sun is setting through the sheers over the window. It casts an orange glow on the white duvet and the light gray walls. The air smells of pine cleaner and the herb garden that rests on the windowsill. It all looks clean and soft and solid.

I feel calmer. I feel happy.

I feel like I know how I got to this moment.


"I felt like I knew how I got here," I tell Dr. Szwick during our next session.

It's coming up on Christmas. I saw the first flakes of the season this morning, small and hard—the worst kind of snow. It's a blustery day, but the heavy damask curtains pulled tightly across the windows muffle the sound of the wind. All that's missing is a crackling fire.

"What happened?" Dr. Szwick asks. He's wearing a navy cardigan with suede patches on the elbows. His beard seems to have gained another inch of his face.

I shrug. "The sun came up the next morning."

"And how did you feel?"

"Like I did when I had my feet off the ground last week."

"Good, good."

"It didn't feel very good."

"No, it's not supposed to."

"If you say so."

"I do." His scratchy pen spikes across the pages. "So, Anne, I'm curious. . . . why did you write that article about arranged marriages?"

"Oh, you read that?"

"I did."

I look into his straight-on gaze. My heart stutters the way it used to do when the vice principal caught me using bathroom passes to skip class.

"I didn't mention Blythe and Company."

"I noticed that. And, of course, if you had, you wouldn't be here today."

"Is that a threat?"

"No, Anne, just a reminder that you've agreed to keep the process confidential."

"I haven't forgotten."

"Good. So, how did you come to write the article?"

I wipe my sweaty palms on my thighs. "I, um, got thrown the column at the last minute, and since I was already doing some research on the topic, you know, just looking into it generally . . ."

Jesus. You'd think I was talking to Ms. Cooper.

"Are you sure that's the real reason?"

"I was curious to talk to people who've had an arranged marriage. Wouldn't you be in my situation?"

"Perhaps. Did you find the answers you were looking for?"

"Maybe. The second woman I met was educated and had options. She seemed happy, settled. She seemed to have what I want."

"Which is?"

"To find that person who everything feels right with. Where the two of us together feels bigger than the sum of our parts."

"And why do you want that?"

"Don't most people want that?"

He taps his fountain pen against his notebook. "Not enough to use Blythe and Company."

"Right, good point."

"To return to a topic from our last session, why do you think that hasn't happened until now?"

"I'm not sure."

"What about your last relationship? Why didn't you marry . . ." He glances down at his notes. "Stuart."

My shoulders tense at the sound of his name. "That's an easy one. Because he treated me like crap."

"Why did you let him treat you like that?"

"I don't know."

He shakes his head. "Come on, Anne. Yes, you do."

"Why don't you tell me why, then," I say sullenly.

"Because I can't do all the heavy lifting. Tell me, why did you let him treat you like that?"

A question I've asked myself a million times.

"I honestly can't tell you. But I'm happy to hear any theory you might have."

He considers me. "Is it part of the fairy tale we were talking about?"

"How could it be part of the fairy tale? People don't treat each other badly in fairy tales."

"Don't they? Doesn't the heroine always get treated badly so that she needs to be rescued? Cue the hero?"

"So you're saying I let Stuart cheat on me so I'd need to be rescued, because if I didn't need to be rescued, then the hero would never show up?"

"Does that sound right to you?"

"I'm not sure. If it is, how come I left him?"

He smiles. "You rescued yourself. You were your own hero."

I slide deeper into the chair, letting my head rest on the back. "But if I'm my own hero, does that mean I end up alone?"

"No, it means you're ready to accept someone who's an actual match for you and not some heroic fantasy."

"Blythe and Company isn't going to find me a hero? Damn. What am I paying so much money for, then?"

His beard twitches. "To begin a new story."

"And how's this one going to end?"

"We'll see soon enough, Anne."

I spend the next three weeks in a fog of happiness caused by my book deal, interspersed with outbreaks of nerves when I remember I'm waiting for a call from Blythe & Company. Christmas comes and goes. The windowsill below the bay window fills up with the smiling faces of my friends' families. I briefly contemplate sending out a card with my "baby" on it—a screen shot of the first page of my manuscript—but use the money it would have cost to buy gifts for my nieces.

I spend New Year's Eve with William at a big anonymous party in someone's loft. Sarah and Mike join us near midnight looking glowy, a cocoon of love around them. Midnight is celebrated with chaste kisses on my cheek from William and Mike. A new year. My year, I tell myself, as I sip my flute of champagne. Good things are going to happen.

And in a flash it's two weeks later, the night of the getting married/getting published party, and I'm standing outside the bar, shivering inside my coat, waiting for Richard to pay for the cab.

I'm here with Richard because he caught me in a giddy moment. Apparently, book deals don't make you smarter.

Once we're inside, I scan the room for Sarah and Mike. They're talking to Sarah's parents and younger sister. I introduce them to Richard.

Sarah raises her eyebrows in surprise. "He's cute," she mouths to me, looking pretty in a wine-colored dress, her curls shining.

"He's boring," I mouth back. Sarah suppresses a giggle.

Mike, tall and slightly beefy, with light brown hair and matching eyes, plants a kiss on my cheek. "Congratulations, Anne."

I thank him and return the congratulations. He smiles happily and puts his arm around Sarah's shoulders.

"Doesn't Anne look wonderful this evening?" Richard says as he drapes his arm across my shoulders, mimicking Mike.

I'm wearing a dark blue satin dress that ties around my neck and leaves my back bare. My book-deal dress for my book-deal party. It's too fancy for the occasion, and as Richard's cold fingers graze my skin, sending the wrong kind of chill down my spine, it's a choice I'm regretting.

I duck out from under his arm and spend a few minutes catching up with Sarah's parents. Then, with Richard deep into telling Mike what he does for a living, I escape to the bar. William's there, paying for a drink. He's wearing a striped dress shirt above a fashionably distressed pair of jeans. His hair stands up from his head like an exclamation mark.

"A.B., you look wonderful!"

"Thanks."

He takes my hands and holds my arms away from me. "No, I mean it, Anne. Being successful agrees with you. You're glowing."

"I think that's the glow of exasperation." I motion over

my shoulder to where Richard's still expounding on the thrill of reviewing thirty-page contracts or some such nonsense. I order a martini from the bartender. Two olives, straight up.

"That's not Richard, is it?"

"Who else?"

"Why did you bring him?"

"Fear of dying alone surrounded by cats?"

"Good point. Too bad I'm not remotely attracted to you."

"Yeah, it's too bad that *you're* not attracted to *me*."

We grin at each other.

"Anyway," I say, "tonight I want to celebrate the greatness of me and the happiness of Sarah with someone who'll buy me a few drinks."

The bartender places a martini glass in front of me. He's made a generous pour. The glittering silver liquid reaches right to the rim.

William raises his glass. "I hear you. So tonight and tonight only, I celebrate the greatness of you."

"Thanks, buddy."

"Hello, dear," my mother says behind me. "Aren't you cold in that dress?"

Icy calm, Anne, icy calm.

I put my drink on the bar and turn toward my parents. Gil and Cathy are behind them. My dad is an older version of Gil, but with my eyes. My mother keeps her chin-length hair the same color as mine, although it's our only common feature. Her eyes are a milky brown, and her face is round, without angles. She's wearing a 1940s-style fur coat she inherited from her aunt. She's always looking for an excuse to wear it. I'm not sure why.

"No, Mom, I'm fine. Hi, Dad."

"Hi, sweetheart, sorry we're late." My dad hugs me, holding me tightly against his scratchy camel winter coat.

"That's okay," I tell him. "Hi, Gil. Hi, Cath."

"Hi yourself, Cordelia." Gilbert chucks me under the chin. "I'm really proud of you, little sister."

My throat constricts at the emotion in his voice. "Thanks."

"Where *is* everyone?" my mother asks, looking around.

"At the back." I wave toward the balloons and streamers Sarah and I put up earlier.

We walk toward the CONGRATULATIONS! sign, and I talk and drink and get congratulated. Janey, Nan, and Susan arrive with their husbands, full of happiness for me and funny stories about motherhood. My agent comes in with a whirl of talk about royalty rates and finalizing my book deal. I direct her toward Gilbert. Time slows and contracts. I'm happy, I'm nervous. I drink several martinis, filling up on olives. I drift away from the group again when I hear my mother say, "Well, you know she gets the writing gene from me. I have drawers full of little scribbles that I always meant to put together someday."

I try in vain to catch the bartender's eye, but he's flirting with a girl who looks barely legal. An Alicia Keys song is belting from the radio, and I don't feel like yelling.

"Can I help?" says the man standing next to me. His voice is medium-low and sexy.

I look at him and my stomach flips. He's tall, slim, and has short black hair feathered in the "hot guy from *Sixteen Candles*" way. In fact, he looks very much like that boy fast-forwarded to his early thirties, with blue eyes and a slight ski jump to his nose. He's even wearing a red and blue plaid shirt over a crisp white T-shirt.

The martinis make me feel bold. "Do you think you can get the bartender to ignore that girl for a few minutes?"

"For you, anything," he says, looking directly into my eyes.

Oh, boy.

He puts his thumb and index finger in his mouth and makes a quick, piercing whistle that gets the bartender to look up. It's a move I'd normally find boorish, but tonight, from this man, it seems appropriate, sexy, even. As the bartender ambles reluctantly toward us, the handsome stranger smiles mischievously at me and asks what I want to drink.

"A vodka martini."

"Coming right up."

We watch him mix our drinks. My new companion pays and hands me mine.

"Thanks."

"Welcome. Cheers."

I take a sip. The drink doesn't bite the way it should. I should definitely stop drinking after this one.

"I've always wanted to know how to do that," I say.

"You mean this?" He raises his thumb and finger to his lips. "It's easy. You just put your lips together and blow."

I laugh. "Bogart fan?"

"I try."

"I never caught your name."

"Aaron. You?"

"Anne."

He ponders this for a second. "Anne. I like it."

"Kind of boring, huh?"

"Are you boring, Anne?"

The edges of our arms are touching. I can feel the rough fabric of his shirt and the warmth of his skin beneath it. "I hope not. You here alone?"

"I'm supposed to be meeting a friend, but he's late. You?"

"I'm with them." I wave my drink toward the balloons and the people gathered underneath them.

"What are they celebrating?"

"Me, I guess."

"You getting married?"

"No, that's my friend Sarah."

"What's there to celebrate about you?"

"You can't see what there'd be to celebrate about me?"

He looks me up and down. "I can see all kinds of things to celebrate about you, but they don't involve streamers and balloons."

My face feels hot. Definitely the last martini. "My book's getting published."

"That's great. What's it called?"

"*Home.*"

"What's it about?"

"This group of friends going to their—"

"Anne?"

Shit.

"Hi, Richard."

He eyes Aaron warily and asks me, "What're you doing all the way over here?"

"I was getting a drink."

Aaron steps away. My arm feels cold, exposed.

"Your mother was asking where you were."

Even better.

"You were talking to my mom?"

"Sure. She introduced herself."

"Of course she did."

"What's that supposed to mean?" He sounds more puzzled than angry.

I look away, scanning the room for Aaron. He's at the other end of the bar talking to a man wearing a peacoat—the friend he was waiting for, presumably.

"Nothing. Let's go back to the party."

I glance over my shoulder and catch Aaron's eye. He toasts me with his half-empty glass.

As the evening waxes on, I keep stealing glances at him, tracking his progress around the bar. Sarah catches me at it. "Is that Tadd?"

"What? No!"

"Looks just like him. Do you know each other?"

"I was talking to him earlier. Do you really think he looks like Tadd?"

She squints. "Half Tadd, half Stuart."

I look at Aaron again. Sarah's kind of right. Damn.

"Do you know any women our age?" I say to her.

"Why?"

"Because I need a new best friend."

"Pht. Who'd point out the obvious if I weren't around?"

"True."

Her eyes are shining with love and contentment. "Thanks for organizing this."

"No, thank you." I reach out and hug her. She even smells happy. "I'm really glad for you, you know."

"I know. Me too."

We break apart. My eyes settle on Aaron. Part of me would like to give him my phone number. Part of me is terrified that I only want to do this because he looks the way he looks. But didn't we have a few minutes of good conversation? Good flirting, anyway?

In the end, I let it go. I'm feeling tired and decide to tell Richard I want to leave. I walk through the crowd, searching for him. So like the wrong man: never around when I need him.

"Anne?" Aaron puts his hand on my shoulder.

The right man, on the other hand . . .

He has his coat on. The dark blue fabric matches his eyes exactly.

"Can I give you my number?" he asks.

"Okay."

"Great." He hands me a business card. "It's easiest to get me on my cell."

"It was nice meeting you."

"It was nice meeting you too, Anne."

I watch him walk away as if we're in some silly movie. He looks back at me once and gives me a devastating parting smile.

When I locate Richard, he's talking to my parents. I can tell my father is only pretending to listen, emitting the occasional grunt of acknowledgment. He does this when he's bored, and the grunts match up with Richard's soliloquy only about one out of three times. Richard is oblivious.

"Anne!" Dad almost falls on me in relief.

"Richard, I think I'm ready to go home."

"That's my cue." Richard takes my mother's hand and kisses it, much to my father's amusement. "Mrs. Blythe, it's been lovely talking to you. I hope we have many more opportunities to do so."

"Ah, oh, yes, right," she says vaguely. "Congratulations again, dear."

"Thanks, Mom. 'Night, Dad."

My father's eyes twinkle. "How many dates have you two been on, anyway?"

I smother a laugh. "Tonight's our second."

My mother perks up. "You know, Richard—"

"No one wants to hear that story, Diane. It's time to go."

Sometimes I really love my dad.

"Oh, all right, I'm coming. Say, Anne, was that Tadd you were talking to before?"

• • •

I fend off a kiss from Richard in the cab (there will *not* be a third date) and escape into my apartment. I'm exhausted but too keyed up to sleep. I settle into my semi-comfortable couch and flip through the channels.

As I watch TMZ follow Amber Sheppard around, my mind wanders to Aaron, replaying how he looked at me, how the fabric of his shirt felt on my arm. I retrieve his card from my coat pocket, turning it over in my hands.

It wouldn't hurt to look him up on the Internet, right?

I type his name into Google, and there he is, an investment banker with an MBA and a long list of accomplishments. The photo on his company website is a good one—although, disconcertingly, it makes him look even more like Tadd.

I scan through the other hits. Halfway down, there's one that stops me cold. It's a wedding announcement from under a year ago. Mr. and Mrs. Price are pleased to announce that their daughter, *Anne,* married Aaron Denis, blah, blah, blah. Aaron smiles happily into the camera with a beautiful blonde in his arms.

Shit, shit, *shit.* I guess he wasn't kidding when he said he liked my name. I guess that's why he told me to call him on his cell. I *knew* it. Okay, I didn't. But I should have.

Bastard!

I rip his card into tiny little pieces and toss them into the trash. Goddammit. It's been months since I left Stuart, and my instincts are still for crap. I see a beautiful man and I throw myself at him without noticing anything else. He was probably wearing his wedding ring and I didn't even notice it. Come to that, Richard's probably an interesting guy. Okay, maybe not. But still.

I wander around my apartment looking for something to punch, to hold on to. Instead, I notice the blinking red light of my cell phone announcing a message. I pick up the clear glass paperweight sitting next to it as I dial in to my voice mail. I have one new message. It was left at 5:47 P.M. from a number I don't recognize.

"Hello, Ms. Blythe, this is Samantha Cooper. I'm happy to tell you we've found a match. Please call me on Monday to schedule an appointment. Have a nice weekend."

Barely breathing, I grip the paperweight as tightly as I can. Its smooth glass is unyielding.

They found a match.

I don't need my instincts anymore.

I have Blythe & Company.

# PART TWO

# Chapter 9
## Don't Drink the Water

My plane lands smoothly at the airport in Cancún, Mexico, a month to the day after I got the message from Ms. Cooper.

I collect my luggage, go through customs, and walk into the sweltering heat. The air feels thick in my throat and tastes like dust. The sun glares off the white adobe walls. I shade my eyes, searching for something familiar. Standing among a sea of cabdrivers is a man holding a Blythe & Company sign.

"For Blythe and Company?" he says with a Spanish accent. He looks overheated in his white short-sleeved shirt and long black pants.

"*Sí.*"

"Please go to *autobús* seventy. It is that way." He points toward a long row of minibuses lined up alongside the building. Rivers of pinky-white tourists wearing bright shorts and T-shirts are in front of the buses, looking excited and in need of refreshments.

"*Gracias,*" I say.

There are four women in front of bus 70, sweating in a

ragged line. I take my place at the end and wait anxiously. The woman standing in front of me—late thirties, faded pretty, straw-colored hair—gives me a nervous smile. She might be as freaked out as I am. As we wait, I silently recite the schedule we'll be following for the next two days: orientation, free period, meeting, dinner, bachelor/bachelorette parties, sleep, breakfast, therapy, wedding. It sounds like a mix of camp, high school, and a dream where everything seems real but nothing makes any sense. And the upshot of it all, the thing that's banging around in my mind and pushing my heart against my chest, is that by the end of tomorrow I'll be married.

I went to see Ms. Cooper the Monday after the party. When I was shown into her office, there was a white folder sitting squarely in the middle of her desk. Somehow I knew that whatever information she was about to give me about my potential future husband was in that folder, and I couldn't keep my eyes off it. I eyed it with nervous anticipation, with hunger, maybe even with lust. The corners looked sharp enough to cause a paper cut if not handled properly. And I wanted to handle it properly.

Most of all, I wanted to see what—*who*—was inside.

"I imagine you'd like to read this?" she said, holding the folder casually.

Hey, lady, be careful with that! My husband's in there.

"Yes, please."

She handed it to me with an inscrutable look. I put it in

my lap and ran my hands along the edges. They were as sharp as I'd imagined. My stomach was a pit of nervousness. I took a deep breath and opened it. Inside, there was a single white page containing a typed paragraph that read:

Profile Match for Anne Blythe
Jack H., 34, writer/journalist. 5'10", brown hair, green eyes, parents deceased, no siblings, never married, wants kids, university-educated. First match. Match quotient 8.

I sat staring at the paper. I read it again and again until I'd memorized each word. No matter how long I stared, the information on the page didn't change.

Jack H.—are you the man for me?

"What does 'match quotient eight' mean?"

"It's a metric made up of your personality type and the matching characteristics we use."

"What's it out of?"

"It's not 'out of' anything."

"Then how do I know if it's a good score?"

A flash of frustration crossed her face. "A match can be one through eight. One is least compatible, eight is most compatible."

"So it's a good match?" I persisted.

"Yes, Ms. Blythe. We don't put people together who have less than a seven. That's the reason we're so successful."

"Will he get the same information about me?"

She hesitated. "It's the same information he's received about you, yes."

"*Has* received? He already knows about me?"

"Yes, Ms. Blythe."

My heart started beating wildly. Somewhere in the world, probably in this very office, Jack H. had read a little paragraph about me and thought . . . what?

"Why did he get to go first?" I asked, feeling childish.

"We've found it's better to ensure the man's agreement before we present the candidate to the woman."

I thought it over. "Because men deal better with rejection?"

"I wouldn't say *better*. Just differently."

"So the fact that you're showing this to me means he's agreed to . . . marry me?"

"Yes."

*Thump, thump, thump.* "Did he accept the first match offered, or did he look at several matches?"

"No, you're the first. That's what 'first match' means."

He picked me. He picked me! He doesn't know anything about me, but Jack H. agreed to marry *me*. How is that even possible?

"What happens now?"

"You decide if you want to continue the process."

"So it's up to me?"

"It always has been."

"How long do I have to decide?"

"You can take as long as you like, but . . ."

"I shouldn't expect him to wait."

She gave me one of her thin smiles. "We find it's best not to wait too long. The other party can get impatient."

"And if I agree? Then what?"

"Our next retreat is scheduled for the fifteenth."

She was referring to the resort in Mexico where the weddings take place. Seven sun-drenched days and moonlit nights in a five-star resort. Speaking of which . . .

"Um, you never said. What are the sleeping arrangements?"

"You will have your own room for the week."

"We're not expected to . . ." I stopped, feeling like I did when I was stupid enough to ask a question in health class.

"What you do with your husband once you're married is up to you, Ms. Blythe. I'm sure Dr. Szwick can discuss this in more detail, if you like."

I nodded like a blushing idiot and got the hell out of there as soon as I could.

I spent the next several days barely able to sleep. When I showed up for my next appointment with Dr. Szwick, I was in mid-panic.

"What do you think I should do?" I asked him, perching tensely on the corduroy chair.

"That's not for me to say, Anne."

"Why not?"

"You know why not."

"But if someone else can pick a husband for me, why can't you tell me whether to marry him?"

"All Blythe and Company is telling you is that this is the type of person you *should* marry. But the decision to marry or not, the decision to marry under these circumstances, that's a life choice you have to make." He rested his hands on his knees. "I know you're too intelligent not to see the distinction, so what's really bothering you?"

"I guess this all seemed so theoretical. Something I was trying out that wasn't going to lead anywhere, or at least not so quickly."

"I won't lie to you, Anne. This is happening faster than I'd ideally like. I think we still have some work to do, and in a perfect world, it would've taken longer. But Jack's such a great match for you that—"

I interrupted him. "What do you mean, Jack's such a great match for me? Have you met him?"

He gave me a patient smile. "Of course I have. I thought you understood that. I've been working with him just as I have with you. I see all of Blythe and Company's clients in the city."

"He's been coming here?" I put my hands on the arms of the chair as though I might find something of him left behind, something that would tell me more about him than the scant words on the piece of paper Ms. Cooper gave me.

"Yes."

"What's he like? Tell me everything."

"I can't tell you anything, Anne, you know that. You'll know the answers to your questions soon enough if you decide to go through with the process. But I can tell you I'm happy your first question was 'What is he like?' rather than 'What does he look like?' That shows some progress, I think."

Or not. I really, really wanted to know what he looked like.

"So ... should I marry him?" I couldn't help asking again.

He shook his head. "I want to try something."

"Do you want me to feel discombobulated again? Because I already feel that way."

"No, I want you to relax. Sit back, close your eyes, and count to ten slowly."

I slid back. "What am I supposed to be doing while I count?"

"Nothing, Anne. Just close your eyes and count. Don't think of anything but the counting. Imagine the numbers forming in your mind. Use the numbers to push back any other thoughts. Ready?"

I closed my eyes. I tried to block out all the other thoughts in my brain but the numbers. One ... two ... three ... four ... five ... I visualized each number as I thought it, bright starry things that hurt my eyelids.

"Have you counted to ten?"

"Yes."

"Good. I want you to think back to the moment you decided to go to Blythe and Company. Do you remember where you were?"

"Yes, I was at work."

"What were you doing?"

"I was talking to my best friend, Sarah. She'd just told me she was engaged."

"She told you she was getting married, and you decided to call Blythe and Company?"

"Yes."

"Why? And don't say 'I don't know.'"

I breathed in and out slowly. One ... two ... three ... now the numbers were pastel tones, the crayon bleeding outside the lines as if my nieces had colored them.

"I suppose I wanted what she had."

"Yes. But why call Blythe and Company to get it?"

"Because I didn't know how to get it myself."

"And isn't that still true? Don't you want what she has?"

Six ... seven ... eight ...

"Yeah, I guess so."

"No ambivalent answers, Anne. Do you know how to get what you want?"

"No."

"Do you still want what Sarah has?"

"Yes."

"Should you marry Jack?"

Nine ... ten ... one ... two ... the numbers sparked brightly and disappeared.

"You're saying if I marry Jack, I get what I want even though I don't know how to get it?"

"What do you think?"

"I want to get what I want."

"And so?"

"I want to marry Jack."

"Okay, Anne. Now open your eyes."

I opened my eyes slowly. The light hurt, like it does when you turn on the bathroom light in the middle of the night. I rubbed my eyes with my fists, and when I could focus again, there was Dr. Szwick, smiling at me.

"How do you feel?" he asked.

"Kind of excited."

"That's good, Anne. That's very good."

I left Dr. Szwick's office on a high, and I rode that high right through to Mexico. I cleared my schedule, requested the time off, and told everyone I was going on an impromptu vacation to celebrate my book deal. I stayed up late, night after night, going through the line edits and copyedits for my book. I purchased some beach clothes and got a haircut. And I changed my mind a dozen times, but something always pushed me forward.

On the day before I was scheduled to leave, I bought a dress to wear to my wedding.

I was all set.


I get on the bus and take a seat next to a round woman in her mid-forties who has wild chestnut hair streaked with gray. She's wearing a cream peasant skirt that falls to her ankles and a sleeveless purple linen shirt. She smells like baby oil and lavender.

"Hi," she says brightly. "I'm Margaret."

"I'm Anne."

"Ever been to Mexico before?"

"No, you?"

"Nope. Say, I wonder where all the men are?"

I've been trying desperately not to think that very thing myself. Not to look into the face of every man on the airplane who had brown hair, wondering if he was Jack. Am I really, truly not even going to see this man until tonight?

"Good question," I tell her.

"Maybe they bring them in on a different bus?"

"That must be it."

"What's yours named?"

I feel shy about saying his name to another person. It makes it more real somehow. Though how much realer can it get than this, sitting on a bus on the way to meet him?

"Jack."

"Mine's named Brian. Funny, I've never liked that name. Oh well. I'm sure it'll be fine. Do you like the name Jack?"

"I do, actually."

"What does he do for a living?"

"He's a writer."

"Brian's an accountant. I've always thought that was a really boring profession, but it's nice to know he makes a steady income, you know? Writer. Hmm. That doesn't sound too stable."

My shoulders tense. "I'm a writer."

Her milky brown eyes widen. "Two writers. Wow. Well, I'm sure it'll be fine."

"Why do you keep saying that?"

"What?"

"That you're sure it'll be fine?"

"Do I? Oh well, it's just an expression, you know? I mean, Blythe and Company has such a great success rate, right? I'm sure they've matched us to the right people. Only . . ." She lowers her voice, leaning in conspiratorially. "Do you ever wonder if they make mistakes, you know, mix up the files or whatever?"

"No, I've never wondered that . . ."

Not until now!

She waves her hand dismissively. "Ah, don't worry about it. I'm sure they've got measures, you know, protocols or something, to make sure that sort of thing doesn't happen."

I fucking hope so.

She looks out the window. "Have you noticed how many classic Volkswagen Beetles there are on the roads here?"

"No."

"Look, there's another one!" She punches the side of my arm. Hard. "Punch buggy yellow!"

"Ouch." I rub the place on my arm where she hit me.

"Oh, sorry. It's just a game I play with my son. Sometimes I don't know my own strength."

"You have a kid?"

"Sure. David. He's nine."

"Were you married before?"

"Uh-huh."

"Married in . . . the usual way?"

She laughs brightly. "What, you think only freaks who can't find husbands in the usual way use this service?"

"No, sorry."

"Yeah, well, when my marriage blew up, I decided to take a different approach to things. I was using this Christian dating service when my sister told me the truth about how she met her husband. You could've knocked me over with a feather, you know, but then I started thinking about it, and I could sort of see the possibilities."

"Like what?"

"Cutting through all the dating, the getting-to-know-you, the am-I-pretty-thin-smart-enough-crap and just building a future with someone I can be friends with, you know? I mean, Sal and I—that's my first husband's name, Sal—I don't think we really liked each other, not even in the beginning. And by the time we got married, I was already sick of so many things about him, but David was on the way, and well . . ."

"I get it."

"Anyway, I think it'll be nice *not* to know anything about Brian for a while, right? Leave the surprises and annoyances for later, you know? Plus, I've always found the kind of things that drive you nuts about your partner don't bug you in the same way when it's one of your friends, you know what I mean? Like, who cares if your friend squeezes the toothpaste tube in the wrong way or doesn't put the toilet seat down? I think Blythe and Company's on to something with this whole friendship philosophy of marriage. How'd you hear about them?"

My head's whirling so fast from trying to follow Margaret's logic that it takes me a minute to catch up. "Oh, um—"

"Hey, we're here!"

The bus pulls up in front of the entrance to the resort. It looks like most of the hotels we passed on our way: white and yellow stucco, large glass doors, colorful Spanish tiles on the steps. The ocean lies behind a large strip of impossibly white sand, azure and calm and vast.

We disembark and wheel our suitcases into the lobby, politely lining up at the front desk. The Spanish tiles continue on the inside, brightening the walls below a vaulted white stucco ceiling. The only men in the lobby are the hotel staff, almost indistinguishable from one another in their white uniforms and beige ties. When it's my turn, the man behind the counter checks me in and provides me with an orientation package. He snaps a blue plastic bracelet around my wrist— my pass for meals and drinks for the week—and tells me not to lose it.

I walk with Margaret from the lobby toward the wing where our rooms are. She chats away as we follow a concrete path bordered by bright pink bougainvillea; the air is full of its sweet and acidic smell. I can hear the faint sound of waves breaking on the shore, a soothing hum.

"Hey, this is me," Margaret says excitedly at room 42. "See you at the orientation!"

Another minute brings me to room 58. The floor is a light gray tile. The sunlight dances through gauzy curtains. The coverlet on the king-size bed is a pattern of bright, gaudy flowers. A basket of waxy-looking fruit sits on a round table in the corner.

Feeling grimy and worn out from the flight, I take a shower

in the enormous tiled bathroom. The water is hard and smells faintly of salt, but the spray is strong and hot. When I'm done, I apply a lacquer of sunscreen, put on some beach clothes, and head to the orientation.

The orientation takes place in a glass-enclosed room next to the lobby. I watch a group of men play volleyball on the beach as Ms. Cooper leads the session. She looks out of place in her usual muted grays and taupes among the bright summer colors. As on the bus earlier, there are only women in the room, about twenty of us, ranging in age from late twenties to early fifties.

Ms. Cooper goes through the schedule and explains that Blythe & Company's resort is connected to the one next door, which is full of regular guests on vacation. The blue band around our wrist gives us access if we want it.

"I have a question," Margaret says. "Where are the men?"

"They arrived yesterday. Which reminds me—I would encourage you not to speak to any of the men until after you're matched tonight."

"Why?"

Ms. Cooper gives her a patented frown. I'm glad I'm not the only one who provokes that look. "We've found it best to keep the two groups separated until the formal introductions."

"So that we don't, you know, fraternize with the wrong person?"

"Yes, that's right. Now, as I was saying . . ."

When the orientation is finished, we have the afternoon to

ourselves. We'll be meeting our matches at six. The four hours between then and now seem like a lifetime.

"You want to hang out at the pool?" Margaret asks.

"Sure." I look at the hotel map Ms. Cooper handed out, trying to get my directionally challenged bearings. "I think it's this way."

"Nah, let's go to the other one, you know, next door."

"How come?"

"Do you really want to sit around all afternoon wondering if every man at the pool is your future husband?"

"Good point."

While the resort next door is the architectural twin of ours, it has a much different atmosphere. Our resort is discreet and understated, like Blythe & Company's offices, only Mexicanized. But this resort has a spring-break vibe to it. Music is pounding loudly through the sound system, and topless bathing seems to be allowed. The pool even has a swim-up bar in the middle that's surrounded by men and women drinking their faces off and flirting madly.

We settle into two blue fabric deck chairs. I reapply sunscreen to my too-white skin.

"You gonna take your top off?" Margaret asks.

"That's not really my kind of thing."

"Hope you don't mind if I do. When in Rome, right?" She reaches for the tie around her neck and takes off the top of her red bathing suit. She lies down with her eyes closed, soaking in the sun.

Maybe I should take my top off too? But hold on a minute.

Jack might've had the same idea Margaret did. He might be sitting on a deck chair at this very pool. I definitely don't want his first sight of me to be topless.

I look around. Are you here, Jack H.? Are you that guy with brown hair and light colored eyes that could be green, flirting with the pretty blond young thing across the margarita you're sipping out of a plastic glass? No, he's too tanned; he must've been here for several days. I search the crowd for another candidate. There's a man with a huge eagle tattoo on his back, floating with his arms draped over an inflatable pool mattress. He has brown hair and looks like he could be the right height. Shit. I really don't like tattoos. How come they didn't ask me that on the questionnaire? Isn't that kind of important? Or maybe they did and I simply don't remember.

Jack, Jack, *Jack*. Are you here? Are you just out of sight, looking at me, wondering if I'm the one you read about? Do I look cute in this bathing suit? Are you glad I'm not topless?

Anne Shirley Blythe, you need to calm the fuck down!

I try to distract myself by reading, but as the afternoon wears on, the boom, boom, bounce of the speakers gets louder, and I can't concentrate. I decide to take a dip in the pool and slip into the warm water. I swim a few halfhearted laps, paddle up to the bar, and order a margarita. I suck on the sugary salt around the edge, counting the individual grains.

One . . . two . . . three . . .

Shit, that's not working anymore.

The suspense is killing me, eating away at me, literally aging me, aging my heart. I wish I could fast-forward to tonight, until a few minutes after we've met, when I know what he looks like and a little bit of what he is like. I wish I could fly like Superman around and around the sun and speed up time. That would be cool. Only didn't he do that to go back in time? Jeez, this margarita's strong.

I polish it off anyway and swim a few more laps until it occurs to me that people getting drunk at a swim-up bar might not be too discriminating about where they pee. That's enough swimming for now.

I check my watch as I towel off. The meet-and-greet is in half an hour.

This is it. Showtime.

# Chapter 10
## Promises, Promises

I show up at six on the dot.

I'm wearing strappy sandals and a mint-green summer dress that skims my knees. I let my hair air-dry into waves, and I caught some sun this afternoon, so my nose has a slight pink glow. I think I look okay, but I'm too nervous to tell. Besides, how exactly is one supposed to look when meeting one's about-to-be-arranged husband? Hot? Demure? Sane?

The building where I'm going to meet him is . . . shit. Is this really happening? Am I really doing this? And is he . . . Argh! Stop it. Relax. Look at the room. Notice the details. Okay, right. The building resembles an ancient Greek amphitheater: perfectly round, with concentric rings of white concrete steps rising twenty rows high. There's a flat area in the middle and a bar tucked off to one side. The ceiling is made of white canvas, with spotlights tucked under the peaks illuminating it. It looks pretty and dramatic. Right for what's about to happen.

The room is pretty full already, and there's a tense, expectant vibe. The men and women are sitting far apart from each other on the steps. Clearly, no one wants to risk talking to the wrong person.

Ms. Cooper is standing in front of the bar, holding a clipboard. She's wearing a sand-colored shirtdress. A matching belt is pulled tightly around her small waist. Her hair is down but perfectly in place. I immediately start second-guessing my look.

"Good evening, Ms. Blythe. How are you enjoying your stay?"

Just peachy, thanks. Except for the terrible unending nerves.

"So far, so good."

She checks my name off the list. "We'll be getting started as soon as everyone arrives. Please feel free to get a drink from the bar while you wait."

Good idea.

I order a margarita and sip it as I climb the steps to the next-to-last row. I survey the room. I've got a good view of the men as they walk in. So far, I've counted three people who could be Jack but who I kind of hope aren't. Make that four. God, I really hope it's not that guy.

Damn. What the hell's wrong with me? I already know Jack doesn't look like all the men I've loved before. That doesn't mean he's an ogre or, if he's not much to look at, he isn't a great guy who can make me happy.

"Why are you sitting all the way up here?" Margaret asks, bounding up the steps with surprising agility. She's wearing some sort of Indian sari that she's fashioned into a dress. It loops around her neck and folds back into itself, ending just above her knees. While the bright red color looks good on her and her already browner skin, the overall effect makes her seem shapeless.

"I've never liked sitting in the front row," I say.

"This isn't school, silly. No one's going to call on you."

I smile and shift over to make room. "What'd you think of that pool?" I ask, still obsessively watching every man walking into the room.

"It was relaxing."

"Really?"

"Yeah, I feel really refreshed and, you know, ready."

"That's good."

"What about you?"

Me? I'm trying not to have a heart attack.

"Um . . . I guess so . . ."

"Are you nervous or something?"

"Aren't you?"

"Not really. I *was* nervous the first time I got married. Though, come to think of it, it was probably because I thought I might puke on my dress."

"How come you're not nervous this time?"

"Why would I be?"

"You're joking, right?"

She shrugs. "I trust Blythe and Company."

"You do?"

"Sure. Don't you?"

Potential Jack Number Five walks into the room and says

something to Ms. Cooper. He's attractive enough, though he looks older than thirty-four.

"Are you trying to figure out if that guy is Jack?"

I tear my eyes away from him. "Guilty."

"He's not bad-looking. You could do worse."

"Are you worried about what Brian looks like?"

She shrugs. "I've never been a looks person. I mean, look at me; I can't really be picky, right?"

I stop myself from nodding in agreement. "I am. A looks person, I mean. Or I have been."

"Of course you have."

Before I can ask her what she means, Ms. Cooper clears her throat loudly. "Can I have your attention?" There's instant silence. "Welcome to Blythe and Company's Cancún retreat. We hope you've found your rooms satisfactory and have been enjoying the facilities. Now, we all know why we're here, and I imagine you'd like me to get on with it. I'll call out each couple's names, one by one. Please come down and join your match. Spend the time between now and dinner together. Dinner is in the Italian restaurant at seven-thirty. We'll fill you in on more details at that time. Any questions?"

She scans the room, but no one moves. Every face I see looks scared, a reflection of my terrified brain.

"I'll be here after the matching is done if you want to ask me anything privately." She looks down at her list. "Stephanie F. and Thierry A."

Two startled-looking people in their late thirties stand up, walk down the steps, and meet in the center of the room.

Thierry A. puts out his hand, and after a moment's hesitation, Stephanie F. shakes it. Several people laugh nervously. Thierry waves to the crowd, who respond with light applause, and they leave the room together.

"Candice M. and Michael P." Two more startled-looking people stumble down the stairs and meet in the middle of the ring.

"Amy J. and Olivier G."

"Tanya B. and Eric P."

"Annie B. and Phil M."

"Sara P. and Patrick S."

God, this is torture! I feel like I did in school when we were picking teams. I knew somebody had to pick me eventually, but it was agony waiting for my name to be called.

"Anne B. and Jack H."

This is it. I stand up so quickly I almost topple over. I walk cautiously down the stairs and meet Jack H. in the middle of the ring. Despite my avid door-watching, he isn't one of the men I was scared was Jack. He looks like he's supposed to—five-ten, light brown hair that tends to curl, green eyes a shade darker than my own. Following the lead of those who came before us, we shake hands. His is dry, warm, and firm. I'm hoping mine isn't shaking.

"Shall we?" His voice is medium-deep, unaccented. A good voice.

"Sure."

We leave the amphitheater as Ms. Cooper calls out the next set of names.

"Tasha T. and Chris T."

"Where do you want to go?" I ask when we get outside. The sun has dropped to the edge of the white buildings. Its still-strong rays lick my shoulders.

"I think there's an outside bar by one of the pools. How about there?"

"Sounds good."

"Lead the way."

"Um . . . can you? I'm kind of directionally challenged."

He looks amused. "Follow me."

We walk along a path to the outdoor bar, Jack ahead of me. I study the back of him covertly. From what I can see, there's an average body underneath his blue madras shirt and slightly rumpled chinos. The back of his neck is pink. He could probably stand to lose ten pounds, but the extra weight is distributed evenly over his body.

The outdoor bar is located in the middle of a large courtyard made of concrete pavers. There's a buffet station tucked into the back, and large mahogany pillars frame the space. There's a ceiling made of flowered vines twined through a latticework. White votive candles flicker on round wrought-iron tables. There's a gentle breeze blowing in off the ocean, tinged with salt.

We find an empty table and sit across from each other in canvas director's chairs. The bar is half full of couples just matched by Blythe & Company. Their chatter creates a din loud enough for our conversation to remain private.

I study Jack's face. He has a high forehead and the beginnings of laugh crinkles around his eyes. His nose is small for a man, giving him a boyish look. His teeth are even and white behind his thin lips. A short beard a shade lighter than the hair on his head covers his square chin. Damn. Beards are really not my thing.

We make eye contact, and I realize he's been giving me the once-over too.

"This is awkward," he says, smiling nervously.

I smile back, my own nervous tic. "It really is."

"You know, I don't even know your last name." He extends his hand across the table. "I'm Jack Harmer."

Jack Harmer. I like it. Anne Harmer. Anne Blythe Harmer. Not bad.

Jesus. What am I, twelve?

"I'm Anne Blythe. Pleased to meet you." I shake his hand for the second time. Still firm, dry, warm. Nice.

"Anne Blythe. Why's that name familiar to me?"

"You mean besides the Blythe and Company thing?"

"Yeah."

"I write for *Twist* magazine."

He thinks about it, nodding. "I've read some of your stuff. You wrote that piece about arranged marriages, right?"

"Yes."

"Interesting choice of topics."

The back of my neck feels hot. "Everyone always says write what you know . . ."

"That's what they say."

A waiter arrives to take our drink orders. "*Buenas noches, señor, señorita.* What would you like to drink this evening?"

"*Una cerveza,*" I say.

"*Dos,*" Jack echoes. The waiter leaves. I giggle.

"What?"

"He called me *señorita,* like I'm a young girl."

"You look young to me."

"Thanks. I think. You're a writer too?"

"Uh-huh."

"What do you write?"

"I mostly write for *Outdoor* magazine, and I've published a couple of novels."

"What kind of novels?"

"Different things. My last book was set during an adventure race."

"What's that?"

"It's this seven-day race that combines running, hiking, rock climbing, and white-water rafting."

"Have you done that?"

"Sure. That's what gave me the idea."

"So, adventure racing, *Outdoor* magazine. I guess you're an outdoor guy."

"You could say that. Are you an outdoor girl?"

I think he's flirting with me. Interesting.

"Sometimes."

"What does that mean?"

"This is kind of embarrassing."

He leans toward me. He smells like a mixture of soap and the woods. "Now I need to know."

The waiter returns with our beers. I sip mine nervously, trying to decide what I should tell him, if anything.

"So, are you going to enlighten me?" Jack asks.

In for a penny, in for a pound.

"No big deal. I dated a guy who was into camping, so I spent a lot of time in the woods for a while. But I'm not sure I really like it."

"I was expecting something much worse."

"Oh, you were, were you?"

Two can flirt at this game.

"Uh-huh."

"Such as?"

"Oh, I don't know. That you've been a shut-in for the last three years, and the only reason you're here is that you're hopped up on enough meds that you can't tell where you are. Something like that."

I suppress a laugh. "Oh, yes, right, that'd be the much more obvious thing."

We smile at each other. He has a nice smile.

"So, is this about the craziest thing you've ever done in your life?" he asks.

"Pretty much. You?"

"Oh yeah."

"Good, because anything crazier would put you in the probably-spent-time-in-a-mental-institution category, and I'm thinking that's not marriage potential."

"All of which raises the question . . ."

"What are we doing here?" we say in unison.

"I'll show you mine if you show me yours," I say, surprised at my boldness.

He takes a long drink from his glass. "Well, I've been in some long-term relationships that didn't work out, and I was never really sure why. Plus, I work mostly on my own, so it's difficult to meet people. I always thought I'd be married with kids by now. One day a friend told me he'd met his wife through Blythe and Company. He's still married, two cute kids. I thought about it a lot and eventually decided why the hell not?"

"So you're totally normal?"

He raises his hand to his chest. "I swear, I'm totally normal. What about you?"

What about me? Why the hell *am* I here?

"I ended a long-term relationship with a guy I never should've been with, and I realized I never should've been with any of the guys I've dated. And everyone around me seems to be married, or getting married, and having kids. I want those things and couldn't see a way to get them without some kind of help."

"So you're totally normal too?"

I make an X with my index finger over my heart. "Cross my heart and hope to die."

"How did you hear about Blythe and Company?"

"You're going to think it's stupid."

"Tell me," he says, leaning toward me again.

"I found a Blythe and Company card on the street on the day I broke up with my boyfriend. And later, when I found out what the company did, it seemed like some kind of sign."

"Do you believe in signs?"

"Not really, no."

"You're an odd girl, aren't you?"

"I might be."

He glances at his watch. "It's almost seven-thirty. Shall we go to dinner?"

"All right."

We stand up and walk to the edge of the concrete pavers where the path begins.

"Stay close to me so you don't get lost, Anne," Jack says mischievously.

He holds out his hand, and I place mine in it. He squeezes my hand gently and leads me toward the restaurant. At the front door, a waiter ticks our name off a list and takes us to a table for two with an amazing view of the ocean.

Jack glances around the restaurant at the other couples, all deep in conversation. "What do you think everyone's talking about?"

"Same as us. Trying to get to know each other."

"I wonder how many people are thinking Blythe and Company fucked up?" He picks up his menu and begins to flip through the pages.

Is that his subtle way of telling me *he* thinks Blythe & Company fucked up? But what about the flirting back at the bar?

"Is that what you're thinking?"

"Not yet," he says, his face still angled toward his menu.

"Well . . . let me know." I pick up my own menu, trying to act casual.

"Will do." He peeks over the top of his with an impish look, and I realize he's been teasing me. The shoulders I didn't even know I was clenching relax.

"So, Anne, tell me your life story."

"Really?"

"Sure, it'll help me to get to know you."

"Okay, but I warn you, it's pretty boring."

"I've been warned."

I tell him my life story. I describe my family, my brother, and my childhood. I tell him what schools I went to and when. I tell him about my job. I tell him about Sarah and William and the friends who've moved away. As I talk, we order food— in fact, we order the same thing: decidedly non-Mexican lasagna—and drink our way through a bottle of wine. Our salads have come by the time I get to the present day.

"You have dressing on your chin," I tell Jack, who has dug in to his salad with gusto.

"Frequent occurrence. You should know that about me." He wipes it off with his napkin, a twinkle in his eyes. "So your parents named you after that girl who's always getting into scrapes on the Family Channel?"

"Don't talk to me about that travesty, please! The books are so much better."

"There was more than one book?"

"Yeah, she's the main character in at least eight books, and . . ." I stop myself, hearing the fanatic in my voice.

"Huh. Who knew?"

"Never let my mother hear you say that."

"An avid fan?"

"Not sure. Would you describe someone who named her children after characters in a book an avid fan?"

"I think that makes you a *rabid* fan."

"That would be my mother."

"Can't wait to meet her."

A chill goes down my spine. Jack meeting my parents. Gil. Sarah. William. What the hell is that going to be like?

"So," Jack says, "you didn't mention any men."

I look up in surprise. "You want to know about that?"

"Definitely."

"Why?"

"If I know what came before, it'll help me understand why you're here."

"I thought that was what Dr. Szwick was for."

He frowns. "Ah, yes. Dr. Szwick. We have ways of making you explore your deepest feelings."

"Not a fan?"

"No, ma'am. Now, come on, tell me about the men."

I tell him. I take each man one by one, sketch out the big picture, and fill in a few of the smaller details. Feeling emboldened by the wine, I even confess that I've had only four relationships instead of the six Blythe & Company requires. When I finish telling him about Stuart, he has a pensive look on his face.

"You have a type."

"Yeah, men I don't belong with."

"That too, but I meant a looks type."

Shit.

I refill my glass. "You listen too well."

He chuckles. "No woman has ever accused me of that before."

"First time for everything."

"Today's the first time for a lot of things," he says gently. "Am I right?"

I put my hands up in surrender. "I confess."

"And it's not me, right?"

"No."

He looks philosophical. "Thought so. Just out of curiosity, what's my competition look like?"

"You sure you can handle it?"

"Bring it."

"Pierce Brosnan."

"Isn't he kinda old?"

"It's an old crush."

"Mm. James Bond. Stiff competition."

"Sorry."

"What's there to be sorry about?"

"Oh, I don't know. What about you? Do you have a type?"

Yikes, why did I ask that? He probably goes for girls who are tall, blond, and tanned golden brown by the sun. Do I want to know?

"Not really."

Phew. "Really? No discernible pattern?"

"Nope . . . though if we're talking celebrity references, I guess my last ex sort of looked like Cameron Diaz."

I knew it!

"That's a lot to live up to."

He shrugs. "Didn't keep us together, though, did it?"

"I guess not." Still, I have to know. "If you could've seen a picture of me before tonight, would that have dissuaded you?"

"It would've encouraged me."

A blush of pleasure creeps up my face. "Thanks. And just so you know, I would've been a lot less nervous if I'd seen your picture."

"Were you imagining male pattern baldness and a beer belly?"

"Only on the good days."

The waiter places our lasagnas on the table. Jack leans over his and smells it, clearly enjoying the experience. He catches me watching him. "I have a confession to make," he says.

"What?"

"I love carbohydrates. In fact, I firmly believe life's not worth living if I can't eat potato products or pasta. Please tell me you feel the same way."

I giggle. "I do. I really do."

"Are you just messing with me? Because I take this very seriously."

"Oh, no, I'm serious. Pasta is my life."

"Anne, will you marry me?"

I start laughing.

"No, I mean it. Will you marry me?" His expression is very earnest, and this makes me laugh all the harder. I try to contain it, but I'm not doing a very good job.

I struggle for breath. "Are . . . you . . . being . . . serious?"

"Normally, no, but given the circumstances, sure, why not? Let's do it."

I stop laughing. Does this man I met two hours ago really want to marry me? My heart starts thumping in my chest. "Tell me about yourself first. Tell me your life story."

"Not the answer I was hoping for, but okay."

As he talks about his childhood and school and his eight (!) past relationships, I try to tell whether he's really disappointed that I didn't immediately agree to marry him. If he is, he's covering well. I stop worrying about it as I listen to him. Jack is an entertaining storyteller, though he tends to move his hands in a hazardous way as he speaks.

"Watch your water glass," I warn, swooping it out of danger.

"Thanks. I'm always knocking things over when I talk."

"I'm not surprised. Hey, check out the sunset."

The sky is streaked orange and red over the aqua water. I try to memorize what it looks like, working on the words I'd use to describe it.

"What do you like most about writing?" I ask him.

"Sounds like a job interview question."

"You kind of *are* interviewing for a job, right? We both are."

"Then you should know I'm messy but not dirty, which I think is an important distinction. Also, I snore only three short snores as I fall asleep, which I have on good authority is adorable, and I make a mean egg-and-bacon sandwich."

"I'll keep that in mind, thanks."

"Good. Now, I believe you wanted to know what I like about writing?"

"Can you be serious?"

"Oh, you want serious? Really serious?" His lips are twitching, but he keeps a straight face. "Okay, here goes. I like using words so they convey a feeling or a place or a smell. I like turning one sense, sight, into five, and when I feel like I'm doing that, it's all worth it. Serious enough? Or too corny?"

"Just right. And I know what you mean. When things are going well for me, I feel like a piece of me is coming out on the page. You know, the way you see and hear the world in your head?"

"Pretty cool, isn't it?"

"Yeah. Makes up for the crappy pay."

He looks around him. "You can't be doing too badly if you can afford to come here."

"I could say the same about you."

"True. So . . ."

I look down at my half-empty plate. I feel shy about confessing where the money came from. "I, um, got a book deal, and I used part of my advance to pay for this."

Jack reaches across the table and squeezes my hand quickly. I look up, surprised. He pulls his hand away, looking flustered. "That's amazing, Anne. When's your book coming out?"

"In a couple of months."

"What's it about?"

"A group of friends at their high school reunion."

"Can I read it?"

"Maybe."

The waiter comes over with dessert menus. I decide on strawberries and ice cream. Jack orders chocolate cake. When the waiter leaves, Jack looks at me appreciatively. "I'm glad you eat."

"Do I look like I eat?"

Jack colors. He doesn't know what to say.

"I didn't mean it like that," I tell him. "I'm lucky. I've got a great metabolism."

"Mental note. 'No, honey, you don't look fat in that at all!'"

"That's the right attitude. Keep it up and you might get the job."

He cups his wineglass in his hands, swirling the ruby liquid around. "Well, I don't know. What's the benefits package look like?"

"Too early to say."

The waiter arrives with our desserts. I take a bite: it's cold, sweet, and creamy. Jack seems to be enjoying his chocolate cake, making small humming noises as he plows through it.

I put my spoon down. "Jack, does this feel totally surreal to you?"

He looks up, his mouth full of cake. "It kind of feels fake-real, if that makes any sense."

"Like you're on a reality show?"

"Yeah, exactly like that."

"Is that a good thing or a bad thing?"

His lips curl. "Too early to say."

"Reality shows are one of my guilty pleasures."

"I'll remember that. Tell me some more of your guilty pleasures."

"Not on a first date."

"Ah, but this is also our engagement party."

"True."

Ms. Cooper taps a knife against her wineglass to get our attention, and the room falls silent. "Good evening, everyone. I hope you've enjoyed your dinner and your companion. As you know, tomorrow is the big event. Come and see me on your way out, and I'll give you your time slots for your pre-wedding therapy session and for the ceremony. If you've chosen not to go ahead, please let me know.

"There'll be another group dinner tomorrow evening to celebrate your marriages. For those of you looking to explore outside the resort, there are a number of tours available that can be booked through the travel agent next to the front desk.

"If anyone has questions, I'll be here for the next hour or so. Finally, since we like to inject a little tradition into the proceedings, there'll be buses leaving at eleven for two separate bars, one for the men and one for the women. Have a good rest of your evening, and congratulations."

Ms. Cooper walks to the entrance, clipboard in hand. Couples begin to form a line in front of her, waiting to get their time slots. They look decided. They look ready. Their certainty blows me away.

"What do we tell her?" Jack asks.

"Ms. Cooper?"

"Yes."

"What do you want to tell her?"

He takes a deep breath. "I want to tell her . . . that we're getting married."

Oh. My. God. I think I might actually pass out.

All I can manage to say is "Oh."

"Again, not the response I was looking for."

I need to breathe. Yes, breathing would be good.

"You okay, Anne?" Jack puts his hand on my arm. My skin warms to his touch.

"I'm kind of freaking out."

"Come on, let's go."

"But we need to tell Ms. Cooper whether we're getting married."

"Forget about that. Just come with me."

Jack stands and reaches out his hand. After a moment's hesitation, I place my hand in his and let him lead me to an exit located at the opposite end of the room from where Ms. Cooper is standing.

We walk past the pool and down a set of steps to the dark beach. I sit on a low concrete wall, breathing in and out deeply, trying to get my bearings. I usually love the tangy scent of ocean, but tonight it barely registers.

I take off my shoes, bury my feet in the soft white sand, and think about what Dr. Szwick told me to do if I had doubts. "Concentrate on what brought you here," he said. "Trust in your decision. Trust yourself."

I'm here because I want what everyone else has. I want a

family. I want to be married. I decided to do this. I have to
trust myself. I have to . . .

"Anne? You all right?"

I open my eyes. Jack's standing in front of me, looking
concerned.

"I'm okay."

"You sure?"

"Yeah."

Jack stuffs his hands in his pockets. "Look, I don't want you
to do anything you're not comfortable with. I just thought,
since we're here, and we seem to get along . . . and I felt . . . I
*feel* a connection between us . . ."

I have to trust myself. I have to trust the decision I made.

"I know, Jack. I feel it too."

He smiles. "What do we do?"

"Keep talking to me."

"I can do that." He sits down on the wall next to me so that
we're both facing the ocean. "Looks fake, doesn't it?"

The moon is full, and all around it are thin clouds
illuminated by its glow. The wind has dropped, and the water's
so calm, it's almost flat. A lone palm next to us has a strand of
tiny neon lights wound around its trunk. It reminds me of a
movie set staged for a perfect romantic night.

"You're right, it does."

Jack takes off his shoes and socks, rolls up his pants, and
imitates me by digging his toes into the sand.

"What're you doing?"

"It seemed to do you good, so I thought I might try it."

"You're a strange man, aren't you?"

He grins. "And here I was, thinking I was hiding it."

"Not so much."

"Oh, well. There's always next time."

"Next time?"

"Yeah, you know, your replacement. Match quotient seven."

"You're prepared to take a step down?"

"It's not what I want, but in the interest of preserving the mission, I guess I'll have to learn to cope."

"The mission?"

He grins nervously. "Yeah, you know, Operation Get Married Before I'm So Fat and Ugly, No One Will Have Me. Oh, sorry, guys aren't supposed to think that way, are they?"

I laugh out loud, too loud for the silence surrounding us. He smiles briefly. We sit there staring at the moon, listening to the ocean beat against the sand.

"What are you thinking about?" I ask eventually.

He glances sideways at me. "Why do girls always ask that?"

"Because we always want to know."

"Always?"

"Well, usually."

"You know, I think this is going to work out well."

"How so?"

"Since I'm not trying to impress you, I can find out all the things I've always wanted to know about women but was too afraid to ask."

"You're not trying to impress me?"

"You know what I mean. We don't have to play games—"

"I get it. And I think you're right. In a weird way, there *is* less pressure than usual."

He gives me a hopeful smile. "So you'll tell me what I've always wanted to know?"

"I might tell you the truth about me, but I'm not going to betray the whole sisterhood."

"We'll see."

I watch a small wave crest and break on the shore. My heart feels calmer than it has in a while. There's just one nagging thought I can't get past.

"Jack, do you buy in to this friendship-philosophy thing? Have you really given up on the idea of love?"

He's quiet, pushing his toes around in the sand.

"You don't have to answer."

"No, it's okay. I guess the truth is, I don't know. Do I exclude the possibility of meeting someone between now and death that I'll fall in love with? No, of course not. How could I? But have I accepted that the people I've been with haven't made me happy in the long run? Yeah, I guess I have. And I do believe in friendship. I think you can be happy with a friend who wants the same things you do. Does that answer your question?"

"Yeah."

"What about you? Have you given up on love?"

"I guess that's what I'm struggling with. I know I'll keep meeting people I'm attracted to, but that hasn't gotten me anywhere. I'm thirty-three years old, and I've never been in a good relationship. I don't want to struggle anymore."

We watch the moon and clouds floating overhead.

"Maybe it's *harder* to make it work if you start out in love," Jack says.

"Why do you think that?"

"Because if things change, you remember how they used to be, and you're disappointed. If you don't have any expectations going in, you can't be let down."

"Sounds cynical."

"Maybe. I don't have all the answers. I only know that I don't think Blythe and Company fucked up when they put us together." Jack looks directly into my eyes, and I feel my stomach whoosh in the way it usually does with men who look like Aaron, Tadd, and Stuart.

"What do you think?" he asks gently.

Decision time, Anne. What's it going to be?

"I think we should . . . get married. What do you think?"

"I think I agree with you."

We smile at each other. I like his eyes. The green has a rim of blue around the outside, a trace of their newborn color.

"You know, you never answered me when I asked what you were thinking."

"I was thinking this is a hell of a first date."

"That's sweet."

He looks troubled. "It's not the way we're supposed to be thinking, though, is it?"

"I guess not. Still, you can't erase years of training in one day."

"No."

"Maybe that's what therapy is for. We have ways of making you stop expecting love."

"Dr. Szwick again."

"There's no escaping him."

"I guess not. But still . . ." Jack leans forward and kisses me gently. His beard is softer than I expected. His lips are firm, a good fit. After a moment, he pulls back and looks at me shyly.

"I bought you something this afternoon. It's not much, but I wanted to give you something. You know, if you agreed . . ."

He reaches into the front pocket of his shirt and takes out a silver band. It has a turquoise stone inset across the flat top, which reminds me of the color of the ocean. It glows blue-green in the moonlight.

"It's beautiful," I say.

He slips the ring on my left ring finger. It fits perfectly.

"Will you marry me, Anne?"

"Yes, Jack, I will."

# Chapter 11
## All I Want to Do Is Dance, Dance

Jack and I walk up from the beach to the hotel, where two buses are waiting to take us to our bachelor and bachelorette parties. Ms. Cooper is standing off to the side, talking to one of the couples. Jack goes to tell her we're getting married.

"Nine and twelve-fifteen," Jack says when he returns.

"What's that?"

"Therapy at nine, marriage at twelve-fifteen."

A double whammy.

"Right."

We stand there awkwardly. The spell that the moonlit beach cast is losing its grip.

"I'll see you tomorrow morning?" Jack says eventually.

"Sounds good."

"Have fun tonight."

"You too."

He gives my hand a squeeze and ambles off toward his bus. As I watch him walk away, some of the panic that subsided on the beach worms its way back into my body. I think it starts in my ring finger. Good thing I'm headed toward a drink.

I follow the line of women climbing on the bus and take a window seat.

Margaret slips into the seat next to me. "Hi, Anne!"

The bus jerks forward and turns onto the same street that brought us here from the airport what seems like ages ago.

"This is going to be fun!" she says.

"I guess. Do you know where they're taking us?"

"Somewhere called Señor Frog's, I think," she says in a bad Mexican accent. "How did it go tonight?"

"With what?"

"Meeting your husband-to-be, silly."

Right. My husband-to-be, Jack. I'm going to marry Jack. I just agreed to do that on the beach.

"Good, I think. You?"

"Yeah, it was really good."

"What did you talk about?"

"My kid, his kid. Nothing much."

"But you had an easy time talking?"

"Of course. We wouldn't be a good match if we didn't."

"Isn't that a flawed argument?"

She looks puzzled. "What do you mean?"

"You could've had a good conversation without being a good match, right?"

"I guess."

"One good conversation doesn't mean anything."

A trace of uncertainty crosses Margaret's face. Shit. What am I doing? She's happy, and I'm using her as a sounding board for my inner turmoil.

The bus slows down and turns in to a parking lot next to a brightly lit disco. A green neon frog crouches over the entrance as a line of women and men stream through the door.

After paying a cover charge to an enormous bouncer, we enter the steamy bar. The music's pulsing rhythm is so loud that I can barely hear myself think, but that might not be a bad thing. The strobe lights flick around at odd angles, illuminating the black walls and a large dance floor covered in twentysomethings glistening with sweat as they bounce to the beat. The air smells like too many people, old alcohol, and dry ice.

I order a margarita for me and a piña colada for Margaret from a bartender who's wearing a black mesh top. We clink glasses and down our drinks.

As the alcohol seeps into my bloodstream, I can feel my shoulders loosening, the tension beginning to lift.

"Let's dance!" Margaret yells into my ear.

All the wine, stress, and margaritas make this seem like a good idea. I set my empty glass on the bar and follow her onto the dance floor. She immediately starts flinging herself in all directions, like the whirling dervishes I saw at a Dead concert I went to a few years before Jerry died. I dance more sedately next to her, letting myself meld into the music. I don't know if it's the heat or the alcohol, but my body's moving more fluidly than it usually does. I might actually be having fun.

"Can I buy you a drink?" asks one of the men dancing near me. He's wearing a white T-shirt, loose cargo shorts, and sandals. He's tall and slim, with dark hair and light eyes. If

I squint, I might mistake him for Pierce Brosnan, circa 1985. Only younger.

"Sure."

I follow him to the bar, and he orders me a margarita.

"How'd you know what I was drinking?" I yell over the music.

"I saw you order one before," he says into my ear, his breath tickling my skin.

Oh boy. He's gorgeous, and he's been checking me out, and he looks like he's twenty-two. This has trouble written all over it. I take a step back.

"Well . . . thanks."

"Welcome. I'm Tom."

"Anne."

"First time here, Anne?"

"That's right."

"You here alone?"

I motion to where Margaret is still at it on the dance floor. "I'm kind of here with her."

He laughs. "Really? She a friend of yours?"

"Um, yeah, sort of. How old are you?"

"I'm twenty-two. You?"

"What do you think?"

He sizes me up. "Twenty-six."

Ha! This guy is so trying to get into my pants. Too bad I'm not remotely interested.

"How old do you *really* think I am?"

Wait, that's interesting . . .

He shrugs. "Twenty-eight, twenty-nine."

This guy's my type . . .

"Good try."

"Am I right?"

. . . and clearly into me. But . . .

"A lady never tells."

He leans in closer. He smells like beer and the beach. "You wanna dance?"

. . . I'm really not interested. Not even a little bit.

"Sure."

I follow him onto the dance floor, amazed at my newfound immunity to the Stuarts of the world. We face each other and start to move to the beat, laughing as we watch Margaret being free to be you and me.

"Can I cut in?" a familiar voice says. Jack's voice. He looks a little angry. Or jealous. Maybe both.

"What're you doing here?" I ask him.

"The men's bar was lame."

"This bar's pretty lame too."

He eyes Tom. "Looks like you're having a good time."

My heart gives a weird little beat. "I was just dancing."

"Okay."

"You're not jealous, are you?"

"What? I can't hear you."

I yell louder. "You're not jealous, are you?"

The music cuts out at precisely this moment. I'm yelling into a quiet room.

Tom puts his hand on my shoulder. "Everything okay, Anne?" He looks at Jack with a challenge in his eyes.

I shrug his hand off me. "Everything's fine. Tom, this is my, um, fiancé, Jack."

Tom's eyes widen. "You didn't say you had a fiancé."

"Well, she does."

Tom looks back and forth between Jack and me. "Nice to meet you, Anne."

"You too, Tom. Thanks for the drink."

"No problem."

The music comes back on, a danced-up version of Imogen Heap's "Hide and Seek." Jack and I stare at each other, uncertain. I move closer to him so he can hear me without my yelling.

"Are you pissed?"

"Should I be?"

"He bought me a drink and asked me to dance. He's twenty-two. Nothing happened, and nothing was going to happen."

"That's what the guys you've liked in the past look like, though, right?"

"Pretty much, yes. But—"

"What am I supposed to do with that, Anne?"

"I don't know, but I wasn't interested in him. I should've been, but I really wasn't." I take another step toward him. The colored lights play across the planes of his face, glinting off his beard. "You know, you look cute when you're mad."

"I do, huh?"

"Yeah."

His face softens. "Good to know."

"Am I forgiven?"

"For now."

"You want to dance?"

I hold out my hand, and after a second's hesitation, he puts his in mine. We walk to a clear spot on the dance floor and start dancing.

We quickly fall into a good rhythm, matching the pulse of the music. He's a surprisingly good dancer, though I'm not sure why this should surprise me. After a few minutes, I can tell Jack's residual anger has melted away. He moves closer to me; our bodies are touching every third beat, and I don't mind. I move to the left and our thighs touch. He moves to the right and our arms brush. A lock of hair slips across my face. He brushes it away. I feel shivery where he touches me, as if a cold hand touched my skin, even though his hand is warm.

The DJ transitions to a slower song—something by Colbie Caillat, I think. Jack places his hands on my hips, and we move together to the pace of the music. I can feel his fingertips through my dress, warm and strong.

I look up. Jack's face is glowing. I raise my hands to his shoulders, and he leans in and kisses me. As we tilt into the kiss, his tongue edges my lips apart. He tastes like beer and mint gum. His hands pull me closer, closer, and now I can smell him too: woods and soap and the salt of his sweat from the hot room.

The music cuts out suddenly, and we fall apart, out of breath. My head's spinning, and I feel like something's been taken away from me, though I'm not sure what.

Jack is looking at me with an expression I haven't seen before. "Anne . . ."

"There you are!" Margaret yells, even though the music's stopped.

"Hi, Margaret. This is Jack."

"You're not supposed to be here," she says to him.

"I thought I'd see what Anne was up to."

"She was dancing with a kid!"

His face slackens. "I saw that."

"Why'd they turn the music off?" I ask Margaret.

"I think it's time to go."

We walk toward the front doors and line up to leave. Jack is standing behind me, close enough so our bodies are touching. I check the big clock over the exit. It's one in the morning. One in the morning on our wedding day.

"We still getting married today?" I ask quietly.

He puts his hands around my waist, holding me tight. "Why the hell not?"

# Chapter 12
## Just Friends

I wake up with a start at six-fifteen. It's way too early to get up, but I can tell by how awake I am that I won't fall back asleep, so I kick off the covers and pull back the drapes. It looks like it's going to be a beautiful day. No clouds in the sky, and the ocean is still calm.

A nice day for a wedding.

I open the closet and look at the dress I bought the day before I left. It's cream-colored cotton, with a light brown pattern of leaves and vines running over it. A black ribbon ties around the waist. The skirt is loose and flowing and falls below my knees. It's not the wedding dress I always imagined, but it's pretty enough.

I look at the clock by the bed. Six-twenty.

Christ. This waiting is going to be torture.

I put on a baby-blue two-piece, a cover-up, and some flip-flops and leave my room. It's already hot, despite the early hour, and the heat is bringing out the aroma of the bougainvillea. I breathe in the lemony scent as I slip down the path.

The pool is a large kidney shape surrounded by deck chairs and palm trees. White-uniformed staff members are pouring chemicals into it. They tell me they'll be finished in ten minutes, so I sit on a deck chair and close my eyes, trying to block out the waves of panic that keep creeping up on me. I concentrate on feeling the sun on my skin and remember the kiss Jack gave me last night at my door—a duplicate of the one on the dance floor. A kiss that kept me up for hours.

When the pool is open for business, I stand on the edge and test the water with my toe. It feels cold, but I bite the bullet and jump in.

The water is much colder than the pool next door was yesterday, and I surface sputtering from the shock. I do a couple of laps of crawl, then hoist myself out and wrap my towel around me, finger-combing my hair. A woman in her mid-forties is sitting in the deck chair next me, frowning at her BlackBerry. Her expression reminds me of Sarah. I miss her. I wish I could've told her why I was coming here and had her support. She wouldn't have actually supported this decision, but still, it would be good to hear her voice.

I glance at my watch. It's not too early to call. I pull my cell phone out of my pool bag and dial.

"Hello?" Sarah answers in a muffled, sleep-filled voice.

Crap, maybe it is too early to call.

"Hi, Sarah, it's me. Sorry, did I wake you?"

"Anne? No, it's okay, I was just waking up."

"You're such a liar."

"I should be awake."

"How come you're not?"

"Late night at the office. I was planning on sleeping in."

"Go back to sleep, I'll call you later."

"No, no, I'm awake now. What's up?"

I'm getting married today. I'm freaking out. I need you to tell me what to do.

"Nothing. Just hanging by the pool. I thought I'd call you and gloat."

"Are you sure? You sound funny."

I clear my throat. "I was at a club last night. I'm fine."

"*Clubbing* . . . Good for you, Anne. What's it like down there?"

"Hot."

"Any nice men?"

"Um, kind of. I think I met someone yesterday."

"You *think* you met someone?"

"Okay, I did meet someone."

"Already?"

"Yeah, maybe."

"What's in the water down there? Clubbing, meeting men." You have no idea.

"Must be all the margaritas."

She laughs. "Aha. So what's he like? Is he from here?"

"Yes, Mom."

"I just don't want you to waste your time on something that can't go anywhere."

Sarah, Sarah, always the voice of reason. If only I could put her voice in my head.

"I know, Sarah. Thank you. Anyway, yes, he lives near you, in fact, and he's really nice."

"What's he look like?" she asks, her voice full of suspicion.

"Not like what you think."

"I'm glad."

My heart skips a beat as Jack walks around the corner. His hair is mussed from sleep, and he smiles when he sees me.

"Listen, Sarah, I've got to go."

"Hot date by the pool?"

"Something like that."

"Okay. Have fun. Don't do anything I wouldn't do."

Fat chance!

"Bye." I close my phone and look up at Jack, shading my eyes from the sun. "Good morning, Jack H."

"Is that my name forever now?"

"Maybe." My voice squeaks like it does before I have to give a speech. Nice.

"I can handle it."

He looks relaxed and rested (how is that even possible?), and he's wearing red swimming trunks that are too big for him. He has a streak of what looks like zinc oxide across his nose.

"Where did you get that stuff?" I stand up and wipe some of the zinc off his face with my thumb.

"Isn't this what everyone wears?"

"Uh, no."

He shrugs. "I had it kicking around in my apartment, so I packed it."

"Kicking around from an expedition to Everest?"

"A man's got to be prepared for any eventuality."

I pull my hair back from my face and tuck it into an elastic. "I'm going to get some breakfast. Want to join me?"

"I just ate. But I'll see you at nine for therapy, right?"

"Right."

We stand there staring at each other. My mind wanders back to our kisses last night. And maybe his mind is wandering there too.

"I'm going to go swimming now," he says.

"I'm going to go to breakfast now."

Jack flashes me a grin, then turns and takes a running jump into the pool, creating a giant wave that nearly drowns an older man doing laps. "Sorry, man, sorry," Jack apologizes as he surfaces.

I watch him horsing around in the pool. He looks thinner without his clothes on, though his body is far from the lean, fit bodies of the men I've always fallen for. I remember in particular how cut Stuart's abs were and the thrill I always felt looking at them.

I shake that thought from my mind. I'm not going to gain anything by comparing Jack to my standard-size man.

At the buffet in the main dining room, I fill my plate with an assortment of smoked salmon, French toast, and fresh fruit and make a disgusting-looking mix of freshly squeezed papaya, watermelon, and green melon. I'm going to feel virtuous after drinking this, but I may also need to spend some extra time in the bathroom.

I run into Margaret at the end of the line. She's wearing a long linen shirt and flip-flops.

"Where's Jack?" she asks.

"He's in the pool."

"You should keep an eye on him. He's cute."

"Thanks." I feel kind of proud. As if I had something to do with creating him. "Where's Brian?"

"Waiting for his omelet." She points to the special-order grill line, where—there's no other way to say it—an enormous man is standing with a plate in his hands.

"Oh. He's, ah . . . he looks nice."

"He's huge," Margaret says matter-of-factly.

What can I say? He *is* huge.

"But you don't care about looks, right? You said yesterday."

Ah, hell.

Margaret seems unperturbed. "Nope. I don't care what he looks like."

"That's good. And you said you had a great conversation . . . I'll bet you're a good fit."

"Of course we are. Say, you and Jack had it going on last night."

I blush. "I don't usually do things like that."

"Having sexual energy already is great. It's way ahead of schedule."

"What schedule?"

"You know, *the* schedule."

Jack walks by the window, wrapped in a striped towel. He gives me a smile and mouths, "I'll see you later." I wave at him and feel my nerves return, taking away my appetite.

"You want to sit with us?" Margaret asks.

"We have our therapy appointment soon, so I think I'm just going to wolf this down, but thanks."

"Sure, see you later."

I carry my plate to an empty table. I take a few bites of everything, but it all tastes the same, except for the disgusting colon-cleaning juice concoction, and that's not a taste I'm enjoying.

I push my plate away and look at my watch. Not even eight yet.

I can't take this anymore. I feel like pieces of me are about to fly off in every direction, as if I'm being held together by gossamer, the tiniest little thread.

I need to kill some time and some nerves before the therapy session. I need to relax. I need . . . a massage. Yeah, that would be perfect. I abandon my food and hurry toward the spa, praying there's a vacancy. I'm in luck—the first appointment of the day hasn't been booked. I sign some forms and am escorted into an all-white room. There's a Japanese waterfall in the corner and a massage table in the center. I lie down on the soft, warm mattress, and the masseuse places a white sheet over me that feels like it has a thread count of a thousand. She turns on some generic Muzak that's a synthesized version of streams and wind and trees, and she goes to work relieving the knots in my back, neck, and legs.

The forty-five minutes pass quickly. And when we're done, I feel ready to have my head examined.

...

Dr. Szwick is sitting in an armchair in his room, looking relaxed. He's wearing Bermuda shorts and a bright Hawaiian-print shirt.

"Jack, Anne," he says when we enter. "Good to see you again. Please sit down."

We sit in the two chairs facing him. Jack's leg is bouncing up and down, the first real sign of nerves I've seen in him.

"So, Samantha tells me you've decided to go ahead. Correct?"

Samantha? Oh, right, Ms. Cooper. Somehow the name Samantha seems much too . . . human.

"We have," Jack answers for both of us.

"Very good. I've been working with each of you individually, but from now on our sessions will be together. As you know, Blythe and Company believes every couple should do a year of therapy after they get married.

"I know that in order to come here, you've already put aside many conventions and preconceptions about your life and about love. In fact, you might think you've already come as far as you need to in order to succeed. You're wrong. You've made a good first step, but you don't really know yet what you've gotten yourself into. Marriage takes work, and commitment, and effort. And this kind of marriage is going to be even harder in some ways. You're flouting convention. You'll be hiding the truth about how you met from those closest to you. You've been told the person you're with is the right person for you, but you'll wonder at times, maybe even often, if that's really the case. These are just some of the reasons you'll need to be in therapy and committed to it.

"You'll see me once a week for the next year. During our sessions, we'll work on creating a foundation that will keep you together, and on any specific issues that might arise. Right now, however, we have a simpler task: to prepare you for the step you're taking today. And that's how you should think of it, as a step. Any questions?"

We shake our heads.

"All right. I want to discuss a few specific issues I've zeroed in on from your separate sessions. Have you two talked about living arrangements?"

"No," I say.

Dr. Szwick looks back and forth between us. "Well?"

Jack shrugs. "I live in a studio apartment."

"Anne?"

"I guess . . . Jack can move in with me."

Dr. Szwick frowns. "Why did you say 'I guess,' Anne?"

I can feel Jack looking at me, waiting for my answer.

"You're not going to let me get away with saying, 'I don't know,' are you?" I say.

"You should know better than that by now. Come on, Anne, what is it?"

I look down at my feet. I obviously should've thought about this before, but somehow, in all the rush, excitement, and nerves between Ms. Cooper's phone call and the plane ride, I didn't. And I can't quite place my finger on the reason why I care where we live. I know only that I have a funny feeling in my stomach, like a warning.

"We can get a new apartment if you want," Jack says, taking my hand.

I meet his eyes, and now I have a different feeling in my stomach. A better feeling.

"Thanks."

Dr. Szwick interrupts our moment. "That should work. Have you spoken about kids?"

Jack's hand tightens on mine. "No."

"You both indicated that you wanted kids, maximum two. You wouldn't have been matched if you had a difference there, but have you discussed timing? Jack?"

He shrugs. "I thought we should get to know each other first."

"I'm sensing what you really mean is that you have no time frame in mind, am I right?"

"How can I have a time frame in mind when I only met Anne yesterday?"

"Most people have a time frame for when they want kids, regardless of whether they're with someone."

"Well, I don't, okay?"

Dr. Szwick turns to me. "Is that okay with you, Anne?"

"Yeah, I'm in no hurry."

"Really? You're thirty-three years old."

"I know how old I am. I have plenty of time. Certainly enough time to get to know Jack first."

I squeeze Jack's hand to show him I'm on his side. He squeezes back.

"At least you seem to agree. That's a good start." He looks back and forth between us. "I sense you're both feeling hostile toward me right now, correct?"

"What gives you that impression?" Jack asks in a biting tone.

Dr. Szwick clucks his tongue disapprovingly. "We've spoken about this before, Jack. I'm here to push you off your center, to make sure you're telling me what you're really feeling and not hiding behind answers that would satisfy your drinking buddies."

Jack drops my hand. "Yeah, I get it."

"Are you sure you do? Or are we wasting our time here? Are you wasting Anne's time?"

"Of course not."

"I hope not. Now, I'm taking a wild guess, but judging from your previous answers, you haven't discussed finances either, am I right?"

"No," I say.

"May I ask what you *have* been talking about since yesterday?"

"We've been talking about lots of things. Our lives, our past relationships. First-date stuff."

"What do you mean by 'first-date stuff'?"

Kissing. Jack convincing me to marry him. That kind of first-date stuff.

"Oh, I don't know, I didn't mean anything by it—"

"She means we've been covering the basics, like you do whenever you meet a stranger," Jacks says.

Dr. Szwick considers us. "Tell me, did you kiss last night?"

Jack hesitates. "Yes."

"More than once?"

"Yes."

Dr. Szwick puts his pen down. "I have to say, I'm a bit concerned about you two. You're a great match—a perfect match, almost—but you don't seem to be taking this very seriously, either of you. You're getting married in a few hours. *Married.* You're about to create a life together. And instead of talking about the real issues, instead of taking this time to make sure you really want the same things, you're acting as if you're dating, trying to see if you can fall in love. This is a recipe for failure. As I've told you, the process is not about falling in love. It's about building a future based on friendship, and that's created through shared experiences, shared goals, and a foundation of compatibility.

"I don't want to—as my kids would say—freak you out. You do seem to have created some kind of bond, and that's encouraging. You'll need to bond in order to face this unique experience together. But if you keep resenting my input and ignoring my advice, this is not going to end well."

He looks at us intently, and we stare back silently. I feel like I did in high school when someone did something bad in class and the teacher punished everyone because no one would admit who did it.

Dr. Szwick walks to the desk in the corner and takes a piece of paper from a folder sitting on top of it. He hands it to me. "Before you get married today, I want you to go through these questions together. As you do, I want you to have a serious talk about why you're doing this and what you expect. Okay?"

"Okay," I say in a small voice.

"Jack?"

He takes a deep breath and expels it. "Yeah, okay."

"Do you think we should call this off?" I ask.

"Only you can answer that question, Anne. Go talk things over with Jack. Use the techniques we've been using in our sessions. You can figure this out."

We leave the room and walk down the stairs to the beach, both of us deep in thought. Jack stares at the waves for a minute, then begins walking purposefully away from the resort. I catch up with him at the water's edge. The wind has picked up, swirling my hair around me.

"Jack . . . will you wait for me? Jack?"

He stops, balling his hands into fists. "Jesus fucking Christ."

I walk around to look him in the face. The waves slap at my ankles, drowning my flip-flops. "Are you all right?"

"I think I hate that guy."

"I feel like that sometimes too."

He looks down at me. His eyes are dark and troubled. "At least we're on the same page."

"Are we?"

Instead of answering me, he puts his hands on my shoulders

and pulls me to him. I tilt my head up, and our mouths meet. Like last night, there's a hard heat between us as we kiss and kiss. He moves his hands down my back and rests them on my hips. I step closer, wanting his body against mine, wanting no space between us.

A large wave crashes against us, wetting our legs to the knees. Jack moves his hands back up to my shoulders.

"Is this the page we're on?" I ask, fighting for breath.

"Looks like it."

"Is that a good thing or a bad thing, do you think?"

He tucks a strand of hair behind my ear. "I don't see how it can be a bad thing."

Another wave hits us and I pull away. "Shouldn't we do the exercise Dr. Szwick suggested?"

"Probably."

I walk away from the water and sit down on the beach, letting my heels dig into the sand. I pat the space next to me. "Have a seat." He plops down, and I pull the list out of my pocket. "Looks like he already asked us most of these questions, but here's one we didn't answer. How are you with money?"

"Okay, I guess."

"What does that mean?"

"It means I kind of live by the seat of my pants, financially speaking."

"You never said how you could afford to come here."

He bites his lip. "My aunt died, and I got a small inheritance. That covered it, but things are going to be tight when I get back.

I don't get my next advance until I turn in the manuscript I'm working on."

"How about doing more freelance work?"

He pulls a face.

Ah, shit. I must sound like his mom. Only he doesn't have a mom anymore. Double shit.

"Sorry, I'm not trying to nag you."

"It's okay. I do some freelance, but it takes a lot of time drumming up business, which doesn't leave much time for actually writing. I sound like a big fucking baby, right?"

"Maybe a little, but I know what you mean."

He runs his hands through his hair. "I can try harder at that, though. And we'll save some money living together."

"But we should probably keep my apartment. Moving is expensive."

"You sure?"

"It's just an apartment, right?"

He kisses me hard on the mouth. "That's great, Anne. Okay, what's the next question?"

The next question makes me blush.

"Well?" Jack says. He tucks his chin on my shoulder so he can see for himself. "'What role do you believe sex should play in your marriage?' Huh. That's an easy one."

I lean away from him. "Oh?"

"Of course. I'm pro-sex. Aren't you?"

"Well, I . . . I mean, yes, of course, but . . ." I catch a glint of amusement dancing across his face. "Dammit, Jack, that's not funny."

He chuckles. "Sorry, couldn't resist. Do you want to talk about it?"

"Um, well, I guess we probably should." I look down at my toes, thinking about Margaret's comment in the buffet line about Jack and me being ahead of schedule, sexually speaking. Did she have access to some pamphlet I didn't get?

"I think . . ." Jack clears his throat. "It will happen when it should. You know, naturally."

"Yes. That sounds right."

A couple on a Jet Ski buzzes through the waves and lands on the beach. The man driving it cuts out the deafening engine. His girl is clinging to his waist, resting her head on his back. He turns and says something to her, the words swallowed by the waves. She smiles and ruffles his hair.

"Was that it?" Jack asks.

"Mmm?"

"The questions? Are there any more?"

"Oh, right." I look down the list. There's only one left, and it's a biggie. "'Why are you really here?'"

"Good fucking question," says Jack. "You know the answer?"

"Nope . . . only . . ."

"Only what, Anne?"

I turn to face him. "The only answer I have, the only thing that's keeping me sane, is that I *am* here. I took this huge chance, I made this huge decision, and it must've been for a reason, right?"

"Everything happens for a reason? Do you believe that?"

"No, I don't."

"You really are a strange girl, aren't you?"

"I warned you before."

"That you did."

Jack picks up a flat shell and skips it into the water. It disappears in the white foam. Another shell lost to the sea.

"What about you, Jack? You got any answers?"

"Not really. I've spent hours turning this over in my mind, and it doesn't make any sense, but I still seem to want to do it."

"Maybe you want to do it *because* it doesn't make any sense?"

"Would that make me crazy?"

"I don't know. You'll have to ask Dr. Szwick."

"Pass."

I smile. "He really gets under your skin, doesn't he?"

He throws another shell toward the water. "I don't usually spend much time thinking about this kind of stuff. And it bugs me how he won't accept anything I tell him."

"I think he does that to push us off our guard, to make sure we answer him honestly."

"Maybe, but all it does is piss me off."

"That was clear."

"Oh, it was, was it?" he says playfully, pulling me into his lap.

"Crystal."

Jack kisses the space between my neck and my shoulder. I hold his head in my hands and look into his eyes. They're the color of beach glass—a green bottle that's been smoothed by the ocean.

"Jack, are you sure this is a good idea? Should we really be doing this?"

Jack holds my gaze. "What's the worst that can happen?"

"We kill each other in a bitter *War of the Roses* dispute over the furniture we picked out together?"

He laughs. "Yeah, maybe. So what? Lots of people have failed marriages. But at least we'll have tried."

"Let the process work? Take it one day at a time?" I say in my best Ms. Cooper voice.

"Right. Or why don't we try to do what Dr. Szwick said?"

"What's that?"

"Be friends and see how that goes."

"You want to do something Dr. Szwick said?"

"He has a good idea every once in a while. What do you say?"

Friends. I like the sound of that. Only what about the kissing? What about the fact that I'm sitting in his lap right now, our faces inches apart, and I'm having trouble thinking about anything but kissing him?

"Friends, huh?" I say.

"Maybe more than friends . . ." he replies, kissing me gently.

# Chapter 13
## To Have and to Hold

Jack knocks on my door at noon.

"Anne, it's me. Are you ready?"

I check myself one last time in the mirror. I'm wearing the cream-colored dress, and I've pulled my hair back from my face, leaving the rest loose and wavy. My eyes look wide and scared.

Here I come, ready or not.

I open the door. "Ready."

He looks me up and down, his hands behind his back. "You look great."

He's wearing a tan suit and a light green shirt. His hair is still slightly wet from his shower, and it curls tightly on his head. He's even shaved. He looks younger without the beard, more vulnerable.

"You look nice too."

"Thanks." He brings his hand from behind his back. He's holding a small bouquet of colorful flowers. "I thought you might like to carry these . . . unless you already have some?"

I'd decided not to have a bouquet, not to make too big a

deal out of this. Out of today. That's fantasyland, but I can pretend with the best of them.

I bring the bouquet up to my nose. It smells like summer. "Thank you, Jack, they're beautiful."

"Shall we go?"

With my heart in my throat, I walk with Jack, hand in hand, to the lobby. We ride the elevator to the fourth floor and follow the signs to the room where the weddings are taking place. Ms. Cooper is standing at the entrance with her usual clipboard in hand. She checks off our names. "You can go right in."

Jack thanks her, but I can't speak. Is this really about to happen?

Jack squeezes my hand tightly as we enter the room. There's a wall of windows at the far end, looking out over the cerulean ocean. The view is spectacular, beautiful, peaceful. A classical processional plays quietly—Pachelbel, I think.

We walk slowly down the aisle toward a small altar. A dark-skinned man in his mid-forties stands in front of it, holding a small black book. He introduces himself as Pastor Rodriguez and asks if we're ready to begin. When we nod, he begins reading the simple ceremony. I feel an odd urge to laugh, which I try hard to contain.

Jack notices me struggling. "What is it?" he whispers.

"Nothing."

Pastor Rodriguez keeps going, repeating the ageless words. I'm barely listening. Then he says something that gets my attention.

"Do you, John Graham Harmer, take this woman, Anne

Shirley Blythe, to be your lawfully wedded wife, to have and to hold, in sickness and in health, for richer and for poorer, and forsaking all others as long as you both shall live?"

"I do," Jack says firmly.

"And do you, Anne Shirley Blythe, take this man, John Graham Harmer, to be your lawfully wedded husband, to have and to hold, in sickness and in health, for richer and for poorer, and forsaking all others as long as you both shall live?"

I look at Jack. He takes my hands in his and looks into my eyes. I feel weak in the knees. But I take a deep breath and say, "I do."

"Do you have the rings?"

Jack reaches into his suit jacket. He takes out a small ring box that contains two simple silver rings and hands one to me. I hold it tightly in my right hand.

"Now repeat after me. 'With this ring, I thee wed.'"

"With this ring, I thee wed." Jack slips the ring onto my finger. It slides into place next to the one he gave me yesterday.

"Now you, Anne."

"With this ring, I thee wed," I say, my voice barely above a whisper, pushing Jack's ring onto his finger.

The pastor smiles. "I now pronounce you man and wife. You may kiss the bride."

Jack puts two fingers beneath my chin and tilts my head. He kisses me like he did the first time yesterday, gently, but longer. His lips are dry and warm, and that same tingling feeling starts to flow through me.

We break apart.

"Congratulations," says Pastor Rodriguez.

"Thank you," we say together.


Jack and I stroll in a fog to one of the smaller restaurants in the resort. We take a seat among several other dressed-up couples with dazed looks.

My ring finger feels strange under the weight of the two silver bands. I keep twisting them around, trying to make them sit comfortably. We eat our lunch slowly and make small talk about the people we see out the window, trying to distract ourselves from the hugeness of the occasion. We just about manage it.

"Hey, look, there's another one," I say, pointing to a large woman wearing a T-shirt printed with a fake slim body in a bikini. "They must sell them in the gift shop."

"Lady, that's so *not* making you look thin."

I push the leaves of my salad around on my plate. "Jack?"

"¿Sí?"

"Did we just get married?"

"I think so."

"So this isn't some insane dream I'm having?"

He frowns. "It isn't that bad, is it?"

"I didn't say bad, I said insane."

"My insanity threshold shifted the minute I walked into Blythe and Company's office."

"Good point."

"What's the matter?"

"Oh, I don't know. I guess . . . this wasn't what I thought my wedding day was going to be like."

"Not the groom you imagined?"

"No, no. I just always thought I'd be with my friends and family."

"And wearing a white dress?"

I smile. "Yeah, maybe. Did you ever think about that? What your wedding would be like?"

"You do remember I'm a man, right?"

"Yes, yes."

He takes a swig from his beer. "Well, maybe. That my parents would be there. I guess I always thought that."

"How did . . . Was it a long time ago?"

"Yeah. When I was twenty-three. Car accident."

"I'm sorry."

"Thanks." Jack puts a piece of his burrito in his mouth, chewing thoughtfully. "I have an idea."

"What?"

"Why don't we try *not* freaking out and see how that goes?"

"What do you mean?"

"We've both had our moments—you last night on the beach, me this morning on the beach—so I was thinking, it's not really helpful to overanalyze this, right? The deed is done. Let's try to enjoy ourselves."

"And you can do that? You can just . . . not think about it?"

"I'm not sure. But aren't you sick of thinking about this sort of stuff all the time? Isn't that part of the reason you did this?"

"Yes, it was part of the reason."

"So are you with me?"

"Just shut off my brain and have fun, huh?"

"You think you can do it?"

"I can try."

He grins. "That's my girl. Hey, there's another one!"

I turn and watch a three-hundred-pound woman walk by inside the T-shirt body of a woman less than half her size.

"When do I move in?" Jack says.

My head snaps around. "What?"

"Should I move my stuff into your room now or after dinner?"

"Are you being serious?"

"Is there a reason I shouldn't be?"

"There're probably a hundred reasons, but sure, why don't you move right on in and we can have—wait—you're pulling my leg, aren't you?"

Jack starts laughing. "I didn't mean to pull it that hard."

My face turns red. "I'm very gullible."

"I noticed."

"Please don't take advantage of me."

"Not without getting you liquored up first."

"Nice thing to say about your wife."

He wrinkles his nose. "Wow. That's weird."

"I *know*."

"Okay. Moving on. I saw catamarans down by the beach. Do you want to go sailing?"

"I don't know how to sail."

"That's okay, I do."

I hesitate. "I'm kind of afraid of open water."

"That's cute."

"No, it's pathetic."

"It'll be fun, I promise. And if you don't like it, we'll come back."

"Okay, then."

Jack rubs his hands together. "Great! And then afterward, I'll move my stuff in."

"Jack . . . Shit! I almost fell for that again."

"God, you *are* gullible."

"I told you not to take advantage of me."

"Sorry, it won't happen again."

"You're such a liar."


When I get to the beach, Jack is already there, wearing the same red bathing shorts he had on this morning and a fresh layer of zinc on his nose. He's standing near a black and yellow catamaran, talking to one of the resort staff. The staffer—a young guy in a pair of blue swimming trunks—says something that makes Jack throw back his head and laugh. He looks so relaxed and happy, it's infectious.

I walk up to them.

"Miguel, this is my . . . wife, Anne." Jack smiles in a shy way as he says the word "wife." I smile back, feeling happy.

We exchange nice-to-meet-yous, and Miguel gives Jack a few final instructions. We buckle the plastic straps of our orange life jackets, and Jack shakes Miguel's hand and helps me into the boat. Jack takes the tiller, and Miguel pushes us off into the ocean. There's a good wind blowing, and the boat skims quickly over the water toward Isla Mujeres, an island a few miles off the coast.

I grip the edge of the rubber hull with my hands, making sure my feet are tightly secured under the black canvas straps. Jack controls the large white sail with a thick rope that he lets in and out with his right hand.

The pontoons hit a wave. The boat rises and falls with a loud *thawp*. I lace my hands through the cords holding the hull to the frame. "Um, Jack. We're going pretty fast."

"You want me to slow down?"

I nod, and he turns the boat away from the wind. We slow to half speed.

"How's that?"

"Better, thanks."

I start to relax and look around me. The bay is dotted with other boats and people on Jet Skis. There isn't a cloud in the sky, and the water is very blue, chopped by small waves with the first signs of whitecaps. I glance back at Jack. He's leaning back so far, his head touches the water.

"What are you doing?"

He brings his head up and shakes the water out of his hair. "Taking a dip."

"Shouldn't you be paying attention to where we're going?"

"Don't worry, I've got it under control. Why don't you stretch out on the deck?"

"Will you keep the boat going slowly?"

"Of course."

I unhook my feet and scamper forward, stretching out so I'm looking back at Jack. I place my life jacket under my head and close my eyes, letting the rocking boat soothe me. I fall into a half-drowsy state while the sun licks my skin.

"Having fun?" Jack asks.

I prop myself up on my elbows. "Yeah, I am."

"Too bad we didn't bring any beer."

"*Dos cervezas por Señor Harmer, por favor.*"

"Impressive."

"*Gracias.* Though that's about all the Spanish I know."

"Could've fooled me."

I look over Jack's shoulder. Our hotel looks small and far away.

"Jack, I think we should turn around. We're really far from the beach."

"We're not that far."

"Doesn't it take a long time to go back across the wind?"

He cocks his head to the side. "I thought you didn't sail."

"That doesn't mean I don't know anything about sailing."

"Pretty *and* smart. Well done, Blythe and Company. Okay, get ready, I'm going to turn around."

"Wait, let me get back in." I take a seat next to Jack and hook my feet under the straps.

"I'll need to speed up to make the turn. Don't freak out."

Jack turns the catamaran so the wind is behind us and lets out the sail. We pick up speed, and Jack pulls the tiller toward him in a jerky movement. "Oh, shit!"

The left pontoon dips beneath a wave and stays there. A moment later, the right pontoon does the same thing. My heart starts to pound as the back of the craft leaves the water, tipping up toward the sky. Something squeaks and whistles toward me and—*smack!* The boom clocks me in the side of the head and sends me careening into the water.

"Motherfucker," I hear Jack saying as I break the surface, coughing and disoriented.

My ears are ringing with the blow from the aluminum boom. A white wave breaks over my head, half drowning me. I kick my legs hard, gasping for breath, cursing myself for taking off my life jacket. I bob once, twice, and Jack's arm circles my waist, pulling me out of the water and against his wet skin.

"Are you all right?"

"Jesus, Jack, I told you to go slow—"

"I'm so sorry, Anne. I don't want to hurt you."

"It's okay. I'm not hurt."

"Are you sure?"

"Yeah."

"Miguel told me not to jibe. Fuck." He splashes the water with his hands in frustation.

"Hey, you're splashing me."

He reaches up and wipes the water out of my eyes. "Sorry, babe."

My anger melts. "Babe?"

"Do you mind?"

"No, I don't mind."

He smiles and leans toward me. His mouth is cold, his tongue rough against mine.

"You taste salty," I say when we break apart.

"And you're turning blue. We'd better get this boat up."

"Tell me what to do."

I follow his instructions, and we lever the turtled catamaran right side up. He drags himself back into it, reaches down, and grabs my arms to pull me in beside him. He kisses me again, holding me to him until our lips are warm.

"You know, I think blue's a good color on you," he says.

"Can we go back to shore now?"

"Aye, aye, Captain."

We spend the rest of the afternoon lounging by the pool, trying the different concoctions listed on a handwritten sign above the bar, from Bahama Mama to Tequila Sunrise. By the time the sun goes down, the buildings are starting to soften around the edges.

At seven, we get back into our wedding clothes and go to the Blythe & Company reception. It's being held in the same restaurant as the dinner last night, though it's been reconfigured with larger group tables. There's a band in the corner wearing matching glittery outfits, and the room has been decorated with centerpieces, soft lighting, and candlelight. We check the seating plan. We're sitting at a table with Margaret and her husband, along with two other couples.

Margaret introduces us to Brian, who's a soft-spoken guy

with kind brown eyes beneath his round glasses. She chats away brightly as he eyes the breadbasket.

Over dinner, Jack entertains us by telling the table about our sailing adventure. I fill in some of the details. It feels like we're already a long-time couple with a pocketful of similar stories, even though we have just the one.

After dinner, the band starts playing typical wedding songs—mashups of ABBA, the Village People, and the Jackson Five. A few couples throw their hands up in the air until the band transitions into sappy love songs. This is that time at weddings when the emcee usually asks all the couples in love to go to the dance floor. If you're in a couple, good, bad, indifferent, you have to answer this siren call; you have to act like you're in love and dance. Tonight there is no emcee, but the tables empty anyway, leaving behind white cloths stained with crumbs and spilled wine.

"Wanna dance?" Jack asks, slurring his words.

"Sure."

Jack guides me to the middle of the floor and takes me in his arms. The band is playing "Endless Love." We turn in circles to the schmaltzy music.

Jack leans back. His face is flushed, and he's obviously having trouble focusing. "You look pretty."

"You're drunk."

"I may be drunk, but you still look pretty."

Jack brings his lips to mine, pressing firmly, urgently. Dr. Szwick's admonishment flashes through my brain, but I quickly dismiss it. This feels too good to be wrong. I kiss him back, closing my eyes and slipping my hands from his waist to his neck. He puts his tongue against my lips, running it along my teeth, and soon my tongue is tangled with his, our bodies tight against each other. Feeling woozy and exposed in this roomful of just-married couples, I pull back. We look at each other as we spin slowly. The band is playing a sweet song about mockingbirds. This singer's voice is raspy.

"I can never remember who sings this," I say.

He concentrates, listening. "It's Bob Dylan. 'I'll Be Your Baby Tonight.'"

"Really? I thought he only sang angry songs about women."

"Such as?"

"I don't know. 'Don't Think Twice.' That's a pretty angry song. Or 'Idiot Wind.'"

"I guess it depended on his mood." He starts singing quietly along with the song, a line about a big, fat moon. He has a good singing voice, rich and deep.

"You can sing."

"You sound surprised."

"I've never had a man sing to me before."

"And?"

"I kind of like it."

Jack rubs the small of my back. His fingers feel hot, or maybe that's my skin.

"You want to get out of here?" he asks.

"Yes."

Outside, the air is warm, and there's a gentle breeze blowing. The pool is lit up by tiki torches. The water reflects their acrid flames. Jack wraps his arms around my waist from behind. I lean back against him, enjoying the feeling.

"Where do you want to go?" I ask.

"How about your room?"

A shiver runs down my spine. My room's a very tempting option.

"Jack . . ."

"I was kidding. Sort of. Let's go to the beach."

We walk to the place we went last night, where we had our first kiss. The moon is still nearly full, and the beach looks like a film set. Jack stumbles at the edge of the sand and falls on his knees. I try to help him up, but he loses his balance again, this time landing ass-down on the sand.

He looks up at me. "Hello, wife."

"That sounds weird." I put my hands on his shoulders. "Hello, husband." I run my hand along his chin. "You know, I like your shaven face."

"Oh, you do?"

"Yeah."

"So, what are you doing all the way up there?"

"Where should I be?"

"Down here with me."

He tugs at my arms, and I fall on top of him. Laughing, I shift over so I'm lying on my side, facing him. He props himself up on one elbow. "Much better."

I watch his lips as he talks. I want them closer. I want him kissing me.

"What're you doing all the way up there?" it's my turn to say.

"Nothing."

I reach for him, and his tongue is in my mouth, soft and rough at the same time. I press myself to him. He runs his hand down my side, brushing his thumb over my breast. I jolt away.

"What's the matter?"

"That tickles."

"What tickles?" He runs his thumb over my breast again, slower this time. "That?"

"Yes."

He shifts his hand to my waist, rubbing the edge of my stomach lightly. "That better?"

I nod, and we kiss, kiss, *kiss*. I can feel his chest rise and fall, his breath quickening, matching mine. His fingers start playing with the edge of my underwear through my dress.

"Jack . . ."

"Mmm-hmm?"

I put my hands on his shoulders and push him away gently. "Stop for a minute."

He lifts his head from my neck. "Did I tickle you again?"

"No, it's not that. I think maybe . . . we're moving too quickly."

Jack sighs and rolls onto his back. "You're right. I'm sorry."

"Don't apologize."

I put my head on his shoulder, letting my hand rest on his stomach. He plays with my hair, twisting it around his fingers.

"Is it okay that I really want to have sex with you right now?" he says.

"I'd be disappointed if you didn't."

I hear his laugh through his chest, deep inside him.

"What about you?" he asks me.

"Ditto."

"I'm glad."

We lie there and watch the black clouds float across the moon, listening to the crash and boom of the ocean. I feel drowsy from the alcohol and last night's lack of sleep.

"Anne?"

"Yes?"

"This is one hell of a second date."

I giggle. "Sure is."

"Dr. Szwick wouldn't be very happy with us right now."

"Probably not."

Jack kisses my forehead gently and holds me close.

We lie there like that in the sand until we fall asleep.

# Chapter 14
## Anything Goes

We wake up the next morning at sunrise, covered in a fine mist of salt spray. My left side has fallen asleep, and my hair is stuck to my face. My head feels like it's been hit with a thousand booms, and my stomach is as choppy as the morning sea.

Jack is stirring next to me and moaning. "My head. My fucking head."

I turn on my side to face him. Oh, boy. My stomach did not appreciate that.

Jack is squeezing his eyes shut. His hair is caked with sand.

"You okay?" I ask.

He cracks an eye open. What should be white is lined with red. "That has yet to be determined. You?"

"So-so."

"If you feel anything like me, that's a huge understatement."

I sit up. The world starts spinning. "You might be right."

We sit there for a few minutes, waiting for the world to right itself. When it doesn't, we stagger back to our respective rooms for showers and sleep.

I take off my very wrinkled wedding dress and stand in the spray of the shower, letting the heat leach the toxins from my body. When I'm done, I wrap myself in a bathrobe and towel-dry my hair, working the cricks out of my neck. I put on some thin cotton pajamas, slip between the cool, unslept-in sheets, and rest my aching head on the soft pillow.

In the moments between awake and asleep, I think back to the things I let Jack do to me last night with the same odd mixture of pride and embarrassment I used to feel in college after some half-regretted hookup at a dorm party.

Did I do that?

Oh, yes, I did.


Around noon, I find Jack dozing in a deck chair by the pool, a book across his chest. He's wearing plaid shorts and a navy polo shirt. His eyes are hidden by a pair of aviator sunglasses. His forearms are starting to turn brown.

I sit in the deck chair next to him and open my own book, waiting for the sun to wake me fully.

He pushes his shades up. "Hey, you. When did you get here?"

"Just now."

"Why didn't you wake me?"

"You looked peaceful."

He sits up and rolls his shoulders. "God, I really screwed up my back last night."

"That'll teach you to fall asleep with a strange girl on the beach."

"Yeah, I should've learned that lesson by now. But I think an exception can be made when the strange girl is your wife."

"I didn't notice that exception in the rules."

"It's right there on page three of the brochure. It's one of the tenets of the friendship philosophy of marriage."

I giggle. "Really? Dr. Szwick never mentioned it."

The side of his mouth curls. "I could've sworn he's the one who pointed it out to me. It's what convinced me to go through with all of this, actually."

"What do you think Dr. Szwick would say about our sleeping arrangements last night?"

He swings his legs around so they're hanging off the edge of the deck chair. His feet are long and white. "Not sure. Then again, I'm not counting to ten."

"Did he do that chair thing with you too?"

"Annoying, wasn't it?"

"Totally."

We grin at each other.

"So . . ." I say.

"So . . . I signed us up for an excursion this afternoon."

"You did? Which one?"

"We're going snorkeling."

"Cool. I haven't done that in a long time."

"The boat leaves at two, so we have enough time to eat."

"Is that your way of telling me you're hungry?"

Jack rubs his belly. "I could eat."

We settle on the restaurant next to the pool. We order a large plate of nachos covered in beef, onions, tomatoes, and cheese sauce. When it arrives, we dig in. For a few moments the only sound between us is that of our mouths munching fatty food.

"I think I can feel my ass expanding," I say, pushing the nearly empty plate away.

Jack puts his head under the table. "Looks okay to me."

"Get out of there, silly."

He pops his head back up, grinning like a little boy. "Want a beer?"

Just the thought of it makes me queasy. "Don't think so."

"You'll feel better once you have one."

"Isn't that how people end up in rehab?"

"Probably."

I wipe my hands on a napkin and notice the book Jack dropped on the table. It's David Sedaris's *Me Talk Pretty One Day*.

"Any good?"

"Very funny. Ever read him?"

"Nope, but my friend Sarah keeps telling me to."

"She's right, you should."

"What's your favorite book? No, wait, don't tell me . . . *On the Road*?"

"How'd you guess?" he says, surprised.

"Because all guys love that book. It's like that Peter Sellers movie."

"You mean *The Party*?"

"I bet you love that movie, right? That and *This Is Spinal Tap*."

"Otherwise known as the Funniest Movie Ever."

"I *knew* it."

"You don't like that film? Damn you, Blythe and Company." He shakes his fist at the sky.

"No need to take it to eleven."

Relief floods Jack's face. "Oh, thank God. I take it back, Blythe and Company. I'll never question you again."

"Are you sure? Because I have a confession to make: I've never read *On the Road*."

"That's pretty serious, but we can remedy it. I'll even lend you a copy, which I just happen to have in my room."

"Of course you do." I smile at him indulgently.

"Good thing too. You never know when an *On the Road* emergency might occur."

"Right."

"So I'll lend it to you, but only if you let me read your book first."

"Really?"

"Yeah, I want to read it."

"We'll see."

"I'll be able to buy it at the bookstore soon," he points out.

"I know, but that's a couple of months away. You'll know me better then."

"What's that got to do with it?"

"It'll be harder for you to tell me you hate it."

"Better toughen up, Anne. Somebody's not going to like it. Those are just the odds."

"I know, but you're not somebody."

He smiles. "I like the sound of that."

"Yeah?"

"Yeah."

We spend the afternoon snorkeling, our backs getting burned as we float facedown in the salty water, watching the fish swim by. The highlight of the afternoon is when I spot a large gray shark weaving back and forth below us—okay, maybe "highlight" isn't *quite* the right word. I've never swum so fast in my life, though we laugh about it afterward, lying spent on the deck of the tour boat.

We have dinner in the Mexican restaurant, then go to the lobby bar to enjoy an after-dinner drink. Rehab might be required after this break from reality.

"So," Jack says, "I checked out the evening program here at Boringland. Cards, don't you know, and I'm thinking not. But over in the land of the hedonistic twentysomethings, they have something called Anything Goes that sounds like it might be fun."

"Do you ever take anything seriously?"

He takes my arm and kisses the inside of my wrist. "I take some things very seriously."

I swat him away. "What do you think 'Anything Goes' means?"

"Why don't we go find out?"

We walk down the long walkway that separates Blythe & Company's resort from its twin and arrive at an amphitheater identical to the one where we met. It's been a hot day, and the air underneath the white canvas feels thick.

"It looks like *Beyond Thunderdome* in here," Jack says.

"You saw that movie?"

"Didn't everyone?"

We take seats halfway up one side, squeezing into place between a young couple and a group of giggling girls who look barely eighteen. A thin woman with bleached-blond hair picks up a mike. She's wearing a tight black tank top and short jean shorts.

"Ladies and gentlemen, my name's Jill and this is Anything Goes night, where, literally, anything goes. Now, those of you who're uncomfortable with nudity, drinking, or general mayhem probably shouldn't stick around. You should also know there's only one rule on Anything Goes night: Once you're in, you're in. So, anyone who isn't up for an adventure should leave now."

"Do you think she's serious?" I whisper to Jack.

"She seems pretty serious. You wanna go?"

"Not unless you do."

"I'm good."

I watch a few people get up and leave, looking embarrassed. I feel nervous about our decision to stay, but hey, what's the worst that could happen?

Hmm. I seem to be saying that a lot.

"Now that the losers have left, let's play some strip bingo! The rules are simple. Everyone gets a card. If a number's called and it's not on your card, you have to take off an item of clothing and place it in the middle of the ring. If you have the number, you get to keep your clothes on."

I glance down at what I'm wearing: tan shorts, a blue tank top, my bra, underwear, and flip-flops. A grand total of five items—or six, if I count each flip-flop as one item. Which I'm pretty sure I'll be doing. Even so, I'm so going to end up naked.

"Bet you wish you'd brought a sweater," Jack whispers in my ear.

"I don't have a problem with nudity."

"Oh, you don't, huh?"

"Well . . . maybe a little."

Jill brings out a large spinning cage full of balls and passes out bingo cards and markers. When all the cards have been distributed, she turns down the lights so we're sitting in semi-darkness.

Maybe this won't be so bad. Maybe I *can* take my clothes off in front of this room full of strangers and this man who knows how to kiss me just so.

I glance at Jack. He raises his eyebrows suggestively, clearly happy with the thought that I might be naked in a few minutes.

On second thought, maybe I need to win this game.

"B12," Jill calls out.

Dammit!

I take off one of my flip-flops and put my foot on the cold concrete.

Jack slips off both of his sandals. He wiggles his toes at me. "Cheater."

I stick out my tongue at him.

"N19."

Yes! I mark the square off with my pen. Jack whips off his shirt.

"Exhibitionist," I tell him.

"*I* really don't have a problem with nudity."

"O39."

Off comes my other flip-flop as Jack marks his card, looking disappointed.

"Come on, people, you're supposed to be putting your clothes in a pile in the middle of the room. Don't be shy. Bring them down here!" Jill commands.

Several already mostly undressed people climb down the stairs in the gloom and drop their clothes into a pile. I stay put, keeping my shoes where I can find them.

"G23."

Shorts or top? Shorts or top? I settle on top. Sitting in your bra's like being in a bikini. No problem.

I take off my tank top and place it next to my shoes. Jack slips out of his shorts, scrunches them up, and tosses them into the middle of the ring. He's wearing a pair of white boxer shorts.

"Good luck finding that," I say.

"Oh, yeah?" He scoops up my tank top and throws it into the pile.

"Hey!"

"Rules are rules, Anne. You don't want us to get in trouble, do you?"

"I17."

I *knew* it. I stand up and unbutton my shorts. I hold them on my lap tightly as Jack tries to grab them from me.

"Quit it." I slap his hand away.

"I25."

Now, this is going too far!

"Bingo!"

Please don't let that be a false alarm.

I sit there nervously while Jill checks the card of the woman who yelled "bingo."

"We have a winner!" The room erupts in applause. "Now we're going to turn out the lights, and everyone has to try to find their clothes!"

I give Jack a dirty look. He smiles at me reassuringly. "Don't worry about it, I'll find our stuff. Stay here."

He walks quickly down the stairs and is back in a moment clutching our clothes. I slip into my shorts and top while Jack does the same next to me.

"This kind of blows, right?" he says.

"I wish we'd left earlier."

"Let's leave now."

"But they said we couldn't."

He grins. "Gullibility becomes you. Follow me."

We walk up the dark stairs to the edge of the canvas. Jack pulls it back, revealing an emergency staircase.

"How did you know this was here?"

He taps the side of his head. "I have an enormous brain."

"Blythe and Company left that off your description."

"I'll have to talk to them about that."

We walk down the stairs and away from the amphitheater. We can hear shrieks coming from inside.

"I feel like such a chicken," I say.

"You married a stranger yesterday. You're definitely not a chicken."

"Yeah, good point. What now?"

"Walk on the beach?"

The beach. The scene of the crime. What the hell.

We kick off our shoes and stroll toward a distant patch of lights at the other end of the bay. Jack wades into the water. Every few minutes a large wave rolls in, and he leaps up, trying to avoid it.

"You know they had to suck all this sand off the ocean bottom after the last hurricane?" he says.

"I heard that."

"They used these big suction machines because the beaches were down to bare rock."

"Yeah, that's what I read."

"Sorry, am I boring you?"

"Not at all. Why?"

"I don't know. Do you feel like today is kind of anticlimactic?"

"How can you call any day where we saw a shark and played strip bingo anticlimactic?"

He smiles. "That was a big fucking shark."

"It starred in *Jaws*, for sure."

"Seriously, though . . ."

"You mean because we did this huge, life-changing thing yesterday, and nothing's that different today?" I ask.

"Yeah."

"What did you expect to be different?"

"I'm not sure. Forget I said anything."

"Do you want anything to be different? I mean, do you want me to be different?"

He turns toward me. "No, Anne. You're great. I think it's just post-anticipation syndrome. You know when you're anxious for some big event and then it comes, you always feel sort of let down afterward. Not that I feel let down . . ."

"It's okay. I know what you mean. We've done the big part, and now comes the hard part: living the rest of our lives."

"I hope it's not too hard."

"Me too. Besides, didn't we agree not to think about this kind of stuff anymore?"

"You're absolutely right."

The lights at the end of the beach turn out to be two giant pirate ships docked at a marina, ready to take passengers on a night tour of the bay.

"What do you suppose they do on those boats?" I ask.

"They go out into the middle of the bay and have a mock battle."

"I should've known."

He looks sheepish. "I read all the brochures to kill time when I got here."

"You weren't skulking around, trying to figure out who I was?"

"That too," he says, one corner of his mouth turning up.

"How did you manage?"

"I picked right."

"You picked me out of all the women here?"

"Uh-huh."

"Bullshit."

"Swear to God."

"How?"

"I told you before, I have an enormous brain."

"Yes, yes. Come on, tell me how you really did it."

"There was only one real redhead in the right age bracket, even adjusting for under-overs."

"Under-overs?"

"You know, women who look twenty-five but might be thirty-five and vice versa."

Music starts to blare from the pirate ships as the passengers file on. We watch the flashing lights and throngs of people pushing their way up the gangplank.

"And which am I?"

He puts his hands on my waist. "Under, definitely. Not a day over twenty-five." He pulls me toward him, and now our hips are touching.

I tuck my hands into his back pockets. "You're teasing me now, aren't you?"

"I'll never tell." He brushes his lips against mine.

"Do you think we should've stayed at that thing tonight?"

"You having a bad time?"

"No."

"Good. Now how about Anything Goes, the private edition?"

"We'll see."

He kisses the side of my face and my neck. The music blaring down the beach recedes.

"Jack."

"Hmmm?"

"We saw a shark today."

I can feel him smile against my skin. "A big fucking shark."

I pull him closer to me, my hands still in his back pockets.

"Da-dun, da-dun," he sings into my collarbone.

"Da-dun, da-dun," I breathe into his ear.

# Chapter 15
# Don't Feed the Animals

I'm sitting next to Jack on a bus, trying to get through *On the Road* while he reads my book. He's been bugging me daily to read it, and I finally gave in this morning, handing over the pages I got from my editor before I left. I was supposed to read them one last time, but I've been a little preoccupied.

We're on our way to a lost Mayan city a few hours from our hotel. We've spent the last two days hanging out by the pool, reading, eating, drinking, talking. I've turned various shades of red, while Jack turns browner by the day. At night, we've spent hours . . . "necking" is the only word that comes to mind, with all that implies. In fact, I frequently feel like we're in high school. I've had too much to drink, eaten too much food, blurted out all kinds of things I'd never say when sober, and my lips hurt from kissing.

Jack arrived at my door at six-thirty this morning with a backpack on his back and a large to-go cup in his hands. The dark aroma wafted into my tired brain.

"Oh, thank God. Where did you score this?"

He handed me the cup. "One of the staff took pity on me. Watch it, it's hot."

I took a large sip anyway, scalding my tongue. "Shit."

"Told you."

"Fuck it. It was worth it."

"Junkie."

"You know it, baby."

"You're in a good mood this morning."

"I guess I am."

He gave me the crook of his arm. "Shall we, my dear?"

With my arm looped through his, we walked to the front door of the hotel. The air smelled different on the other side of the hotel: dustier, less salty, hotter. I hesitated on the threshold. "Do you realize we haven't left this place for days?"

"Scared?"

"No, I just have that feeling I get when I've been holed up in my apartment, writing. You know, when you go outside for the first time and everything around you looks new or different, like something has shifted slightly while you were away."

"Deep thoughts for so early in the morning."

"Forget it."

"You ready to see what's out there?"

"Sure."

We met our tour guide for the day—Marco—in the parking lot. He's in his early forties, has light brown hair, and is wearing a white Puma baseball cap. He speaks English well but with the local accent.

We clambered onto the bus, tossing our backpacks in the overhead bins above our seats. And now it's an hour into a bumpy ride.

I'm too nervous to pay attention to Sal Paradise on his speed-driven journey. I glance over at Jack. He's wearing a khaki desert shirt and a Panama hat that's a little too small. My manuscript is in his hands. He smiles, and then a few minutes later, he laughs out loud.

"What do you think?" I ask.

Jack lowers the manuscript. "Anne, I've told you a million times, I'm not going to tell you until I've finished it."

"Just give me a hint. Please?"

Jack brings my hand to his lips. "Read your book."

I read another page, but the words are floating around instead of drawing me in. I close the book with a sigh. When I look up, Jack is smiling at me.

"What?"

"Come here a second."

He puts his hands on either side of my face and kisses me briefly. He moves his lips to my ear. "It's good, Anne."

"Really, really?"

"Really, truly, truly. Come on, you know it's good."

I wrinkle my nose. "Some days I think it's good. Others, I think it's shit. Or small. Or too personal."

"The personal is what's good. What makes you think it's shit?"

"Reading other people's books. Seeing good movies."

"Like what?"

"Like *Brokeback Mountain*. I almost stopped writing after I saw that movie."

"You're truly a strange girl, Anne Blythe."

"So you keep saying."

Jack gives me a weary smile and smothers a yawn.

"Oh my God. My book *is* boring. It's putting you to sleep. I *knew* it."

"Relax, Anne. I just haven't been sleeping that much lately."

"Oh? What's been keeping you up?" I look out the window at the passing scenery and try to calm down. We're on some secondary dusty road. The bus jostles and jolts its way along.

"I think you know what's been keeping me up," Jack says. "And what would make me sleep better."

I turn back to him, my face aflame. "You want to talk about that *here*?"

"Why not?"

Because I'm not sure I'm ready to sleep with you yet, and if we don't talk about it, then I don't have to think about it?

"How about we talk about your novel? When do I get to read it?"

He looks disappointed, but only briefly. "I brought a copy with me."

He gets his backpack out of the overhead bin, takes out a book, and hands it to me. It has a forest-green cover featuring

a picture of a craggy, snow-covered mountain range. Its title—
*Race to the Finish*—is scrawled across it in bold white lettering.
I turn it over to read the synopsis on the back. There's a black-
and-white photo of Jack smiling at the camera.

"This is a really good picture of you."

"Deceiving, isn't it?"

"I didn't mean it that way. Can I read it now?"

"Sure. But I want a rain check on the 'Sleepless in Mexico'
conversation."

"We'll see." I snuggle down in my seat, crack the spine, and
start reading.

I like it straightaway. He writes in crisp sentences, and
I'm immediately sucked into the story. It's about a team of
adventure racers and maybe—I can't tell yet—a romance
between the narrator and the only woman on the team.

"Jack."

My manuscript is lying across his lap, and his eyes are
closed. "Mmm?"

"How can you sleep knowing I'm reading your book?"

He cracks an eye open. "I'm keeping my mind off it by
fantasizing about us on the beach."

"Jack!"

"Can I go back to sleep now?"

"Okay."

"Thanks, 'cause you look hot in this fantasy."

I whack him with the book, and he rubs his arm, laughing.
Then I settle into my seat and let Jack tell me a story.

• • •

"Ladies and gentlemen, hello," Marco, the tour guide, says. "We're almost at Cobá, so I want to give you some information before we get there. First, so we can all find each other today, I will be calling you Pumas, like my hat." He pronounces the word in an elongated way—*Pooommmaaas*—as he points to his baseball cap. "So when you hear 'Pumas,' please make sure to come to me. Everyone got that? Pumas, come to me. Pumas, come to me."

He looks around the bus expectantly, and I smother a laugh.

"Okay, next, we need to order our lunch when we get off the bus. We'll be going to an authentic Mayan restaurant, and there are three choices. First, there is armadillo. Armadillo tastes like chicken. Second, there is snake. Snake tastes like pork. And finally, there is alligator. Alligator tastes like beef. So when you get off the bus, just tell me armadillo, snake, or alligator. Okay?"

"Anne, please tell me you're not being taken in by this?"

I totally am. I was just thinking I don't want to eat *any* of those things.

I square my chin. "Of course not."

"Uh-huh."

"Kidding, Pumas, kidding," Marco says. "The choices are chicken, pork, or beef. Tell me which when you get off the bus. Okay, so we are coming to Cobá, site of the highest Mayan pyramid in the Yucatán Peninsula." He pronounces the word "Mayan" in the same way as "Pumas": *Maaayyyaannn.* "People think the pyramid at Chichen Itza is higher, but they are wrong. Also, you can't climb the pyramid there anymore, so you chose the right tour today, Pumas."

"Where did they find this guy?" Jack asks.

We pull into a parking lot full of tour buses and disembark. We get our tickets and follow Puma Marco on a two-mile hike through the jungle. The canopy is thick, blocking out the sun and trapping the humidity steaming up from the ground. Though I know the noises are real, the air is filled with what sounds like a fake jungle soundtrack.

We stop at the ruins of a ball court where the ancient Mayans played pok-ta-pok, a primitive ball game. Marco explains that it's commonly believed the players who lost were killed, but, he adds, "There is no evidence of human sacrifice at this site. There is only evidence of self-sacrifice. Seelllfff-saacccrriifiissse," he says again, making a motion like he's trying to commit suicide by cutting his wrists. "This is also why you chose the right tour, Pumas: you are getting the truth today."

The weathered gray stone pyramid we've come to see is 138 feet high—as tall as a ten-story building—and stands in the middle of a clearing. A line of tourists is scrabbling up and down the central staircase with the aid of a rope.

"Race you?" Jack asks, a glint in his eye.

"Oh, I don't know . . ." I bend down to tie my shoe, then sprint away from him toward the steps.

"Hey!"

I keep my head down and concentrate on making it up the stairs as fast as I can. Jack catches up to me about thirty steps in. We weave between the large-bellied and blistered tourists. It's 120 steps up, and my calves start cramping on step 83.

"Come on, Anne! You're not going to give up so close to the top, are you?" Jack yells beside me, panting.

"Ne . . . *ver* . . ."

I find a last reserve of energy and take the final three steps in one giant leap before collapsing on the square platform at the top.

"I win," I say as triumphantly as I can.

Jack drops down next to me. His face is bright red and there are sweat stains across his shirt. He's struggling for breath. "If you're that fast . . . maybe you should do the next adventure race with me . . ."

"Not a chance." I turn toward the view and catch my breath. The near–heart attack was worth it. We can see for miles. Other ruins poke up through the jungle. The people down below look tiny. I'm glad I remembered to bring my camera.

A few pictures later, I hear Marco bellowing from below. "Come on, Pumas . . ."

We struggle to our feet. I look down the steps. Big mistake.

Jack grabs my arm to steady me. "Don't look down, Anne."

"Too bad you didn't tell me that a few seconds ago."

"You gonna make it?"

"What goes up must come down."

"Hold on to the rope, and take it one step at a time. I'll be right beside you."

I grab the rope. It's slippery with the sweat of a million

tourists. I step gingerly on the first step like I used to do when I was three years old. First foot, second foot, stop. First foot, second foot, stop.

Jack stays with me step for step. When we get to the bottom, I feel almost as triumphant as I did when I reached the top.

We follow Marco through the jungle back to the parking lot, climb onto the bus, and drive a mile to an "authentic" Mayan restaurant. Tables for twenty are set up family-style within the large dark wooden structure. There's a thatched roof above. We sit at the end of one of the rough-hewn wood tables. Jack grabs two beers from a big ice bucket in the middle of the table. "So you made it." He clinks his bottle to mine.

"Thanks to you."

"Anytime."

"Do you mind if we sit with you?" Margaret asks. She's wearing a long, shapeless cotton dress. Brian is sweating quietly behind her in jeans and a white T-shirt.

I catch a warning look from Jack and ignore it. "Of course not."

They sit down. Brian reaches hungrily for a bottle of beer.

"Where did you come from?" I ask. "I didn't see you on the bus."

"Oh, we're on a different bus," Margaret answers vaguely.

"What did you think of the ruins?"

She shrugs. "Not as impressive as I thought they'd be."

Jack looks nonplussed. "What do you mean?"

"I thought they'd be taller. You know, like the Egyptian ones."

"I don't think you can compare the two."

"Why not? They're both pyramids."

"Yes, but they didn't have the same technology."

"What's technology got to do with it?"

"Have you ever heard of a little thing called the wheel?"

I place my hand on Jack's arm. "Well, I was impressed."

A waiter comes to our table to verify who's having chicken, beef, or pork.

"I'm having the armadillo," Margaret says.

"Otherwise known as the chicken," Jack murmurs, rolling his eyes at the waiter.

"Are you going to the Mayan village this afternoon?" I ask.

"Yes," Margaret says with relish. "I can't wait to see their houses and the little children. I hear they're super-cute."

"We go into their houses?"

"Yeah, to see how they live, you know. We get to go right in and look at their stuff."

The waiter arrives with our food. The chicken is very tender from having been cooked in a clay oven with tomatoes and spices, and it smells delicious. We pass around family-size portions of rice, salsa, and tortillas.

Jack cracks open another beer and leans back in his seat. He has a hint of mischief in his eye. "So, Margaret, how do you like Mexico?"

"It's fine, I guess. Not as good as China, though."

"China?"

"Yeah, that was brilliant. The Great Wall, now, that was impressive."

"You can't really be comparing China and Mexico."

"Why not?"

"Because no one says, 'Should I go to Mexico or China?' You don't go to those places for the same reasons at all."

"They're both places to visit, aren't they?"

"Yes, I guess. But really, if you think about it . . ."

"I don't see the difference."

Jack shakes his head. "If you can't see it, I can't explain it."

Margaret spears a piece of meat on her fork and holds it up. "You know, this armadillo really does taste like chicken."

"Now, Pumas, we are going to see an authentic Mayan village. The families who live here make about a hundred and fifty dollars—yes, a hundred and fifty dollars—a week. Where you come from, you would pay a hundred and fifty dollars *not* to get out of bed in the morning, eh, Pumas? But here, that is a good wage.

"One thing, though, Pumas—it's important not to give money to the children, no matter how cute they are. They learn bad habits that way. We had to cut one family from the tour because the children got too aggressive asking for money. So please, please, don't give them any money. Candies, yes; money, no. Okay, Pumas?"

Jack leans toward me. "What do you think he means when he says, 'We had to cut one family from the tour'?"

"I don't know. Maybe it's like Mayan Disney World and the village is fake?"

"Ah, but Pumas, it's supposed to be authentic!" Jack says.

Marco continues. "You know, Pumas, they have a great health care system here, second only to Cuba. There are many great things in Cuba. Health care, education." He shrugs. "The people aren't free, but you can't have everything."

Jack's shoulders are shaking with laughter. "Whatever we paid for this tour, it wasn't enough."

The "Mayan" village is a collection of ten corrugated iron shacks along a very dusty road. Two little girls, brown from the sun, are sitting in the doorway of the first house. They're wearing white peasant blouses and brightly patterned ruffled skirts. They wave and smile at us with extremely white teeth.

Inside, the house is lit by a single bare lightbulb. A woman in her mid-forties sits at an ancient Singer sewing machine. A fire sputters in the corner. The room is filled with acrid smoke that makes my eyes water.

"You wanna get out of here?" Jack asks, looking as disconcerted as I feel.

"Yes."

We duck out the front door and walk up the road in silence. A ten-year-old boy whizzes by us on his bike, his friend riding pillion behind him, laughing with delight.

Jack turns to watch them fly down the road, kicking up a cloud of dust. "This place looks like the opening sequence of a movie about a South American revolutionary."

"I know what you mean."

"I don't like this. I don't think it's right that we're here."

"Me neither."

"Okay, Pumas, back to the cantina!"

"Hear, hear."

Back at the hotel, Jack tips Marco heavily, and we separate to clean up. An hour later, Jack picks me up for dinner wearing a light lime-green shirt and linen pants. The tan on his face has deepened over the course of the day. I don't know if it's the memory of his hands on my skin or the addictive nature of his scent, but he's looking better to me by the day.

"What was it like growing up named after a character in a book?" Jack asks as we linger over dessert.

"It was harder for my brother, Gilbert. He had girls following him around, hoping to play out some romantic scenario they'd read about."

"Doesn't sound too bad."

"That's because you're assuming hot girls are obsessed with Anne of Green Gables."

"Weren't you?"

I smile. "That's different. When I was young, I thought the books were written about me: that someone had written what my life was supposed to be like."

"And now?"

"I'm trying to write my own life."

"Aren't we all?"

"Speaking of which . . . who's Kate?"

"Kate from my book?"

"That's the one."

"She's no one. It's fiction."

I watch him fiddle with his fork, chasing a scrap of chocolate cake around his plate. "You still like her."

"I do not."

"I thought she didn't exist."

He raises his hands in surrender. "All right, all right, you win."

I feel my stomach fall. "You do still like her?"

"No, no. I meant yes, she exists. We dated, but it didn't last. It was no big deal."

"That's not what it seems like in the book."

"It's fiction, Anne."

"Based on your experiences, right?"

"Yeah, that's what I do, but it doesn't mean I don't have an imagination."

"Sorry. I guess I wanted to be sure there isn't some unresolved issue there."

He puts his hand over mine. "You and I both have a past, Anne, but there's nothing to be jealous about. We were together, it didn't work out, we broke up. Anything else you want to know?"

"I think I'm good for now."

"All right. Would you like to go to the activity tonight?"

"I assume you mean the activity next door, where the kids play?"

"Of course."

"What is it?"

"Some kind of drinking competition, I think."

"Hasn't this whole week been a drinking competition?"

"My point exactly. We have to put our training to good use."

"I'm kind of tired, actually. I thought I might head to bed early. Do you mind?"

"No, of course not."

I stand to go, and he rises as well. "Why don't you stay? Finish your beer. I'll see you in the morning," I say.

"Are you sure?"

I kiss his brown cheek at the edge of where his beard is growing back in. "I'll see you in the morning."


Two hours later, I'm lying in bed feeling an odd mixture of exhaustion and being keyed up. Every pore of my body is screaming for sleep, but my brain won't shut down. It keeps spitting out a kaleidoscope of Jack. The way he looked reading my book, a small smile on his face. The way he looked on the catamaran, boyish and happy. The way he looked at me when we'd been kissing so long it felt like kissing forever.

I turn on my side, hold one of the extra pillows to my chest and squeeze my eyes shut, willing sleep to come. And this works, after a fashion. In fact, I'm on the edge of slipping away when there's a soft rap at my door.

"Anne? It's me."

I feel a moment of disorientation, like I might be dreaming.

"Jack?"

"Yes."

"Hold on."

I slip a thin cotton robe over my T-shirt and underwear and tuck my hair behind my ears. I snap on the light in the hall and ease open my door. Jack is leaning against the doorframe, swaying slightly.

"What's going on?"

"I came to kiss my wife good night."

"Are you drunk?"

He concentrates. "I may be a tiny bit drunk."

"Mmm. I thought when I turned thirty, I was done with drunk guys showing up at my door."

"Maybe you can make an exception . . ."

"I'll consider it."

"And the kiss?"

"That you can have."

"Good."

He rests his hands on my hips and pulls me toward him with that look in his eyes, the one that was keeping me awake. He tastes like beer; his mouth is wet and soft. My arms are around his neck, and my back is pressed against the doorframe, though I hardly feel it. I'm still half asleep, half full of the dreamy thought of us kissing, so now that we are kissing, hungrily, all tongues and teeth and weak knees, it feels unreal.

His lips glide toward my ear. "Shall we go inside?"

"Yes," I say. Yes. I can feel his smile as he bends down and sweeps me into his arms.

"Not our wedding day, but close enough," he says playfully.

He carries me into the room and kicks the door shut with his foot. He walks to the bed and sets me down. The light in the room is dusky.

He kneels in front of me and reaches for the tie on my robe. "This okay?"

"Yes," I say. Yes.

He tugs on it, pulling aside the folds of fabric and slipping it off my arms. He runs his hands up my bare arms till his thumbs brush across my breasts, loose under my thin T-shirt.

"This okay too?"

"Mmm-hmm."

His hands slide to the edge of my T-shirt and under it. His fingers are gentle and strong against my ribs. His features are softened by the alcohol. I watch him, waiting, as he slides his hands down my legs, laying them flat. The tips of his fingers graze the inside of my thighs. I twitch away from him.

"What?"

"It tickles."

He grins, and his mouth is on mine again. We kiss, kiss, kiss until I can't tell where my mouth stops and his begins. He pushes me back, settling himself between my legs, kissing my face, my neck, the lobes of my ears. He mutters things to me, half sweet, half sexy. I can't speak. All I can do is think.

Jack, Jack, *Jack.*

"Jack."

"Umm." He moves to another inch of my skin.

"Jack." I put my hands on his shoulders, rolling him off me.

He turns on his side, his face inches from mine. "You want me to go?"

"No. I just want to talk about what we're doing for a sec."

"Don't worry, I have something."

"Good, but that's not what I meant."

"Then what did you want to talk about?" He tucks his head down and begins kissing my neck.

I put my hands on his shoulders. "I can't concentrate when you're doing that."

"I know."

"Jack."

He brings his face back up to mine. "It's not too fast, Anne, it's just right."

"Are you sure?"

"It was bound to happen sometime. Just let go."

"Just let go?"

He brushes his lips against mine. "Yeah."

"Just let go," I murmur against his mouth. "I can do that."

I start working on the buttons of his shirt, undoing them one by one. I let my fingers run over his chest and the tangle of light, curly hair that covers his breastbone. His skin feels hot against mine through my T-shirt.

Jack stands up, pulling me with him. He strips off all his clothes but his boxers, then pulls my T-shirt over my head. We are so close against each other we feel like one skin. All I can feel are his hands, his breath, touching every part of me.

"I want to be inside you, Anne," Jack mumbles into my ear.

I nod, and in a moment he's taken off my underwear and his.

And then he's inside me and I can't think anymore.

## Chapter 16
## I Am Aglow

I wake up the next morning feeling like I've spent the night in that song "Your Body Is a Wonderland." We're all legs and sheets and blankets, and my body feels loose, stretched out. The balcony door is open. I can hear the waves crashing against the shore, playing in the bright sunlight.

I look over at Jack. His eyes are squeezed shut like those of a little boy who doesn't want to be woken from his nap.

"You asleep?" I ask.

"Mmm."

"You want me to be quiet?"

"Mmm." He pulls the covers up, wiggling over until he's closer to me. He starts kissing my bare shoulder. "I like the smell of your skin."

"Yuck. I must smell disgusting."

"Noooo. You smell like us."

"I think us might need a shower."

He flips on his back and slips his arm beneath me, pulling me into the space between it and his chest. I settle my head on his shoulder, feeling peaceful and happy.

"You sleep all right?" he asks.

"Yeah. You?"

"Better than I have all week."

"Must be the release of tension," I tease.

"It's certainly relieved. Though, it could build again if you'd like."

"That's such an adolescent pass."

"Every man's a fourteen-year-old boy underneath the surface."

"How discouraging."

He kisses the top of my head. We lie there like that for a few minutes, Jack stroking my hair.

"What are you thinking about?" I ask eventually.

"There's that question again."

"I'm sorry, was it ex-rated?"

"Actually, I was thinking about whether I want to get up."

"Any decision?"

"Didn't get that far. You?"

"I was thinking how having sex shifts the air between people. How everything is different afterward, no matter how many people you've slept with."

Jack laughs softly. "You really do have deep thoughts in the morning."

"It's when I usually write."

"I usually write in the afternoon."

"I thought we were supposed to be compatible."

"We feel pretty compatible to me."

"I guess you're right."

"Of course I am. Come here."

"Here?"

"Mmm-hmm."

We're having brunch much later when Jack asks, "What do you want to do on our last day in paradise?"

"Sit on our asses by the pool?"

"So you can complete your transformation into a lobster?"

"There's a little bit of brown coming through."

He picks up my left arm and examines it. "The only brown I see are freckles."

"I think we have an appointment with Dr. Szwick first, anyway."

"Joy."

I look at my watch. "Crap. I totally lost track of time. Our session starts in five minutes."

"Let's get it over with."

We walk to Dr. Szwick's makeshift hotel-room office. Jack twines his fingers through mine, and I start to skip like I used to when I was a little girl, swinging his hand. Jack laughs, and I pick up the pace, tugging him behind me. We get to Dr. Szwick's door right on time.

"Therapy in the middle of vacation is a total buzzkill," Jack says.

"Agreed." I knock on the door.

"Come in."

Dr. Szwick is wearing another garish Hawaiian-print shirt.

"Jack, Anne, welcome. Please sit down." He watches us sit, taking us in. "You both look relaxed."

"Thanks," I say.

"You got married?"

We nod in unison.

"How are things going?"

"Well."

"Do you agree with that, Jack? Have things been going well?"

"Sure."

Dr. Szwick watches us for a moment. "Oh, I see. You've slept together."

"Why do you think that?"

"Am I wrong?"

"No, you're right," Jack says. "We've slept together. Is that a problem?"

"Do you think it's a problem?"

"Why would I think it's a problem?"

"Isn't it part of your pattern? Sleeping with women before you're sure you want to make an emotional commitment?"

What?

Jack's mouth is a thin line. "That's not what's happening here."

"Are you sure?"

I look at Jack, trying to catch his eye, but he's staring Dr. Szwick down.

"I think Anne wants to know the answer too, Jack."

"I've made a commitment, haven't I?"

"Of a kind."

"What's that supposed to mean?"

"Until you fully commit to someone, emotionally as well as physically, you won't be able to make another person happy."

Jack's face reddens. "That's what I'm trying to do. That's what I am doing."

"I feel like you're still holding something back, Jack, something important."

"I don't feel like that," I chime in. "I think he's been doing what you said, trying to be friends, trying to forge a connection."

Jack shoots me a grateful look.

"I'm glad to hear that, Anne. And I hope you're right. Let me make one thing clear to both of you. I'm not the enemy. I'm here to help you succeed, not to tear you apart. But if you don't do the hard work now, then you'll go to pieces later on down the road, just like all your past relationships have done, no matter how compatible you are."

"Do you think it's a problem that we slept together?" I ask.

"Not necessarily. I just want to make sure you don't start repeating patterns without noticing it. Think of me as your institutional memory. I'm here to point out the warning signs that you're going back to your original programming, so to speak."

"So we become Anne and Jack two-point-oh?" Jack asks.

"If you will."

I bite my lip. "And one of Jack's warning signs is sleeping with someone too early in the relationship?"

"Yes."

"Is that true, Jack?"

Jack sighs. "Yes."

I meet his eyes. "Can you tell me that's not what's happening between us?"

"I don't think it is. I meant what I said last night. It wasn't too soon."

Jack holds my gaze, and Dr. Szwick recedes into the distance as I remember the connection we formed in my bed last night.

"I agree," I say.

Jack smiles and turns to Dr. Szwick with a hard expression. "Can I ask you something? How come you get to bring up things from our individual sessions? Shouldn't you be keeping those confidential?"

"In normal therapy, you'd be right. But this isn't normal therapy. I only saw you alone to prepare you for the process and to gather information that would be useful in these joint sessions. Everything you told me there is fair game, Jack. That's how this works. And it's the only way it works. Understood?"

"Yes," we say together.

We spend the rest of the day by the pool. I stare at the fluffy white clouds as Jack scribbles in his notebook next to me. For the first time in days, I can feel the pull of my real life, and it's starting to freak me out.

I eye Jack over the rim of my margarita. "Have you given any thought to what you want to tell everyone when we get back?"

He closes his notebook. "I thought we'd use the standard 'met on vacation, fell madly for each other, got married while very drunk one night, will live happily ever after.'"

"Right, but what night did we get married? Who married us? How come we didn't get it annulled when we woke up the next morning?"

Jack's eyes grow wide.

"I know I sound nuts, but I also know my best friend, and she's going to be asking these questions. We need to have a detailed story."

"Why's she going to be so curious?"

"Because she's a girl, because this whole thing's really not like me, because she's a lawyer. Take your pick."

"All right. Let's see . . . we'll say we met on the first night here, spent hours talking, had a good connection. We went out to a club and ended up making out on the dance floor, after I rescued you from a punk-ass twenty-two-year-old who was all over you. You wanted to jump me, but me being the gentleman I am, I turned you down and told you there was plenty of time for that."

Jack just manages to dodge the swizzle stick I throw at him.

"We spent the next day and each day after that talking all day and kissing all night . . . and on our second-to-last night here, we had a long, romantic dinner where several bottles of wine were consumed." He snaps his fingers rapidly three times.

"And later, suitably liquored, we stumbled into somebody else's wedding and decided to pull a Britney Spears and Jason Alexander. We woke up with sore heads but happy hearts and agreed to give it a go. I think that about covers it. What do you think?"

"I think I'm glad I'm not your mother dealing with you as a teenager. Tell me, how did you know the name of Britney Spears's first husband?"

"I've told you a million times, I have—"

"An enormous brain. Yeah, yeah. Okay, that's our story, but I think it's more believable if you were the one all over me on the dance floor."

"What about that twenty-two-year-old I had to peel you away from?"

"That's not jealousy I hear, is it?"

"I'll never tell." He lies back in his chair and closes his eyes.

A few minutes later, Margaret wanders over to my deck chair. She's jettisoned the top of her bathing suit once again, and her hair is in beaded cornrows. Her breasts lie long and flat against her skin, bright white in contrast to the tan she's accumulated over the last week.

Jack returns her vague hello with a perfunctory "hi," mutters something about needing a beer, and leaves.

"Can you believe the week is already up?" she asks. "Brian was just saying how fast it's all gone."

"Are things going well? He seems so quiet."

"He's not when he's alone with me. I think Jack intimidates him."

"Really? Why?"

"He's so sarcastic."

"He is?"

"Very."

"What are you doing on your last night?"

"Not sure. Maybe we'll have sex."

A snort escapes me before I can stop it. "That sounds like a good idea."

"I wonder if it'll be any good."

"Um . . ."

"I really like him, you know?"

"I'm glad. Tell me, have you thought about what you're going to do when you get home? How you're going to tell your family and friends about this?"

"I'll probably just tell them the truth."

"Doesn't Blythe and Company insist on secrecy?"

"Who cares? I'm not lying to my family, especially not my kid." Her voice turns fiercely protective. "Besides, my sister already knows."

"Couldn't you get in trouble?"

"How could I get in trouble?"

"I don't know, maybe they'll kick you out of the program or something." I feel my intelligence slipping away, as it always does when it comes to Blythe & Company.

"Anne, we're married. They found us a match. They've already done everything they can for us. Hey, have you got a piece of paper?"

"What for?"

"I want to give you my email address. So we can keep in touch."

Do I want to keep in touch with Margaret? I'm pretty sure Jack doesn't. But it's only email.

"Yeah, okay, hold on." I spy Jack's notebook lying on his deck chair. I rip out a clean sheet, take his pen, and scribble my email address on it. I hand it to Margaret. "Here."

"Thanks." She writes her email address on the bottom, rips it off, and hands it to me. "You looking forward to going home?"

Sarah's sure-to-be-shocked face flashes before my eyes. "I guess . . ."

"I sure am. Things seem good with you and Jack. Am I right?"

"Yeah. It seems to be working out."

"That's great. I'll see you around?"

"Bye."

She wanders off. A moment or two after she leaves, Jack comes back with a beer in each hand.

I shade my eyes with my hand. "Were you just waiting for her to leave?"

"How well you know me already."

"She's not that bad. In fact, I kind of like her."

"You're a very tolerant woman." He looks at the notebook paper with Margaret's handwriting in my hand. "What's that?"

"We exchanged email addresses. I tore a page out of your notebook. I hope you don't mind."

"I kind of do, actually."

"It was only the last page. What's the big deal?"

He sits on his chair silently, sipping his beer. "Here's the thing. The only thing I'm really private about is my writing. I don't let anyone see it, not even a little bit, before it's finished. So I guess I'm asking you not to touch this or any of my notebooks. I know it sounds crazy, but it's kind of a compulsion, and it's pretty important to me." He gives me a big smile, trying to diffuse the awkwardness of what he just said.

I feel myself getting mad, and a little jealous, that he wants to keep something from me. Then again, I might have things I want to keep private too. What he's saying isn't unreasonable.

"Okay, Jack. I'm sorry."

"No, I'm sorry for being such an asshole."

"You're not an asshole."

"I'm keeping that one for later."

"Margaret says that Brian thinks you're sarcastic and that you intimidate him."

"Do you think that?"

"No."

"That's all that matters." Jack glances at his watch. "I'm getting hungry. Ready to go?"

I look around me at the sunburned guests sitting in the blue deck chairs. A waitress is weaving among them, carrying a tray full of drinks. It rests heavily on her shoulder. A large woman in one of those faux-slim-girl T-shirts lights a cigarette and waves the smoke away with her hand. Above it all, the sun shines brightly, ruthless.

I turn back to Jack. This man I met a week ago. My lover. My friend. My husband.

"Lead the way."

# PART THREE

# Chapter 17
## Crickets

Our flight gets in after seven. We wait half an hour for a customs official to stamp our passports, then collect our luggage and take a cab to my place. After a quick tour of the apartment—this is where I eat, this is where I write, this is where I watch too much TV—we order in Chinese food and spend the rest of the night in my bed.

I'm awakened the next day by Jack gently shaking my shoulder.

"Wake up, sleepyhead!"

I poke my head out from under the covers. Jack is dressed in grubby jeans and a faded T-shirt.

"What?"

"It's nine. Time to get up."

I pull the covers back up. "I thought you said you're a late riser."

"I said I write in the afternoons. I reserve my mornings for torturing the woman I'm sleeping with."

"Nice. I didn't get much sleep last night, you know."

"Can I help it if I'm a godlike lover?"

I pull the covers back down, giving him an incredulous look. "Godlike? That's pushing it."

"Okay, who's my competition?"

I make a face.

"Strike that, I don't want to know."

"What's the hurry, anyway?"

"I want to move my stuff in today. We have to pick up the U-Haul in an hour."

"When the hell did you reserve that?"

He looks sheepish. "I booked it online at the resort after we agreed . . . after you said I could move in here."

"How much stuff are you bringing?" I look around the bedroom at the furniture I rearranged until it was just right.

"Don't worry. Most of my furniture's crap. I'll only bring my clothes, my typewriter, my leather club chair, my books, and my flat-screen."

"You write on a typewriter?"

"I highly recommend it. The sound effects alone are worth it."

Freaky.

"I was saying that very thing recently."

"So you understand. Anyway, let's get this show on the road."

I get up, shower quickly, and get dressed in old jeans and a ratty sweatshirt. The sight of my cell phone sitting on the dresser reminds me that I haven't checked my voice mail in a week. I dial in for my messages. I have a couple from work and one from Sarah.

"Anne-girl. Where are you? Aren't you getting back tonight? Hope you had an awesome time in Mexico! I want to hear all about this man you may have met. Thought we might have drinks with Mike tonight at the bar. I'm on my cell. Call me."

I erase Sarah's message while chewing my lip. "Jack?"

He pops his head through the door. "What's up?"

"You up for meeting my best friend tonight?"

"Is this the best friend who's going to be asking for all the gory details?"

"The very one."

"Do you think that's a good idea?"

"I'm going to have to face her eventually. I want to get it over with."

He mulls it over. "Yeah, okay. You ready to go?"

"Let me make a call first." I dial Sarah's number and get her voice mail. "Hey, Sarah-girl. I'm back. Sorry I didn't call you last night; I was tired. Anyway, meeting for drinks sounds great. I have some news about the man. His name's Jack. Um, anyway, he's going to come tonight, so you can meet him. Maybe we can meet alone first? How about seven-thirty? Text me to let me know. I've got a bunch of shit to get done today. Love ya."

I hang up and stare at my phone. Sarah's not going to take this well. Well, there's not much I can do about that now.

"You ready, babe?"

"Ready."

• • •

We spend a large part of the day moving Jack's possessions out of his apartment and into mine. Thankfully, the nearly-March weather cooperates. The sun shines weakly as we hastily pack his books into boxes and his clothes into garbage bags. He was right about the state of his furniture—it's left over from someone else's college days. We leave it for whoever ends up taking over the lease on his apartment.

"Do you think it's going to take long to sublet this place?"

"I've already gotten five offers since I posted it on craigslist."

I look around the 650-square-foot studio apartment. There are large squares of dust where Jack's club chair and flat-screen used to reside. The one window gives onto a brick wall and could use a good Windexing. Without Jack's framed movie posters on the walls, it feels claustrophobic and abandoned.

"Is the real estate market really that tight?"

"Nah, I just write awesome descriptions. 'Real estate gem, original details, steps from everything you need to live your bachelor existence. Act now!'"

"Confident man."

"You know it." He kisses my forehead and tapes the last box shut.

We find a parking place for the U-Haul steps from my front door. I clear out a few drawers in my dresser and make some room in the closet, creating piles of clothes to give to charity. Jack reinforces the wall in the living room with a two-by-four so it can hold his flat-screen and speakers. I'm not sure how

I feel about having a giant television take up half my living room wall, but I know I can't keep things exactly the way I like them if this marriage is going to work.

Around four, we face a crisis regarding our respective book collections. Jack neglected to mention that he has about twenty boxes of books, which are definitely not going to fit into my already overloaded bookshelves.

"I don't see why we need two copies of anything," I say, holding up his copy of Donna Tartt's *The Secret History*.

"But that's my copy. It has my notes."

"Your notes?"

"Thoughts I get when I'm reading something. I like to keep them."

"For what?"

"I just like knowing they're around."

"I guess I could get rid of my copy."

He frowns. "Is that a book you want to reread at some point?"

"Yes, why?"

"I don't really like people reading the notes I make."

"Is this like your notebook/writing thing?"

"Kind of."

"There goes that solution out the window."

He stares at the wall behind the quasi-creepy couch. "Why don't I build shelves to cover this whole wall here, and we'll have plenty of room."

"Build shelves?"

"Sure. I took some woodworking classes. I know what I'm doing."

"What do we do in the meantime?"

"I'll put them here in the corner. I'll start on the shelves next week."

I watch him stack several boxes. "Um, Jack?"

"Yeah?"

"Do you only want to keep your books separate in case this doesn't work out?"

He walks over to me and puts his hands on my shoulders. "Where's this coming from, Anne?"

"I don't know. Reality hitting, I guess. I think I'm nervous about telling Sarah."

"Having second thoughts?"

"Noooo . . ."

"That fills me with confidence."

"All this just happened so fast, and here you are, moving your stuff in, and the last time I lived with someone, it didn't go very well."

"Anne, it's just stuff. It took me a few hours to move it in, and it would take me a few hours to move it out. Things are good. Let's not Dr. Szwick this to death, okay?"

I meet his eyes. They're filled with assurance. "Yeah, okay."

"Good." He ruffles my hair. "You're filthy. Why don't you hop in the shower and I'll fix us some drinks."

"Good idea. You'll be nice to Sarah, right?"

"Of course."

"I want her to like you."

"And I want to like her. C'mon, enough. Shower."

• • •

I arrive at the bar twenty minutes early, beating Sarah there for once. I sit at a table for four, facing the door so I can see her come in. I made Jack promise to show up no later than eight, which gives me half an hour to spill the beans. I do better with deadlines.

I order a beer from the waitress and sit there sipping it, trying to stifle my nerves. Every few minutes I take off and then put back on the rings Jack gave me.

Sarah walks through the door fifteen minutes later, wearing a belted trench coat over a tight pair of jeans and knee-high boots. She's holding her BlackBerry to her ear. I can tell by the tense set of her shoulders that she doesn't like what she's hearing. I slip my hands under the table and take off my rings, shoving them in my pocket.

She ends her call with a curt "Later" and says to me, "Hey! You look great. You actually got a tan."

"Miracles do happen. How're things?"

She drapes her coat over the back of her chair. "Busy, busy, busy. Planning a wedding is a full-time job, but I think I've finally gotten everything under control. How was Mexico?"

"Mexico was—"

The waitress comes to our table and takes Sarah's drink order. When she leaves, Sarah looks at me expectantly. I take a deep breath and start again. "Mexico was great. Beautiful weather, beautiful ocean, beautiful beaches."

"Who cares about that, silly? Tell me about this man you met. How come you never called me back?"

"I was so busy relaxing, I forgot."

"Yeah, right."

"Okay, okay. His name's Jack. He's a writer. He's smart and nice. I don't know. What else do you want to know?"

"Uh, everything!"

"I told him you'd want to know everything."

"Of course I would. But why were you talking about what I'd want to know?"

Oops.

"No reason. I was just telling him that my best friend is a very curious person and always wants to know all the details about my life."

"Is that a bad thing?"

"Of course not."

"So, tell me everything."

I think back to the story Jack invented on the deck chairs. I can almost taste the salty-sweet tang of margarita on my tongue, the force of the sun on my skin. "We met the night I got there. We got to talking and really hit it off. We sort of started spending all our time together, and um, he's great, and smart . . . I told you he was smart, right? Right, I did. So, where was I?"

A furrow appears between Sarah's eyes. "Anne, what's up? You're acting funny."

I gulp. "I'm just really nervous."

"Why?"

"Because something kind of huge happened, and I'm worried about how you're going to react."

"What, did you sleep with him on the first night? I know you think I'm uptight about that kind of stuff, but it's just for myself, really. It's okay if you did. I'm not going to judge you."

"No, that's not it. I mean, I did sleep with him, but not the first night."

"What's the big deal? It's not like you got married, right?" I remain silent. She stares at me in disbelief. "What? You what? Anne, this isn't funny."

I clear my throat. "We did get married."

The color drains from her face. "You're joking."

"No, I'm not. We did."

"Jesus." She picks up her martini glass and takes a long drink. She looks unhappy and upset. "What the hell, Anne? What were you thinking?"

"We were, uh, kind of drunk. But not *that* drunk. It's really romantic, in a way. We stumbled into this other couple's wedding, and the minister jokingly asked us if we needed his services, and we sort of looked at each other, and next thing we knew, we were getting married."

"You got married while you were drunk? Well, we can use that. Right, okay. I can put you in touch with a guy I know. He's handled these kinds of things before. If you were drunk, it'll be much easier."

"Much easier to do what?"

"Get the marriage annulled. If it was even legal in the first place. I'm not sure what the law is in Mexico, but I can find out." Sarah pulls out her BlackBerry and starts scrolling through her contacts.

"Sarah." She doesn't look up. "Sarah."

"What?"

"I'm not getting the marriage annulled. We decided we're going to make a go of it."

Her head snaps up. "What? Are you crazy?"

And you don't even know the half of it.

"No," I say in a small voice.

"If you don't get it annulled now, you'll have to get divorced later. Annulments generally work only if you apply close to the beginning of the marriage."

"So I'll get divorced. Or maybe it'll work out."

Sarah gives me a hard look. "Be serious, Anne."

"I *am* being serious. Jack moved his stuff in today."

"Christ." She slumps in her seat, looking defeated.

"Look, I know this is a shock. I'm kind of in shock too. But I think I might've done a good thing. I think it might work out. But I need your support. I need you to back me up."

"I'm not sure I can do that."

"Why not?"

"I wouldn't want you to support me if I were doing something stupid."

"How do you know it's stupid?"

"Anne, come on."

I can feel my anger rising. "What if I thought Mike was a creep? Would you seriously want me to tell you that?"

"Yeah, I would. That's why I told you about your ex-asshole's extracurricular activities, if you remember. You think Mike's a creep?"

"No, Mike's great. What happened with Stuart was different. That's more than not liking someone. And you stuck by me when I was with him, even though you didn't like him. We were sitting right here, remember, the night we broke up, and you told me you'd kept your feelings about him to yourself because you thought it was better if I had someone in my corner looking out for me. And that's what I need, Sarah. Someone in my corner."

Sarah smiles ruefully. "How can I argue against you when you quote me to me?"

"Really?"

"Yeah, I guess. But I'm concerned, Anne. I know you've been feeling down and lost, but latching on to the first man who comes along isn't a solution to your problems."

Ouch.

"I know it seems like that's what I'm doing, Sarah, but it's really not. Can you just meet him and see? He's really different from the other men I've been with."

She looks skeptical. "How so?"

"For one thing, he doesn't have black hair and blue eyes."

"That's progress, I guess. Tell me more."

"I don't know. I feel like . . . this is the first time I've been with someone I can really be friends with. And I think he feels the same way."

"Friends, huh?" she says sarcastically.

"Yes, friends. He's a great guy, Sarah. I'm really lucky." I reach into my pocket and pull out my rings. "Look, he bought these for me."

She touches the ring with the blue stone, looking the opposite of how I know I looked when I saw her engagement ring.

"Are you sure he's different from the other guys you've been with?"

"Yes, I'm sure. You'll see."

"This is just really hard to accept."

"I know. And I love you for being concerned. But can you reserve judgment until you've given him a chance?"

"I'll try. But tell me. Do you honestly think you love this guy?"

Jack walks through the front door with Mike right behind him. I feel a rush of warmth when I see his freshly shaved chin above his worn bomber jacket.

I wave to them both, and they realize on the way to us that they're coming to the same table. They exchange names and a handshake. The simple greetings of men.

"Sarah, this is Jack Harmer."

She gives him a once-over and frowns. "Hi, Jack."

"Nice to meet you, Sarah." He gives her his widest grin. She softens slightly.

Jack sits down next to me, and Mike sits next to Sarah. They order beers from the waitress. We all look at one another awkwardly.

"Mike, Jack and Anne got married in Mexico," Sarah says into the silence.

Mike doesn't know where to look. "Oh."

"It's okay to freak out, Mike," I say. "Sarah just did."

He smiles. "Thanks. I was wondering what the appropriate reaction was."

"Shock and awe, I think," quips Sarah.

"Not as bad as the bombing of Baghdad, surely?" Jack says.

"I don't know about that." Her frown is back. "It is kind of *the* conversation ender, isn't it? I mean, you could stop any conversation in its tracks by saying, 'I got married to a stranger a few days after we met in Mexico.' Guaranteed crickets every time."

"I'd have thought it was a conversation starter, really. Think of the ink spilled every time a celebrity does it." Jack gives her his big smile again, but it doesn't work this time.

"You and Anne aren't celebrities."

"True. And you aren't lying unconscious in a pool of your own blood."

"I don't follow."

"No bombs here. No permanent wounds either."

"Touché." She turns to me. "He has a conditional pass. For now."

Mike tips his glass at Jack. "You got off lightly, buddy."

Jack takes a long drink from his beer. "Doesn't feel like it."

"You should see what she does to people in court."

"I can imagine."

"Shall we order?" I ask, my stomach rumbling now that the tension's dissipated.

Everyone agrees. We summon the waitress and place our orders.

"So, Jack. Tell me how you convinced my best friend to marry you."

Jack catches my eye across the table. I mouth, "I told you so."

A wicked grin plays across his face. "Actually, it was her idea . . ."


We're in the bathroom, later, brushing our teeth.

"One down and three to go," I say around my tooth-brush.

"Three?"

"William. My brother. My parents."

"Can't you combine your brother and your parents?"

"Maybe. What about you? When do you start telling your side?"

Jack spits into the sink. "No parents to tell, as you know, and my best friend's on some six-month around-the-world odyssey, and I don't think this is the kind of news you drop in an email."

"What about that guy you were telling me about? Your editor?"

"We don't have that kind of relationship."

"He sounded to me like a father figure."

"Only if father figures come in verbally abusive packages.

He's more like one of those teachers who get excellence out of their students through fear."

He rinses his mouth and pulls me toward him. He looks boyish and cute in his white T-shirt and boxers. He starts kissing my neck.

"Don't you have any other friends?"

"Sure I do. Drinking buddies, mostly. I'll tell them the next time I see them. No big deal."

"You think I'm being too melodramatic about all of this?"

"No, I think you're being a girl. Girls need to talk things over and analyze them. Nothing wrong with that. It's just not a guy thing. Take Mike's reaction tonight. Good guy, by the way. Anyway, his response was 'Oh.' That about sums up what I think most of my friends will say."

"And the battle of the sexes rages on."

"I was hoping for a meeting of the sexes, actually."

I touch my nose to his. "Oh, you were, were you?"

He rubs his nose across mine. "Yes. Yes, I was."

Back at work on Monday morning, I go through a week's worth of email and organize my calendar of deadlines for the week. I get a phone call from Dr. Szwick's assistant early in the day to schedule our first couples therapy appointment for Friday afternoon. When the Fashion Nazi leaves for a meeting, I call Gilbert.

"*Hola*, Cordelia, welcome back," he says.

"Hey, Gil."

"How was your trip?"

"Pretty good."

"So much detail."

"What do you want to know?"

"Attend any wild parties?"

"It wasn't spring break."

"Could've fooled me."

I toy nervously with the telephone cord. "Listen, Gil, I have some news."

"What's up?"

"I, um, met someone in Mexico."

"And you're finally coming out of the closet?"

"Gilbert!"

"Sorry, sorry. You were saying?"

"Right, well, I met someone, his name's Jack, and um, well, *wegotmarried.*" It comes out all in a rush.

"Pardon?"

"We got married."

There's complete silence on the line.

"Gil? You still there?"

Gilbert whistles into the phone. "Mom and Dad are going to freak out."

"I know."

"How did this happen?"

"How do you think? A guy asked us some questions, and we said 'yes.'"

"You know what I mean."

"I don't know. It's all a bit of a blur."

"Ah, I see. A margarita ceremony."

"Something like that."

"I know a good guy who can work this out for you."

"God, Gil, that's just what Sarah said. I'm not calling you for that. I'm not getting the marriage annulled. He moved in, and we're giving it a go."

"Relax. Just trying to protect my little sis."

"Thanks."

"This is crazy."

"I know. I want you guys to meet him, though. Will you?"

"Let me call Cathy and we'll set something up."

"Thanks, Gil."

"No *problemo.*"

"I was wondering if maybe you could do something else for me?"

"What?"

"Tell Mom and Dad?"

He laughs, a deep belly laugh. "No way. Though I absolutely want to be there when you do."

"Maybe I'll just wait until the next major holiday."

"Chicken."

"Like you'd be so brave if *you* had to tell them you'd gotten married to someone you met on vacation."

"Excuse me?" I look up. William is standing at the edge of my cubicle, two shades lighter than normal.

"Gil, I've gotta go. I'll call you later to set up dinner."

William slumps down in my visitor's chair and stares at me, round-eyed.

"I guess you heard my conversation with Gil?"

He nods slowly.

"So you heard me say I got married?"

He nods again.

"Come on, William. It's not that surprising, is it?"

"Define 'surprising.'"

"Something that's totally astonishing, astounding, or startling."

He makes check marks in the air with his index finger. "Tick, tick, tick."

"Interesting to know your friends think it's impossible for you to do something you have, in fact, done."

"How did this happen, Anne? I told you to relax and have fun, but I never dreamed—"

"I did relax, and I did have fun. I also met a great guy and, well . . . it's a funny story, if you want to hear it."

I fill him in on the agreed-upon details. It feels a little more real each time I say it. William listens without interrupting, likely because he's too gob-smacked to speak.

"I still can't believe it."

"It's true, I assure you."

"When do I get to meet him and find out if he's good enough for you?"

"He's good enough."

Jack turns the corner to my cubicle. "I hope so," he says.

He's wearing a pair of jeans that fit him really well, and his hair's mussed in a good way above a worn blue Oxford shirt. He extends his hand. "You must be William. Nice to meet you."

William stands and they shake hands.

"So you're the man who convinced little orphan Annie to settle down?"

"She didn't need that much convincing, really. Only four or five cocktails."

William gives him a hard look. "She does have a weakness for cocktails."

"I've noticed."

"A gentleman wouldn't take advantage of that weakness."

"Are you challenging my honor?"

"No, defending Anne's."

"All right, then. Will it be pistols or swords?"

William's lips start to twitch. "Oh, pistols, I think."

"Have you met Sarah, by any chance?"

"Of course. Lovely woman."

"I think you'd give her a run for her money."

William's face breaks into a broad grin. "All right, A.B. Maybe you've only gone half mad. I'll leave you two kids alone."

"What brings you by?" I say to Jack after William has gone.

"I was sitting at home trying to write, and I thought, I haven't been raked over the coals by one of Anne's friends yet today." I stand and take a swat at him, which he ducks. "I thought we might go for lunch."

"Sounds great."

"Anyone else I should know about before we leave the safety of your lovely cubicle here?"

"None comes to mind."

"Phew."

I kiss him on the cheek. "You handled yourself very well."

"Thank you, m'lady."

# Chapter 18
## Good Share

We spend the rest of the week settling into the routine of living together. I go to work, Jack meets me for lunch, I go back to work, I come home, we order in and spend the night in bed. I haven't had a decent night's sleep since I went to Mexico, and I'm starting to feel the effects.

I'm especially tired this morning. My complete lack of inspiration for the article I'm writing—on a raging city wide debate about whether natural-grass soccer fields should be replaced by artificial turf—isn't helping.

My phone rings. I tuck the receiver between my ear and my shoulder. "Yello."

"I've figured it out."

"You figured what out, Sarah?"

"Why you married Jack."

The Fashion Nazi walks by, her four-inch stilettos clipping against her heels. With disdain, she takes in my black dress pants and badly pressed shirt. I give her a fake smile and speak as quietly as I can. "I already told you why I married Jack."

She sighs. "Yeah, right, but I think I know what's really going on."

How can she? "Okay . . ."

"I've been mulling it over a lot this week, and I think it might be kind of my fault."

"Your fault?"

"Not my *fault* exactly, but because I'm getting married, you were feeling left out and jealous, so you went and got married."

Her words hit me like a punch to the stomach. "Excuse me?"

"I know this sounds really self-involved, but I think if you examine your actions since I told you I was getting married, you'll see I'm right."

I try to control my voice. "What actions in particular are you talking about, Sarah?"

She hesitates. "Just the one, really, but it's a pretty big one, don't you think?"

"Of course it's a big one. But I really don't see how it's connected to you."

"You don't? I get engaged, and within a few months you've gone off on some last-minute vacation and married the first man you met there? It's obvious, isn't it? He even looks a bit like Mike."

"What?"

"I said he looks a bit like Mike."

"Sarah, what the fuck are you talking about?"

"Shit, you're mad, right? I knew you'd be mad."

"How did you expect me to react? You call me at work to tell me that one of the biggest decisions I've made in my life is just some jealous reaction to something going on in *your* life, and to top it all off, I'm looking for a man exactly like *your* man. Hey, maybe you even think what I really want *is* your man."

"I've never thought that, Anne, not for a minute. That's not fair."

"What's not fair is being ambushed with this phone call."

"I'm sorry, okay? You know I sometimes speak before I think."

"No, you don't. You always mean exactly what you say, and you always think before you say it."

"Maybe you're right, but I didn't mean to hurt you."

"Sarah, listen to me carefully. I'm not looking for an explanation for why I did this. I'm not looking for a way out. I'm just looking for some support from my friends—or the people I thought were my friends."

"Anne, please. I'm sorry." She sounds uncharacteristically on the verge of tears, which makes my own eyes start to water.

I clear my throat. "I can't do this right now, Sarah. I've got a deadline."

I hang up before she has a chance to say anything more. I wipe my tears away angrily. Fuck, fuck, fuck! Why'd she have to tell me that? Why can't she just let me try to be happy, like she is?

Why does she always have to be so goddamn right?

...

I meet Jack later that day in the lobby of the Telephone Tower for our first post-Mexico therapy appointment.

Jack kisses me on the cheek and gives me a look. "What's the matter?"

I blink rapidly to stop my tears. "I just had a big fight with Sarah."

"About?"

"You, me, us."

"I thought she backed down the other night."

"Nah. She's just gotten started."

"What did she say?"

"I'll tell you later."

He takes my hand and squeezes it. "I'm sorry."

"Yeah, me too. Anyway, we should get up there."

We take the elevator to Dr. Szwick's office. He's left the curtains open. The room feels less cozy with the March rain streaking against the windows.

Dr. Szwick turns to a fresh page in his notebook. "So, Jack, Anne, how are you adjusting to married life?"

"It's going well, I think. Jack moved his stuff in on the weekend," I tell him.

"Ah. The merging of the stuff. Always a tense moment. How did it go?"

"Pretty well. Jack didn't bring much except his enormous book collection."

"Hey, we both have a lot of books," Jack says defensively.

I smile at him to show I was teasing. "We do."

"I'm building shelves. I bought the materials today."

Dr. Szwick nods at Jack like he's a good little boy, then turns back to me. "In Mexico, you seemed reluctant to have Jack in your space. Any second thoughts?"

"I'm adjusting."

"What does that mean, Anne?"

Can't this guy ever let anything slide?

"It means it's an adjustment, but on the whole, I'm happy Jack's there."

"It's all right if you're not happy he's there."

"I know."

"What about you, Jack? Does it bother you that Anne was reluctant to let you move in?"

He flattens his palms on his thighs. "No."

"Come on, Jack. Not even a little?"

"I understand where she's coming from."

"Because you feel the same way?"

"Isn't it normal to feel a little crowded after moving in with someone?"

"Of course it is. But that doesn't answer my question. Do *you* feel crowded?"

Jack gives him a tight smile. "Not really. Anne's gone all day, so I can write. In fact, I've set up my own writing corner, a room of my own . . ."

"We're not on *Oprah*, Jack," Dr. Szwick says.

"It's fine, I promise. Cross my heart and hope to die. Can we move on?"

"All right, but we'll come back to this. How has telling your family and friends gone? Anne?"

"My brother took it pretty well. I haven't told my parents yet, but I've told my closest friends."

"And?"

I take a deep breath, trying to quell the sting of Sarah's words. "My best friend tried to convince me to get an annulment, and today she told me she thought I got married because I was jealous of her."

"Is that why you were so upset earlier?" Jack asks.

"Yes."

Dr. Szwick flips through the notebook, searching for something. "Ah, yes. We've spoken about this before. You called Blythe and Company right after she told you she was engaged, correct?"

"Yes, but . . ."

"But what, Anne?"

"I didn't know what Blythe and Company did when I called. I was looking for a date, not a husband."

"Weren't you? Or was it simply a coincidence that you were willing to go along with the process once you learned what Blythe and Company was about?"

Both Jack and Dr. Szwick watch me, waiting for my answer. "I don't know. Maybe. It *is* why I decided to call the service, but not in the way Sarah means. She thinks I married the first man who'd have me because I couldn't bear to be alone. It wasn't like that."

"Are you feeling resentful that you have to let her think you married Jack on a whim?"

"Yeah, maybe."

"It's difficult, I know, but are you prepared to let her be mad at you, and maybe misperceive your actions, in order to keep up the facade?"

"I guess. If you think it's necessary."

"It is."

"Why is that again?" Jack asks.

"We've found that it's the best formula. As difficult as it is to ask your family and friends to accept that you've done something they see as impulsive, they can relate to it on some level if they think you were caught up in the romance of it all. That people would choose to forgo romantic love for a deep friendship is a much harder sell, believe me."

Jack doesn't look convinced. "If you say so."

"I do. Anne, do you think you can repair things with . . . What's your friend's name?"

"Sarah."

"Sarah. Can you talk things out? Do you have that kind of relationship?"

"I thought we did."

He looks sympathetic. "Give her time, Anne. This is a big adjustment for everyone."

"Right."

"And you, Jack, how has telling your friends been?"

"I haven't told anyone yet."

"Why not?"

He shrugs. "No one to tell, really."

"I find that very hard to believe. You know, this will all

remain make-believe if you don't put it out into the real world."

"It feels pretty real to me."

Dr. Szwick drags his hand across his chin. "Tell me: Why do you keep putting up barriers in here?"

"I don't."

"Yes, you do. You have from the very beginning. And this behavior can and will create walls between you and Anne. We need to work on it and stop it before it becomes a problem." He looks back and forth between us, thinking something over. "For our next session, Jack, I want you to find two people to tell. I don't want any excuses about why you couldn't get it done. All right?"

Jack nods curtly.

"I'll see you next week."

"Class dismissed," Jack mutters.


"How about we go on an adventure?" Jack asks as we drive to Gil and Cathy's house in his beat-up Jeep the following Thursday. We're caught in the snarl of rush-hour traffic. Jack's knuckles are white against the steering wheel as we inch along the expressway. I keep switching the radio between the classic-rock station Jack favors and the top-forty station I usually listen to. Match quotient 8 doesn't extend to song choices, apparently.

"Why the hell does anyone live out here?" Jack asks.

"Backyards. Block parties. Street hockey."

"Those things are overrated."

We exit the freeway near the train station and roll along the service road past a row of small boxy houses built in the fifties. The sun is approaching the horizon. A few leftover Christmas lights twinkle from front porches and bushes.

"Take this next left. What kind of adventure were you thinking about?"

"Have you ever been white-water rafting?"

"White-water rafting? Going down a raging river in a raft?" My voice is all squeaky.

"Yeah," he says enthusiastically.

"I've never felt the need. Turn here."

"Well?"

"Isn't it dangerous?"

"Not in the least."

Near my brother's house, I spy a space between two SUVs and point it out. "Isn't it a little early in the year to be on a river? It'll be freezing."

"The course opens the second week of April, and they have wet suits."

I don't have any more excuses, except "Jack, why are you always trying to kill me?"

He shuts off the loud, knocking engine. "I'm not, I swear. But I like going on adventures. It's a nice break from what I do all day."

"What *do* you do all day?" I tease.

"Sit and stare at a blank page, mostly. So, you want to go?"

We get out of the car and stand facing Cathy and Gil's front walk. I straighten the waist of my skirt. Jack fiddles with his shirt collar.

"When were you thinking?" I ask.

"I called, and they have an opening on the twelfth."

"But that's the day of my book launch!"

"I know. We'll go in the morning and be back in plenty of time for the launch. And before you leave me for your big book tour."

I smile. "It's just a week."

"And it's just a river."

"True enough. Okay, I'll do it."

"Great."

"Ready for tonight?"

He gives me a half grin. "Do I have a choice?"

"Nope."

"Then let's do this thing."

We walk to the front door. Before I can ring the bell, Jane flings it open, jumping up and down.

"Aunty Anne, Aunty Anne! Mommy, Aunty Anne's here!"

I crouch down to hug her hello. She's wearing footie pajamas and smells like she's just come from the bath. She wiggles with excitement in my arms. "Who's that?" she asks into my shoulder.

"This is my friend, Jack. Jack, this is Jane."

He bends down, extending his large hand toward her tiny one. "Hi Jane, I'm Jack."

"Oh, I know who you are. You're Anne's hunnban."

"That's right."

"Who told you that, honey?"

"I heard Daddy telling Grandma and Grandpa."

Great.

"When was that? On the phone?"

"Nah, in the living room."

"In the what?"

"The living room," Gil answers for her as he steps into the hall. He's wearing a gray cashmere sweater, black dress pants, and a gleeful smile. All that's missing is an unlit pipe and an audience to complete his *Our Town* look. "I'm Anne's brother, Gil," he says to Jack, shaking his hand firmly, businesslike. He looks Jack up and down. "You certainly don't look like the right man for Cordelia."

"Gil!"

"I'm the new-and-improved model," Jack tells him.

Gil raises his eyebrows. "I see."

"Gil, are Mom and Dad in the living room right now?" I ask.

He rocks back and forth on his heels. "Yup."

"So when I said I wanted you to tell them, and you said no?"

"Changed my mind."

"And you didn't tell me because . . . ?"

"Much more fun not to."

"What would be more fun, dear?" My mother pokes her head out from the living room. She's wearing a classic pink Chanel suit she inherited from the same aunt who left her the fur coat she wore to my book-deal party. I knew this felt like theater for a reason.

"Anne, what are you doing just standing there in the hall? Come in here. And you, young man, I assume you're Anne's . . . husband." She sniffs the air as if she's trying to smell whether he's a good man.

"Mom, cut out the Rachel Lynde impersonations, please!"

Jack mutters to me, "A character from the *Anne* books, I assume?"

"What else? There's still time to escape," I mutter back.

"It's okay, press on, press on."

I scowl at Gil and follow my mother into the living room. Jane runs back and forth between us, which causes Gil to threaten her with bed. My father is ensconced in Gil's favorite chair, a large Scotch in his hand. He's had a few, judging by the amount of vapors in the room.

I introduce Jack to my parents, and we settle into the love seat underneath the bay window. We sit there, wordlessly staring at one another, until Cathy enters the room. She's wearing a black dress made out of a stretchy fabric that supports her perfect baby bump. Her long blond hair falls loosely down her back.

"What's going on in here? Gil, why haven't you gotten Anne and Jack drinks? They look like they could use one, and so could I." She gives us a big smile. "But since I'm still months away from being allowed to, I'll just look longingly at yours."

Gil guiltily takes our orders and walks to the kitchen to fill them.

Cathy sits on the couch next to my mother and rests her hands on her belly. "So, Jack, tell me about yourself."

"What do you want to know?"

"Where are you from? How did you meet Anne? How did you convince her to marry you? That should do for now. And maybe when you're done, everyone's tongue will have loosened."

Jack steals a glance at me and begins to answer her questions. Cathy listens to him closely as my father nips into his Scotch and my mother affects an air of disinterest while simultaneously listening to every word.

Thank God for Cathy, the most normal of all of us. I catch her eye and mouth, "Thank you."

She shakes her head gently and mouths back, "He's cute."

Three hours later, we're at the front door, trying to escape. Though it's way past her bedtime, Jane is wrapped around Jack's leg. A groggy, awakened Elizabeth is wrapped around mine.

By the time Jack finished answering Cathy's questions, my parents had finally drunk enough to overcome their shyness. Unfortunately. My mother has barely paused for breath in the last two hours, shifting from one story to the next without any pattern, and my father has been asking Jack random questions that rival the ones on the Blythe & Company questionnaire. What was his father's name? What day was he born? Where did he live between the ages of four and six? I finally get him to stop by asking him whether he wants to plot Jack's zodiac charts.

"What? No. I don't even know what that means."

"Why all the bizarre questions, Dad? Why do you care about any of this stuff?"

"Aunty Anne, Aunty Anne, watch me do this flip."

"In a minute, honey."

"How else am I supposed to get to know my son-in-law?"

"Aunty Anne, Aunty Anne, I can flip better than her. Watch me, watch me."

"Girls, please, I'm talking to Grandpa. I don't know, Dad. Like a normal person."

"What's that supposed to mean?"

"That reminds me of when Anne was in choir in the third grade," my mom interjects. "She had the solo, only this other girl, a much worse singer, thought *she* had the solo, and she was about to sing at the same time as Anne, but Anne, such a clever girl, figured out that this girl was about to sing and shushed her and then sang her solo. It was beautiful."

"What's normal? Who's not a normal person?" Dad asks.

I reach down and pry Elizabeth off my leg. "Say good night to Uncle Jack, girls."

"Good night, Uncle Jack," they say together. He gives each of them a kiss on the cheek. They giggle and run away shrieking with delight. Cathy and Gil are in for a long night.

"Bye, Mom, bye, Dad. Thanks, Gil." I shoot him a murderous look, though frankly, I'm glad he did me the favor of telling my parents. Plus, Dr. Szwick will be pleased. An added benefit.

The door closes behind us, and we walk to Jack's car. Away from the city lights, the sky is full of twinkling stars. I search for the North Star, feeling unsteady on my feet.

"You okay to drive?" I ask.

Jack gives me a look. "Better than you."

I stand up straighter. "Hey, it was the only way I could get through the evening."

"And I thought you drank a lot of margaritas in Mexico."

"Bastard."

"I think your father established tonight that I'm definitely *not* a bastard."

We climb into the car. I have trouble doing up my seat belt. Jack takes it from me and clicks it into place.

"Thanks. And sorry about tonight. My parents aren't always that . . . weird."

"Forget it." He starts the engine and backs down the street. "I'll tell you what your punishment is later."

"We'll see. So, did my family scare you off of the whole starting-a-family thing?"

"Your nieces are very cute."

As Jack drives us toward the freeway, I watch the detached four-bedroom houses roll past. We stop at a stop sign. In the house on the corner, the living room is lit up like a stage set, the TV a flickering strobe. Growing up, I always used to imagine what went on behind the curtains of the houses like mine. Could I pick a door and try on a whole new life?

"Have you talked to Sarah yet?" Jack asks softly.

I wince. "No."

"'No' as in 'I'm never talking to her again'? Or 'No' as in 'I haven't had the chance, but I've been meaning to'?"

"Not sure yet. She really hurt me, you know?"

He reaches over and ruffles my hair. "Keep your chin up, kiddo."

"Kiddo?"

"What?"

"Where do you come up with this stuff?"

"I've got a million more where that came from."

"Thanks for coming tonight." I lean in and kiss him on the cheek.

"Anytime."

# Chapter 19
# Ready, Set, Go!

A month passes. I work and hang around with Jack. I make preparations for my book launch and the small book tour I'll be going on afterward. And though I often start to, though I want to, though it's killing me not to, I don't call Sarah. This mix of emotions means I'm having trouble sleeping. I fall asleep easily, tucked into the crook of Jack's arm, but at three A.M. my eyes fly open like clockwork. The only good part is that with all the extra hours I'm getting out of the day, I have more time for writing. But every time I look at the pages the next night, I crumple them up and throw them in the trash.

Tonight I don't even wait that long. Three pages in, I pitch my latest effort toward the metal basket in the corner. I miss.

"I could trip on that, you know," Jack says sleepily from the doorway. His chest looks ghostly in the half light of the floor lamp I'm trying to write by.

"I was going to pick it up. Sorry, did I wake you?"

He yawns and scratches his head. "Nah. I always wake up at four in the morning so I can play bad-story basketball."

"Funny man."

He picks up my pages, smooths them out, and starts to read.

"Hey, no fair reading something I've thrown away. For that matter, no fair reading anything I've written that's not finished."

He sits down next to me. "You're right. But why did you throw it away? It looks okay."

"It's derivative and boring."

"That's a little harsh for the middle of the night, don't you think? Are you always this down on yourself?"

"Only when I'm on five hours' sleep."

"Maybe you should talk to Sarah."

"Maybe you should mind your own business."

He pulls back in surprise.

"Sorry. I don't mean to take it out on you."

He puts his hands on my shoulders, kneading into the hard knots of tension. I close my eyes and concentrate on the warm strength of his fingers.

"Better?" he asks.

"Um, getting there."

He moves his hands along my neck, up my face, to my temples, kneading all the while. "Better now?"

"I'll let you know in a minute."

"If you're this tense, I think there's only one thing that's going to cure you."

I open my eyes and smile. "Oh yeah?"

"Yeah."

"You think you can cure me?"

"I think I can try."

"Try away."

We're driving along a wet, bumpy road an hour past Cathy and Gil's. Through the tall conifers lining the way, I catch a glimpse of the river we'll be hurtling down. It looks wide. It looks deep. It looks fast. It looks full. And most of all, despite the glorious spring day, it looks cold.

"Is it really safe with the river this high?"

Jack glances at me, his eyes hidden behind his sunglasses. I look small and scared in the reflection. "You're not chickening out on me, are you?"

"No, but you know it would really, really suck to die on book-launch day, right?"

"It's safe, I promise you."

We pull into the parking lot next to a log cabin that sits on the side of the glinting black river. There's a group of college kids in board shorts and tank tops playing beach volleyball in a sandpit. A half-dozen women about my age are sitting at two picnic tables, soaking in the sun. Bags of charcoal lie ready next to a barbecue. We go inside the cabin to pay and are handed a release form. Sign on the dotted line, and you have no rights against the rafting company, no matter how negligent. As I read it, I find myself missing Sarah—it's only because of her that I'm trying to read this legalese in the first place.

We sign the forms and are introduced to our guide, Steve. He's an athletic-looking nineteen-year-old with honey-blond hair and a tanned face. He's wearing a red life jacket over a full wet suit. The front of it is unzipped enough to reveal a reassuring set of muscles. He gives us a brief explanation on how to handle ourselves in the boat, then we get outfitted with wet suits, life jackets, and paddles. Jack tightens my life jacket, pulling the straps so snug I don't move at all when he lifts me up by them to test it.

"That'll keep you safe," he says.

"I thought you said it *was* safe."

"It is. Stop worrying."

Fat chance.

We carry the bright yellow raft to the river, which is about fifty feet wide and lined with sharp rocks and green deciduous trees. The water looks blacker up close and smells like powdered rocks, as if it just finished carving out the mountains behind it. I sit in the raft next to Jack, second from the front. Steve pushes us away from the shore and commands us to start paddling. Jack tells me to hook my left foot under the strap running along the bottom, just like in the catamaran in Cancún.

"Oh yeah, that worked out well," I mutter.

"What? You didn't like capsizing?"

"I'm hoping it remains a once-in-a-lifetime experience."

Jack's eyes dart away from mine.

"Jack, why are you making that face?"

He dips his paddle into the river. "What face?"

"Don't change the subject." I think out loud. "Okay, you started making that face when I was talking about capsizing . . . Shit! Are they going to flip the boat?"

"Noooo . . ."

"Jack!"

"The guide flips it when we go down the first rapid," says the man sitting across from me, trying to be helpful.

"Is that true? Jack?"

We're rapidly approaching a patch of foaming white river at the front of a bend. I can't see around it, but I have a sinking feeling I know what's past it. Or what isn't.

"Calm down, Anne. It'll be okay."

"I don't like this . . ."

The boat starts to bump and pitch and roll as the water roils beneath it. We round the bend, and sure enough, the river disappears 250 feet ahead.

"Paddle hard," Steve screams.

"Jack!"

"Paddle hard, Anne, paddle hard," Jack shouts with relish.

I grit my teeth and drive my paddle into the water. My right hand hits the cold river with every stroke. "You're so going to pay for this . . ."

As we plunge over the edge of the rapids, I give up paddling and hold on tight to the side of the raft. Everyone is yelling. I can't tell if the others are screaming with excitement or fear, but I know which camp I'm in.

I glance back at Steve. He has a big grin on his face as he wrestles to keep the boat in the middle of the rapids. And then I see him do it. He deliberately flips the boat by placing his paddle in the water and holding hard against the current.

The raft tips sideways, disgorging us. I try to fling myself clear, but I get caught underneath it as it hurtles down the river.

The shock of cold water pushes the air out of my lungs. I struggle to keep my head above the surface in the air pocket formed by the yellow dome of the raft. I bounce and roll and rock down the bumpy water. There's a loud roar, followed by relative silence as the raft moves into less turbulent water.

The raft is lifted off my head, and I'm pulled into Jack's arms. His face is white with concern. "You okay, Anne?"

My teeth start chattering. "I think so."

"I thought you were done for."

"That's what you get for convincing me to go on adventures. I told you not to try to kill me on book-launch day."

"It'll never happen again."

"Promise?"

"Promise."

I look around me. The river's calmer, and the sun's shining brightly, flashing off the water. The water here feels warmer, less aggressive. I realize that, as scary as flipping was, I'm having fun. I like doing these things with Jack. I kind of *am* an outdoor girl.

"Help me back in?"

"You sure?"

I smile brightly. "Let's have an adventure."


"So you really had fun?"

"I already told you a million times I did."

We're in a cab en route to my book launch, having made it back to the apartment with barely enough time for me to shower, dress, and dry my hair. The nerves I've managed to avoid all day have come back with a vengeance. I slip my hand from Jack's and rest my chin on the edge of the door, watching the traffic.

"Sorry again about the flipping."

"Forget it."

"You nervous?"

"Yeah."

"You'll be fine."

"Maybe you could do the reading for me?"

"I don't think anyone wants to hear me read your book, Anne."

"Probably not."

"Just imagine the crowd naked."

We hit a pothole, and my chin bangs into the doorframe. I rub it, concerned there's going to be a mark. "Does that really work?"

"Search me."

The cab pulls up outside the bookstore. There's a poster in the window with my author photo on it and a blowup of the cover of my book. *Home,* by Anne Blythe. How the hell did that happen?

Inside, there's a woman in her mid-twenties—Shelley, her name tag reads—standing at the counter, looking anxious. I'm ten minutes late. I apologize, and she quickly fills me in on where I'll stand to read, and sit to sign, and stand again to drink and eat appetizers. She leads us up a curved wooden staircase. I can't keep my eyes off all the other books on the shelves, or really believe that mine will be tucked between them soon. In fact, copies of it must already be tucked in here somewhere. Freaky.

Next to the coffee bar, the tables have been cleared away and replaced by folding chairs, a lectern, and a large stack of copies of my novel. I walk to the lectern and wait nervously beside it. Cathy and Gil are sitting in the front row, and Jack takes a seat next to them. My parents are in the row behind. My dad leans forward and starts talking to Jack.

Poor Jack! He's probably being asked for his dental records.

I start as someone hugs me from behind. "Heya, A.B.!" I turn around, and William is beaming at me.

"Thanks for coming," I tell him.

"You kidding? Where else would I be?"

"Drinking?"

"True enough. But the cocktails will wait. There *will* be cocktails, right?"

"Of course."

He sits down with a group of people from work, more people than I expected—even the Fashion Nazi is here. My book editor and publicist are sitting at the back, next to Janey and Nan. Susan sent her regrets. I wave to them, and they wave back excitedly. I try not to look for Sarah, the one person I really want to be here.

Shelley signals to me that it's time to begin. I take a deep breath, step up to the podium, and stare out at the crowd. As my eyes flit from person to person, *I feel naked.*

I clear my throat. "Good evening, everyone. Thanks so much for coming. You have no idea how much it means to me. I wanted to say two things before I read something from my book. And before you all buy two copies."

I pause to cough the nervousness out of my throat. Out of the corner of my eye, I see Sarah and Mike taking seats next to William. Sarah gives me an uneasy smile.

"So, first thing. Writing a book is what I imagine being pregnant must be like. You have an idea of what it's supposed to be like, people tell you what it's like, but you really have no idea. And everyone you tell wants to know all kinds of things about it. What's it called? How big is it? When is it going to be delivered?

"After a while, it becomes all anyone ever asks you about, and you kind of wish you'd never told anyone about it in the first place. It gets bigger and bigger, and you sort of just want it to be over. You want to see what it looks like when it's done. Then it is, and you can't tell if it's beautiful or hideous or somewhere in between. This is probably where this analogy falls apart, but anyway, you show it to your friends, and they tell you it's beautiful. And though you know they're telling you that because they're your friends, it's what gives you the courage to show it to other people. To take a chance. Sometimes that chance pans out, like it did for me.

"So I want to thank the friends who helped me through the pregnancy of this book, but most especially Sarah, who read it more times than I did."

I'm suddenly nervous again. "Okay, second thing. I know

I probably should be telling each of you this individually, but what the hey. For those of you who don't know, I got married recently, and I want to introduce you all to my husband, Jack."

Jack stands up amid a few gasps and a lot of very curious stares, and takes a bow. A few people laugh, and a few people clap.

"All right, enough about me. This is chapter one of *Home*.

"'I know you have a person like this. I do. He broke your heart and you can't forget him. Though you try. And you try. So you wonder about him. Wonder about running into him. How you'll look if and when you do. You want him to want you again. No matter how happy you are with the person you're with, you always wonder what it would've been like if the person who didn't choose you, did. What change would that small thing have wrought? For me it was Ben. We kept in touch for a while after we broke up, and then I lost track of him, or him of me, and so there are important things I don't know about him anymore. Where he lives, who he loves, what he does day to day. But I was always sure I still knew the man underneath the unknown life. Silly that, but there it is. There it is and there it was.'"

"Canapé?"

"Yes, thank you." I take a shrimp roll from the platter and pop it in my mouth. The tangy Asian sauce burns my tongue. I take a large gulp of my white wine, trying to stanch the heat spreading through my mouth.

"Hi," Sarah says. She's wearing one of her blue power-lawyer suits and has her hair pulled back from her face. She looks serious and sad.

"Hi, Sarah."

"It turned out really well."

"My book?"

"The book, your speech. Everything." She waves her hand around the room in a vague way.

"Thanks."

"How've you been?"

"Okay."

"You didn't return my phone calls."

"I know."

"You're not going to cut me any slack, are you?"

"No, I don't think so."

She gives a resigned nod. "I wasn't going to come tonight."

"Why did you?"

"Jack convinced me to."

"Jack?"

"Yeah. He called me. He told me I should be here. He said you'd want me to be."

"I didn't know."

Her voice catches. "I guess he doesn't know you that well, huh?"

She waits for me to say something. And when I don't, she turns to leave.

A glimpse of her sagging shoulders is enough to melt away the little anger I have left. "Sarah, wait. I'm really glad you came. I mean it."

I put my hand on her shoulder, and she turns toward me, relief written on her face. We hug, and I hold her to me tightly. "Maybe the two of us," I say, "can have lunch when I get back?"

She wipes a tear from the corner of her eye. "I'd like that."

"And maybe you can give Jack a chance?"

"At least ten."

"Make it an even dozen, and we have a deal."

Much later that night, after dinner with Sarah, Mike, William, Janey, Nan, Gil, and Cathy, and wine, wine, wine, I'm fumbling with the key to our apartment. On the third try, Jack takes the key from me.

"Here, let me do that." He concentrates and, in a smooth motion, fits the key into the lock. He pushes open the door, straightens up, and gives me a sloppy grin. "See, it was easy. You must be drunk."

I put my arms around his neck. "Why is it so sexy when you do that?"

"Do what?"

"Put a key in a lock. Open a door for me."

"What else is sexy?"

"I don't know. Other manly things?"

He bends down and swoops me up into his arms. "How about this?"

"Definitely."

He carries me over the threshold and into the living room,

putting me down on the couch. He puts my feet in his lap, takes off my heels, and starts massaging my feet. "And this?"

"Oh, yeah."

I enjoy the feel of his fingers working on my feet, ankles, and calves. Then his hands start to work their way up my legs, and I like that feeling even more. Jack scootches over so my legs are draped across his lap and starts to kiss the hollow of my throat.

"Good turnout tonight," Jack mutters between kisses.

"Um-hmm. Hey, I have a bone to pick with you, mister."

I can feel his grin against my skin. "Interesting choice of words."

I push him away. "You called Sarah. You asked her to come tonight."

"I did."

"Why did you do that?"

"Because someone had to." He undoes the buttons on my sweater and leans toward me.

"I'm mad at you."

"No, you're not."

"I might be."

"Hush," he says into my ear.

And so I do.


My head is resting on Jack's chest as he breathes deeply. Moonlight plays on the hardwood floor. Outside, the city hums.

"You asleep?" I ask.

"Pretty much."

"Thanks for calling Sarah."

"Welcome."

"Did you set the alarm?"

He kisses the top of my head. "I'll make sure you get up, don't worry."

"Thank you for today, Jack."

"Anytime."

I let the rise and fall of his chest lull me to sleep. And then, as I'm on the verge of slipping away, I hear myself say, "I love you."

Jack's arms stiffen around me, and I can feel the quickening of his heart. Or maybe it's my own. Those words seem to crash down on me like the cold water in the river this afternoon, and I'm having trouble breathing.

Why did I say that? And what is Jack thinking? Why hasn't he said anything?

This isn't what we agreed to, his silence implies.

Love is not what we agreed to at all.

## Chapter 20
## It All Makes Sense Now

Jack drives me to the airport the next day. We talk of trivial things on the way: my itinerary, how many book signings I'm doing in each city, what we might do on the weekend after I get back. Jack promises to water the plants and plan something adventurous but not too adventurous. He sounds excited and chats away while I chew my nails and look out the window and try not to ask him about what I said last night.

"So you're going to write?" I ask distractedly.

"Yeah, I told you. I'm in a good groove right now."

"Right, sorry. I wasn't listening properly."

"You okay?"

I sit up straighter. "Sure, I'm just preoccupied."

"Nervous?"

"A little."

"Do what you did last night, and you'll be fine."

My heart skips a beat, but he means the book launch, not last night in bed. When I told him I loved him. Stupid, *stupid* thing to say.

He stops the Jeep in front of the sign for the airline I'm flying and puts it in park. We get out, and Jack pulls my suitcase from the back, setting it on the concrete. I check my purse for my ticket, wallet, and cell phone. Everything's where it should be but me.

"You afraid of flying?" Jack asks.

"No."

"You're acting kind of strange."

I'm having trouble looking him in the eye. "I'm just tired."

He places his hands on my shoulders and waits for me to look at him. When I don't, he takes my chin and lifts my face so I don't have a choice.

"What's going on?"

I speak through the enormous lump in my throat. "Nothing."

"Is this about . . . what you said last night?"

So he did hear me. I'd been half hoping he hadn't. That I'd only imagined the rigidity of his body or the implication of his silence.

"Oh, that," I say, and try to laugh. Instead, it sounds like I'm choking. I clear my throat. "I had too much to drink, and old habits die hard, I guess. It didn't mean anything."

"Anne—"

"Just forget I said it." I kiss him hard on the mouth to cover what I'm feeling. If only I knew what it is I'm feeling.

He breaks the kiss. "Will you just listen to me for a second—"

"I'm going to miss my plane."

"Come on, Anne—"

"I can't right now, okay? Can we talk when I get back?"

I smile at him to show him I'll be fine. I can see his indecision.

"Yeah, all right."

"I'll call you tonight."

"Sure. Good luck."

"Thanks."

I grab the plastic handle recessed into the top of my suitcase, and it clicks into place. I pull the suitcase along behind me, clacking over the concrete toward the sliding glass doors.

And when I turn back, Jack's gone.


I spend the next three days talking, smiling, signing my name, and reading the first chapter of my book over and over, until I have it nearly memorized. My state of mind isn't helped by reading aloud the things that make you start falling in love for the first time. Things like the way the wool of a boy's sweater smells. The way you see, just in a flash, how he'll be when he's a man. And the flashes are so short you think you've imagined them. But something between you changes. Some thread connects you, and you both know it's there.

You can feel its pull.

"So how did the day go?" Jack asks during our fourth nightly phone conversation.

I'm lying on the bed in my hotel room with the phone propped under my ear. "Hi, my name is Anne Blythe. What? Yes. That's right. Anne Blythe. Yes, like in the *Anne* books. No,

I'm here to read from my book. Yes, my mother was obsessed. Oh, you too? Yes, it's funny that I have red hair and green eyes. My mother has magical powers. No, my husband's name is not Gilbert, that's my brother. Yes, my mother *is* odd. Right, so, here we go, chapter one."

"Sounds like another excellent day."

"I wanted this, right?"

"This and a lot more."

"I sound like a brat."

"You sound tired."

"I am."

"Why don't you turn in?"

"I'm going to. But first I need something to eat. I'm starving."

"I'll let you go, then." He sounds disappointed.

"Sorry, I'm just really hungry."

"It's okay. I'll talk to you tomorrow. And see you in two days."

"Right. 'Night, Jack."

"'Night, Anne. Sleep well."

I hang up the phone, collect my room key, and go down to the hotel bar to shake off the day. It's one of those English-hunting-scene places, with a mahogany bar and forest-green walls. There's a fire in the fireplace, and the burning-wood smell almost covers up the years of spilled beer and malt whiskey. The room is empty except for a female bartender in a white shirt and black apron. She's wiping down the top of the bar, looking bored, while she listens to the radio. Top-forty, by the sound of it. I decide to sit at the bar rather than at one of the small tables scattered about. They look lonely in a way a seat at the bar doesn't.

I order a pint of Harp and a pastrami sandwich with a dill pickle and open the newspaper I brought with me to pass the time.

"Mind if I sit here?" says a man with a British accent.

"Suit yourself," I reply, glancing sideways at him. He has short black hair and an ordinary profile.

He turns toward me. "Thanks. You eating or just drinking?"

I look into his blue, blue eyes. He might look ordinary in profile, but straight on, he looks like a man who belongs with me. "I'm waiting for a sandwich."

He smiles. His teeth are straight, dazzling. "That sounds just right."

He waves the bartender over and orders a Guinness and a roast beef sandwich. While his attention is diverted, I check out the rest of him. He's wearing a very well-tailored black suit and a still-crisp powder-blue shirt. He's loosened his navy tie at the throat and undone the first two buttons on his shirt, showing just the right amount of dark chest hair.

He turns back to me. "So, what brings—"

"A nice girl like me to a place like this?" I laugh. "You can do better than that!"

"You'd think so, but no, I can't." He laughs along with me, a deep, infectious laugh.

Shit, shit, *shit*.

"I'm on a book tour."

He raises his eyebrows. "Not the answer I was expecting."

"What, you thought maybe I was a lady of the evening?" I'm wearing old, loose jeans and a simple black V-neck sweater.

He shakes his head. "My name's Perry."

"I'm Anne."

The bartender brings our sandwiches. As we eat, Perry tells me about his business trip (client development) and his business (corporate investigations), and I tell him about my book (not his cup of tea, but he listens politely) and the book tour (more interest here), and we spend an easy hour together. Between the bites of pickle and pastrami and the next two beers, I decide he looks most like John, but I can't tell whether that's a good thing or a bad thing. All I know is that the noise in my head has quieted down for the first time all week.

"So," he says as I finish the last dregs of my third pint. Our stools are close enough that his thigh is brushing against mine. We've had this much contact for several minutes, ever since we both moved toward each other at the same moment. "Time for one more drink?"

"I should be getting to bed. I've got another round of signings in the morning." I stand up. My feet feel uneven.

"Steady there." He puts his hands on my shoulders. I feel the heat of his hands through the fabric of my sweater, and I understand the look in his eyes. I might have the same look in mine. Everything seems to slow down in this moment, and I feel hyper-aware. I smell old beer and dust. Christina Aguilera is singing on the radio.

Then something shifts, and I'm hit by a wave of déjà vu. My book-deal party. The way everything—even my skin—

was attracted to Aaron. I check Perry's left hand to see if he's wearing a wedding band. His ring finger is bare, but mine isn't.

"Can I walk you to your room?" he asks.

"Sure."

What the hell am I doing?

"Shall we go?"

I turn to leave, and two steps in, I feel dizzy. "Let me go splash some water on my face first. I'll be right back."

"I'll be right here." He sits back down on his stool, a smile playing on his perfect face.

I walk toward the bathrooms at the back of the bar and push through the swinging door. The music from the radio is piped in through a tinny speaker, and it bounces off the tiles. I turn on the water to wash my hands as Christina holds her last note and the music switches to a mellow guitar. A song about mockingbirds flying away.

I recognize it right away. It's the song Jack and I danced to on our wedding night. The song he sang to me.

I look at myself in the mirror as I let the words wash over me. My face looks strange, like a word you say over and over until you're not sure it's a real word anymore.

My God, my God, what am I doing? Why can't I move past the ridiculous, infantile attraction I have to this particular type of man? I'm not like this. I don't cheat. I don't pick up men in bars. Then again, I don't marry strangers either. Goddammit! What do I want from my life? What do I want from Jack? From my marriage? From this day?

I realize I'm crying, and I wipe the tears away. My hands smell like the soap I just washed them with, and it makes me think of Jack. My hands smell like he smells. His soapy, woodsy smell.

I look at myself in the mirror and face the truth. I know what I've been trying to ignore. What I've been pushing away. What I've been afraid of. Why I've been distracting myself with Perry, being an earlier version of myself.

I love Jack.


I slip past Perry, who's flirting with the bartender in my absence (a backup plan?) and return to my room for a hard hour of self-reflection.

At the end of it, I'm stuck with two things: I love Jack, and that scares the shit out of me.

The love part is easier to understand. I've been in love before. Too many times. And Jack and I fit together in a way I haven't with anyone else. But the fear—where does that come from? Am I worried Jack doesn't love me? No. I know with a quiet certainty that he does. Despite his silence the other night, we think too much alike for us not to feel the same. He was probably even trying to tell me he loved me at the airport, and I was too freaked out to let him. And since then, whenever we've spoken, I've kept him at arm's length.

So what is it? Why am I terrified?

God, I wish I could talk to Sarah. But what could I say? I just realized I'm in love with my husband, and that's freaking me out? It wouldn't take more than five minutes for her to strip away my Blythe & Company facade. And as much as I need to talk this out, I have no desire to expose the way Jack and I met.

Speaking of Blythe & Company, emergency phone sessions with Dr. Szwick should really be included in the ten-thousand-dollar cover charge.

What would Dr. Szwick say if I *could* call him? He wouldn't let me get away with telling myself I don't know why I'm terrified. And shouldn't I be able to do this on my own? Shouldn't I know my own mind by now?

I do. I know why I'm scared of love. It's because that's when it always starts to go wrong. When it starts to deviate from the fairy tale. After the happy ending comes . . . disappointment. I don't think I can stand another disappointment. I did this crazy thing, married a stranger, so I could avoid it, so I could get my happy ending.

So save yourself, Anne. One more time.

In the morning, I call the airline and change my flight so I can leave right after my last signing.

I decide not to tell Jack I'm coming home a day early. I want to surprise him. Surprise him and tell him that I don't take it back, that I love him, that I hope he feels the same way.

After ten anxious/happy hours, I push open our front door and call out his name. "Jack?"

My stomach churns with nerves and longing, but there's no

answer. I try to suppress my disappointment as I walk into the empty living room. Jack has set up a sawhorse in the middle of it, but he's made minimal progress on the shelves. I smile as I look around at the mess, because right now I love even his messiness.

I wheel my suitcase into the bedroom and find more chaos. The bed is unmade, there are clothes all over the floor, and Neil Young is whining through the clock radio. I turn off the radio and look around for some sign of when he'll be back. There isn't anything, because he doesn't know I'm coming home today. I think briefly of calling him until I notice his cell phone sitting on the night table. Damn. I can't even let him know I'm here.

Frustrated, I go back into the living room and sit down at the desk he's set up in the corner to write. His appointment book is sitting there, open to today. He's meeting his editor, Ted, for drinks at five-thirty.

I check my watch. It's six o'clock. He probably won't be home for a while. Maybe I should go meet him at the bar. No, no, that's crazy. Relax, Anne, relax.

I sit on the couch, turn on the TV, and flip through the channels. I can't rest on a channel for longer than ten seconds, and after a few minutes, I realize I'm sitting on something uncomfortable and bulky. I reach under me and find a large stack of paper held together with a clip. I turn it over. It's Jack's work in progress, the one he never lets me read.

Its title makes me feel queasy. With shaking hands, I start reading.

## Married Like Me
## Prologue

I was kicking around my editor's office about six months ago, waiting for the inevitable "So, what's your next project going to be, Jackie, my boy?" It was the only reason he'd ever call me in for a meeting.

Great guy, Ted, but in the years we've worked together, he's assumed a role of parental concern about my career, my general lack of drive, and my revolving door of six-month girlfriends. He also has this unnerving ability to call me at the exact moment when I most need a kick in the ass. And since the final proofs for my book were approved two weeks after Jessica, my last six-monther, demanded her key back with a shrill "Never call me again," I knew it was only a matter of time before Ted started talking about the future.

"Jackson, your presence is required in my office tomorrow at two sharp."

"Yessir, Master Ted."

"Knock it off, Jackass. Be here." He clicked off, on to his next problem child.

He has a stable of about twenty of us. All men. All writers of middling success. All in need of his tough love, without which, according to him, we would never get off our "keisters" and produce anything salable. "And then where would you be?"

"So, Jackson, what's the plan?" Ted said, now that he had me in front of him.

"I've been toying with the idea of doing one of those survivalist adventures where they drop you off in the woods for two weeks sans everything."

"Jesus, Jack. Have you been reading women's magazines for inspiration?"

"What do you mean?" I asked, trying to keep my temper.

"Gwyneth Paltrow just did that for *Vogue.*"

Ted's an insomniac, and he reads—and remembers—everything under the sun. He's also a hub of information: celebrities, quasi-celebrities, people who might be celebrities and even average Joes—chances are Ted knows them or knows something about them.

"What about sending me up McKinley? People keep dying there."

"Isn't it called Denali now?"

"So?"

"Why not Everest, Krakauer wannabe?" He knew he was hitting a nerve, and he was enjoying it. I looked at him sitting smugly at his desk, his feet propped up and his head resting on the back of his chair. I realized I was missing the obvious.

"Why don't you just tell me what my next project's going to be?"

"Finally got there, did you?"

"Looks like."

He brought his feet to the floor and leaned forward with an excited look in his eyes. He asked me if I'd ever heard of Blythe & Company. When I told him no, he asked me to close the door. He had a book idea for me that was going to "knock my fucking socks off." All I had to do was one little thing.

"What's that?" I asked with a hint of trepidation.

He paused dramatically. "Get married."

# Chapter 21
## An Unfinished Project

I read Jack's book all the way through, frozen on the couch, barely breathing, barely thinking.

There are so many shocking things in this book, it's hard to know where to start.

But the highlights:

He uncovered a lot of details about Blythe & Company, details I failed to find in my limited search on the Internet. Details that show me to be either a terrible journalist or a stupid girl looking for a fairy tale. Maybe both. But now, thanks to Jack, I know all about the aging guru couple behind it and their enormous house and Swiss bank accounts. Whether Blythe & Company works or not, is real or not, someone's making a lot of money off it.

Jack also tracked down some of Blythe & Company's former clients. Some were deliriously happy and spoke about the company the way people used to speak about the Peoples Temple. Others ended up poorer, divorced, and bitter. They spoke about the "process" like kids talk about their grades in high school: how it was all random, how there was no method to any of it. I can't tell if their relationships failed because it *was* all random or because they'd never given it a real chance. Were they part of the 5 percent? *Was* there a 5 percent?

And then, and *then,* he writes about me, about seeing me for the first time. Oh, he gives me a different name: Diana Barry (c'mon, Jack, couldn't you make up a name instead of using one from the same book I was named from?), but it's recognizably me.

Jack knew all kinds of things about me before we ever met. When he received his slip of paper from Ms. Cooper, he got a friend to hack in to their computer system and learned my full name. Then he Googled me to death and read everything he could find.

The first time he saw me wasn't in Mexico. He followed me around for a day, watched me buy some of the clothes I got for the trip. In the book, he speculates on what a person like me (good-looking, successful, educated) would want from a service like this. Was it my fault all of my relationships had failed, or did I just have bad luck?

He has that freaky ability the best journalists have of remembering conversations verbatim, or nearly so, without taking notes. So every time he quotes me in the book, it's something I said, or it sounds like something I could've said, even if I don't remember saying it. And Jack's accuracy doesn't make it any easier to see it written down on the page, or to be editorialized by him.

By the time I read about our first night together, I'm nearly hyperventilating. And while this is the most restrained chapter, it makes me sick to my stomach to see these moments I thought were so private captured starkly on the page.

Ten pages from the end, I throw the manuscript down and run to the bathroom, throwing up what's left of the lunch I ate hours ago. When I finish, I sit down on the cold porcelain floor and rest my head against the wall. The act of throwing up makes me furious. I hate throwing up. I hate the tangy metallic taste in my mouth and the lack of control and—

I hate Jack. I hate him.

I start to cry.

The cold, hard floor makes my butt ache. And my heart aches, it *aches,* so I cry and cry until there are no tears left in me.

Fuck, fuck, *fuck.* What am I going to do? What am I going to say to Jack? How will I be able to speak to him, see him, share any space with him for longer than one second? I don't think I can manage even that. One second is too much. I need to leave before he gets back. Write a note for him and tell him to get out, that I never want to see him again. Don't contact me, don't call. And don't bloody publish that book, or I'll get Sarah to sue your ass to kingdom come. You think you've been unsuccessful before? You have no idea. I will own you and everything you produce until you die, you asshole motherfucker!

God. What time is it? Jack's going to be home soon. I need to get up. I need to pull myself together.

Get up, Anne, get up.

I hear a key in the lock.

"Hold on a sec, Ted. I think I left it on the couch," Jack says, crystal-clear though he's rooms away. Even his voice is too close.

I hear a murmur of a deeper voice but not the words. Through a supreme act of will, I stand up, run some water in the sink, and wash the grief off my face. Feeling unsteady, I dry myself on a towel. I don't want to see Jack, but mostly, I don't want him to find me in here like this.

"Anne? Anne? Are you here?"

"I'll be out in a second," I croak. "Give me a minute." A little louder, a little stronger.

"I want you to meet Ted," Jack calls from outside the bathroom door.

Are you fucking kidding me? He wants me to meet *Ted*, the mastermind behind this whole shit show? Just the idea of it makes me so mad, I'm filled with a burst of energy.

"In a minute," I say as firmly as I can.

As his footsteps recede, I start formulating a plan, a way I can deal with this and retain (maybe) a small measure of dignity. I look at myself in the mirror. I'm a disaster, but I can fix it. I brush my hair, apply some mascara, and tuck in my blouse. I check my reflection again. I look presentable. I look normal except to myself.

I square my shoulders and leave the bathroom.

Jack is in the living room with a man in his late fifties who's about the same height as Jack, with a large beer belly that protrudes vertically from his body. He has short graying hair and wears glasses that are too big for his face. He's holding Jack's manuscript under his arm.

I extend my hand and put on a pleasant smile. If my eyes are daggers, I can't help it. "You must be Ted. Jack's told me . . . well, not that much really, but I've been reading all about you."

Ted shakes my hand, looking puzzled. Jack comes over and kisses me on the temple. I try not to flinch when his lips touch my skin.

"Hey," he says, "you're back early."

My lucky day.

"Yeah."

"What did you mean when you said you were reading all about me?" perceptive Ted asks.

"Oh, in Jack's book." I motion to the manuscript under his arm.

Their faces turn to shock. Jack's mouth actually falls open. I've never seen anyone do that before, like in a cartoon.

I make myself laugh. "Boys, boys, no need to look so surprised. I read Jack's book, and I know this has all been a big experiment, a project." I wave my hand around the room, as if this room is the project, Jack's half-finished shelves. "So I know. And now you have the ending for your book. It'll come out of nowhere. Whammo!" I smash my hands together. They make a loud smacking sound. "No one will see it coming."

Jack finds his tongue. "Anne, please—"

"Please what? You can explain? Don't even bother trying. I've read the book, remember? Now, Ted, I think you can see that Jack and I have a few things to discuss, so why don't you leave?"

I shoo him toward the door. He opens it and turns to me, a sad look on his face. "Anne, let me apologize . . . I don't think either of us really thought this through before we did it—"

"Don't be ridiculous. Of course you did. You just didn't think about me. Now, why don't you give me that manuscript? No point in reading it if it's never going to be published, is there?"

Like a child who's been busted for stealing candy, he hands it over.

I hold it tightly to my chest. "Goodbye, Ted."

He opens his mouth to say something but decides otherwise. He nods to Jack and leaves. Jack is sitting limply on the couch, his hands loose between his knees.

"Now, Jackson. Or do you prefer Jackass?"

"Anne, babe, please—"

"Don't you dare call me that. Don't you even fucking dare."

Jack stands and walks over to me. His palms are open and facing me as if he's surrendering to the police. His face is his white flag. "What do you want me to do?"

"I'm going to Sarah's. When I get back here tomorrow, I don't want there to be a trace of you left in this apartment. It shouldn't take you long to get your stuff out. Remember what you said when you moved in? A couple of hours should do the trick. And when you're done, I want you to forget you ever met me."

"Anne, can we please talk about this?"

"No."

"Will you just give me a chance to apologize, to explain?"

"No."

He steps closer and takes hold of my arms above the elbow. "Anne, I love you. I know you don't believe me right now. I know you might never believe me, but what I wrote in there, it's just the way I had to write it."

I step away from him. "That's such horseshit, Jack. You didn't have to write anything. And you certainly didn't have to write about *me*."

"No, you're right, I didn't. I started writing it before I met you, and it was too late to change it . . . but I want to. That's what I was telling Ted."

"Jack, stop lying to me, okay? You've been *happy* with the way your book's turning out. You've been telling me that every day."

This silences him. His hands hang limply by his side.

"I thought so."

"Anne, I love you. And I know you love me. We can work this out." His voice is wavering.

My throat constricts. The only reason I'm not crying is that I left all my tears in the bathroom.

"Anne, please. Can't we start over? Can't I do or say something to change all this?"

A small, stupid part of me wants that to be possible. But I can't give in. I can't. I take a deep breath. "No."

His eyes crowd with doubt. "Why not?"

"Because . . . I don't love you." My voice sounds shaky and unconvincing. I try again. "I know I said I did the other night, but I was drunk and tired, and I didn't mean it."

"Anne—"

"No, Jack. It's true. You were just my friend. And now you're my friend who's done this completely shitty thing to me. So I don't need you in my life anymore. I want you to pack up your stuff and go."

His face is filled with sadness, but the doubt is gone. He believes me now.

I take his rings off my finger and place them on the table. They clink against each other, making a hollow sound. I imagine this is what the inside of my heart would sound like if it weren't shattered.

"Anne, please. I know I fucked everything up. I know I've been a complete asshole. But please . . . don't go."

There they are. The words I wanted to hear six months ago from another man. The words that might have kept me in place. But not now. Not today.

"Goodbye, Jack," I say, and then I walk out the door.

When Sarah opens her door, I fling myself into her arms and hold on as if she's a life raft.

"Anne, what's wrong? Did someone die? Anne?"

I can't talk. All I can do is gulp for air. She walks me to her couch and sits me down. "Anne, you're scaring me. Please tell me what's going on."

I wipe my nose with my sleeve and take several shaky breaths. My words come out in staccato bursts. "You're never . . . going to believe . . . you're going to think . . . insane."

"Is this about Jack? Did you have a fight? Fighting doesn't make you insane, Anne, it's normal."

I shake my head and pull Jack's manuscript from my purse. "Sarah, you have no idea."

While Sarah reads, I change into a pair of her pajamas and curl up on the couch to watch a *Gilmore Girls* rerun. It's the episode where Luke and Lorelai finally kiss for the first time. I love this show, this episode especially. It's perfect and romantic and the last thing I should be watching right now. But what can I say? I like fairy tales.

Every page or so Sarah reads something that makes her exclaim "No fucking way" or "You're shitting me." Thirty pages in—I can guess it's when Jack starts speculating about what would make me use a service like this—she says, "Fuck you, asshole," in a particularly vicious tone. I enjoy these exclamations. There's a strange comfort in being involved in this drama, this crazy, sensational story, and listening to Sarah's reactions to it all.

When Sarah is halfway through, Mike comes home and wants to know what's going on. She wordlessly hands him the part of the manuscript she's already read. He sits down on the couch next to her and starts reading. His first "holy shit" escapes about two minutes later. Sarah shushes him and keeps reading. They read through two more episodes (it's a *Gilmore Girls* marathon, apparently), almost never at a loss for words.

Sarah gets to the last page, further than I could. No surprise. She's always been stronger than I. She looks up at me with tears in her eyes. "Oh, Anne, how could you?"

I wrap a fleece throw tighter around my shoulders. "I don't know. I just thought it might work out, you know?"

"But all that money. All your book money."

"It's only money, Sarah. It was for my life, and I was trying to have one."

"You have a life."

"Not the life I want."

"Whoever said you get everything you want?"

"You did."

"Oh, Anne."

I wipe my tears away with my knuckles. "Don't feel sorry for me. Please don't."

"But you fell in love with him, right?"

"How did you know?"

"I knew it when we got into that fight. You weren't just defending your decision. You were defending him too."

"I feel so pathetic. But I thought it would work. I thought it *was* working." I shake my head. "Oh my God, I'm going to have to get divorced."

"No, you're not, Anne."

"What do you mean?"

Sarah bites her lip. "Please don't be mad."

"What is it?"

"Well . . . I contacted that divorce lawyer I mentioned before, you know, in case you changed your mind, and he looked into it for me as a favor. And, well . . . I kind of filed annulment papers for you . . ."

"You did what?"

She cringes. "Shit, you're mad, right? Will you let me explain?"

"I'm listening."

"It was when we had that fight, and I thought you'd come around eventually, and things between you and Jack wouldn't work out. And the idea was, when they didn't, you wouldn't have to go through all the trouble and the waiting time. I thought you'd be happy."

"But that was months ago. Does that mean—"

"No, it's not final yet. You still have to sign the papers. And Jack."

I'm only half listening. Jack and I are two signatures away from being unmarried. Does that make it better or worse? I can't tell.

Sarah is biting her thumb, anxious. "Are you mad?"

"I should be, but . . . I don't know. I'm trying not to feel anything right now."

"I hear you. And I'm sorry."

"It's okay. Do you think Jack's going to publish his book?"

"Not after he gets my cease-and-desist letter, he's not."

Mike looks up. "This guy's a really good writer, you know."

Sarah gives him a look that could kill. "Mike! We're on Anne's side."

"Of course we are. He's a complete fucking asshole. But still. This is well written."

"Mike!"

"I think you're sleeping on the couch tonight, buddy."

He looks rueful. "Taking one for the man team. Got it."

Sarah gives him a loving smile, which she tries to hide from me. "What happened after you found the book? Did you confront him?"

"Yeah. I came home early from my book tour to tell him how I felt about him—can you fucking believe it? Anyway, I found *that* lying on the couch. He was bringing it to his editor, and he forgot it. So I read it, and threw up, and sat crying forever on the bathroom floor. When he came home, we had it out."

"What did he say?"

I reenact the scene, playing my part, then his.

"I'm impressed. I think I would've just curled up into a ball."

"I did curl into a ball for a while, but then I got really mad, and I didn't want to cave in front of him. I'm not sure he bought it, but I'm glad I tried." I start to cry again. Sarah puts my head on her shoulder and strokes my hair. "You were right, you know," I tell her.

"Right about what?"

"I did just do all this because you were getting married."

"That'll teach you to copy me . . ."

We laugh together through my tears.

God, it hurts to laugh.

# Chapter 22
# Shut the Fuck Up!

"That's the craziest thing I've ever heard."

I'm curled up on the couch in William's office with my legs tucked under me and Jack's manuscript on my lap. I just dropped the fake-marriage bomb and am managing to keep my tears in check. So far.

"I swear."

"No. Fucking. Way."

"I promise you it's true."

"Anne, it can't be."

"Do you think I'd make this up?"

William meets my eyes, probing them for any possibility that I might be messing with him. He looks both intensely curious and intensely sad. The tears I've been holding back start to well up.

"To summarize, your marriage was actually an arranged marriage. And Jack, who seemed great and into you, was really just doing research for his latest book, and is so dedicated to his craft that he *married* you for it. And you were totally fooled, and when you came home to tell him that you'd fallen in love with him, you found his book, discovered his secret, and kicked him out?"

"That about sums it up, yes." I pat the manuscript on my lap. "You wanna read all about it?"

"Really?"

"It's a pretty good read, though I hate to admit it."

He stretches out his hand. "In that case, hand it over."

I give it to him. He holds it cautiously, moving it up and down as if he's weighing it. "Is this the whole thing?"

"As far as he got."

Almost as far as *we* got.

"It doesn't feel heavy enough to be so devastating."

"What's weight got to do with it?"

"Not sure. It just seems like there aren't enough words in here to change your whole life."

"It only took two words to change my life."

"Which ones?"

"I do."

"Can you tell Mom and Dad?" I ask Gil later that day on the phone.

"Why am I always your messenger?"

"Because you're the best brother ever?"

He chuckles. "Of course I can, Anne. If you want me to."

"Thanks, that means a lot to me."

"You want me to beat the crap out of him?"

"It's amazing how tempting that is."

"That doesn't sound like the Anne I know."

"I'm not sure the Anne you know exists anymore."

"You want to come over for dinner?"

"I'll think about it."

"Please come."

My throat feels tight, a feeling I'm too familiar with these days. "I've got to go, Gil. I'll call you later."

I hang up and start to clean off my desk, getting ready to go home. I haven't been back to the apartment since I left Jack. Sarah went to pick up some things for me and to confirm that Jack was indeed gone. She came back with my clothes and a letter from Jack.

I stared at the envelope for a long time. Then I put it away, unsure whether I wanted to read what was in it. Instead, we rented a silly action-adventure movie and ordered pizza. When Sarah and Mike went to bed, I finally opened the envelope, unable to resist anymore.

The look of the letter almost killed me. Jack had typed it, so it looked just like his book. A bad choice, even though I didn't think he did it consciously. Still, the sight of the words on the paper, the knowledge that it was Jack who wrote them, suddenly hurt too much, and I couldn't read it after all. I had an urge to burn it. To put it in Sarah's fireplace, set a match to it, and watch it turn to ash, to smoke, to disappear.

I couldn't quite manage that in the end. I needed to have the whole story. The part Jack hadn't written yet. I wanted to know if he could surprise me any more. Turns out he couldn't.

Dear Anne,

I apologize for typing this, but I can't seem to keep my hand from shaking, and I'd like, if you read this, for you to be able to understand what I need to tell you.

Because I need you to know that I'm more sorry for this than for anything I've ever done. I know you can't believe me, that I've done nothing to deserve your trust. I don't know if what I did is forgivable.

You see, all this is confusing to me too. Marrying you is both the worst and best thing I ever did in my life. Actually, the worst thing was writing the book; I can see that now. Because if I hadn't gone through with that, you wouldn't ever have had to know any of this. We could've been happy. I really believe that.

I love you, Anne. I hope you know that and can believe it. What I'm going to have to live with is why that wasn't enough for me. Why it didn't stay my hand from writing. Why I didn't throw my pages away after the first time we slept together.

Why wasn't I strong enough to do that?

The only answer I have is that I'm a weak man. I know I have no right to hope that there can ever be anything between us again. But yet I have to hope. I have to hope that you're both better than me and as weak as me.

I have to hope, Anne. Please forgive me.

Love, Jack

I felt surprisingly numb, reading the letter. Not because I didn't believe him. I do. I know he's sorry, that he cares for me. And that same small, stupid part of me even wants to forgive him, to feel his arms around me, his lips on mine, and to hear him tell me he loves me. That's the part of me that still believes in fairy tales. That's the part of me that's still waiting for the little boy who pulled my pigtails to turn up and be this perfect man. That's the part of me that thought I was in love with Jack.

Halfway home, I change my mind and decide to go to Cathy and Gil's, to put off the sight and smell of the apartment a little longer. I flag a cab and let it crawl its way through the end-of-day traffic to their house, not caring about the sure-to-be-enormous expense.

When we exit the highway, something in me shifts. Rather than the usual alien feeling I get as I cross the county line, I feel reassured. The pitter-patter of rain on the windshield, the slap of the wipers, the smell of the wet concrete and grass coming in through the window feels like home.

I ask the cabdriver to let me off a few blocks from their

house. I don't have an umbrella, but it's a light rain, harmless. I walk past the comfortable houses, looking in at the lit-up lives.

A car splashes through a puddle behind me, snapping me back to the real world. I've spent enough time in fantasyland.

I head up Gil and Cathy's front walk and ring the bell. The ever-vigilant Jane answers it, swinging it open with a flourish. "I opened the door."

"I can see that, honey."

"Next year, at school, I'm going to have a key and come home by myself."

"Somehow I doubt that."

"No, it's true." She stops and studies me for a moment. "Why are you sad, Aunty Anne?"

Oh, to have the perception of a nearly-seven-year-old.

"Because my heart hurts, little one."

"Can the doctor fix it?"

"I don't think so."

She thinks about it. "Maybe Uncle Jack can fix it?"

"No, honey, not him either."

"Can I fix it?"

I bend down to look her in the eyes and feel that time warp back to me at her age. It's funny, because all I remember from then are the times I hurt myself. How I broke my arm at Brownies. How I burned my hand on the stove. How I got food poisoning at school. I don't remember the actual physical pain, only the events surrounding it. But looking at Jane, I *can* remember how excited I was by everything then. How I didn't realize anything *actually* bad could ever happen to me or the people around me.

I pull her to me. Her little arms circle my neck. "Maybe you can, little girl, maybe you can."

We're sitting around the dinner table, finishing off a second bottle of wine and talking about anything other than Jack. Or really, I'm finishing off a second bottle of wine. Gil had a glass, and Cathy pleaded pregnancy.

"Now, Anne. Please tell us the whole story," Cathy says with a serious look.

I shake my head. "Can't do it. But hold on a sec." I walk into the hall, looking for my purse. I locate it in the entryway and bring it back to the table, stumbling as I go.

"I still can't believe it," Cathy says as I plunk the manuscript down on the table.

"I know, I know. Anyway . . . I've written an addendum." I did this last night at Sarah's when I couldn't sleep. The writing isn't up to Jack's, but that's not really the point.

"An addendum?"

"That's right. I can't handle having to tell everyone what happened over and over again, so I've written an addendum to Jack's book. Instead of telling people, I'm just going to give them the package, and they can read it and get the whole story. I won't have to explain anything."

Cathy looks skeptical. "You need to talk to someone, Anne. Maybe a therapist or—"

"No. No more therapists." I drain my glass. "You know, I was reading this article about the fact that, blindfolded, most people can't tell the difference between white and red wine. Do you think that can be true?"

Gil starts clearing the plates. He pointedly picks up the bottle of wine and takes it with him to the kitchen.

"I don't think Gil approves of my drinking," I whisper to Cathy.

She puts her hand on mine. "He's just concerned for you, Anne. He loves you very much, you know. We both do. And so do the girls."

"I know, Cathy. Thanks." I swallow hard. "You want to read it?"

"All right."

I hand her the manuscript and go into the kitchen so I can't hear the exclamations of shock that are sure to follow. Gil is standing at the sink, rinsing dishes and putting them in the dishwasher. I fill my glass with the last of the bottle.

"You know, that's just wasting water," I tell Gil.

"When did you become so concerned about the environment?"

"I'm just saying."

He puts the last dish in the machine, closes the door, and turns toward me. He frowns when he sees the glass in my hand. "Haven't you had enough?"

"You really shouldn't worry so much about me. I'm gonna be okay. I'm strong. I've been through this before. I'll survive."

I like the sound of that. I will survive. Like the Gloria

Gaynor song. Yeah, totally. Don't be afraid, don't be petrified. Dum-da-dum, yeah, that's right . . . I'm going to have to change the goddamn locks, 'cause I forgot to make you give back your key . . . And then some other part, and then the good part, so go, go, go, walk through my door, and don't turn around, no, I won't welcome you here anymore, you think I'm going to crumble, that I might want to die, but no, no, no, I'm going to survive!

"Anne, what the hell are you doing?"

I stop mid-twirl. "Dancing to a song in my head."

Gil takes the glass from my hand. "Definitely enough wine for you."

"Party pooper."

I sit at the breakfast bar and rest my head in my hands. I click my heels together, trying to find the beat again, but the song is gone. My clicking heels remind me of that night so many months ago. The night I found the Blythe & Company card lying on the sidewalk. I clicked my heels together three times, trying to get somewhere else, I'm not sure where. And it worked, after a fashion. Maybe not in a good way, or any way I'd want to repeat, but it could work again. I close my eyes and click my heels. Click, click, click.

"Anne, what are you doing now?"

My eyes fly open. "Wishing on a star."

"You're one crazy-drunk girl, Cordelia."

"Maybe yes, maybe no."

He goes into the living room to watch TV. After a moment I follow him, but not before I hear an uncharacteristic "Fuck me!" from Cathy in the dining room. Hearing her reminds me why I'm here, and the hurt that receded for the brief seconds of wishing and dancing and teasing Gil comes back in a rush and settles on my shoulders like a weight.

Gil is sitting in his favorite armchair, so I curl up on the couch. We sit there together, not talking, watching an episode of *The Daily Show* that Gil has TiVoed.

"You know, I met one of the writers on that show in Costa Rica," I tell him.

"You're full of fascinating facts this evening."

I throw a pillow at him. "Shut the fuck up!"

"Nice language."

"You should hear your wife right now. I'm sure she's saying lots of worse things."

"Anne, shush, I'm trying to listen."

I snuggle back into the couch and don't say another word. At some point, I fall into a half-sleep state where I can hear the TV but can't put together the words or tell whether they're funny. After a long time, Gil—it must be Gil—clicks off the TV and pads across the room. He drapes a blanket over me and kisses me on the crown of my head.

"Sleep tight, little sister."

Don't let the bedbugs bite.

# Chapter 23
# Refund Policy

I wake up the next morning with a crick in my neck and my hair standing out sideways. And in the newness of the morning, I realize I've spent enough time mourning Jack. Enough time crying, talking, or thinking about him. I've known the guy only a few months, for Chrissake! I'm better than this. I've survived worse. I will not let it become my whole life.

I throw back the blanket and sit up, full of energy, ready to face the day. This lasts about thirty seconds before the bottles of wine I consumed last night start attacking me. I have an instant, blinding headache, and I feel like I've got about two, maybe three seconds to get to the bathroom before any food or drink left in my body exits.

I take several deep breaths and concentrate on calming my stomach, and after a few minutes it starts to work. The nausea and the pain recede. I stand up and walk to the kitchen, following the waft of coffee. It smells good, despite the wine doing trampoline tricks in my stomach.

Cathy is standing at the stove, making eggs and French toast. Mary is cooing softly in her playpen in the corner.

"Are you a real person or a robot?" I ask.

Cathy looks at me and laughs. "You look a lot more Pippi Longstocking than Anne of Green Gables this morning."

I put my hand to the side of my head, trying to smooth down my hair, but it won't budge. "I'm voting for robot."

"There's coffee." She motions toward the pot.

"Thanks. I'm trying to decide if it's going to make me feel better or worse." I sit on one of the stools and rest my head on my arms, trying to get the world to stop spinning.

"That bad, huh?" Gil puts his hand on my shoulder and gives me a squeeze as he walks into the kitchen.

"Why, why did you let me drink like that?"

"Pretty sure I didn't."

I sigh loudly and lift my head. Gil is standing behind Cathy. He has his arms around her, and he's rubbing her big round belly.

"Okay, okay, enough with the PDA! You're making me jealous of my own brother."

"Sorry, Anne."

Gil walks over to the coffeepot and pours us each a cup. I wrap my hands around the mug, feeling the heat seep into my hands. I take a few tentative sips and let the caffeine work into my bloodstream. I feel infinitesimally better than I did a few minutes before. I can sense briefly what it will be like when I feel wholly better again.

"So, what's on the agenda today?" Gil asks, eating a piece of French toast with his hands.

"I'm supposed to be at work."

"'Supposed to' being the operative words in that sentence?"

"Yeah."

"Calling in sick?"

"I think that's a given."

Cathy puts a plate of French toast in front of me, and I take a few cautious bites. A bite, a deep breath, a sip of coffee, repeat. I pause after three or four repetitions to make sure it'll all stay down. It does, for now.

Jane and Elizabeth come barreling into the room in matching footie pajamas, full of morning glee. They scamper around, eat their breakfasts loudly, and fight with their mother about what they want to wear. Jane crawls into my lap and gives me a big hug.

"What's that for?" I ask.

"So you feel better. Jeesh." She drops to the ground and runs from the room, her feet going *pat, pat, pat* on the floor, her red hair flying behind her.

I thank Cathy for breakfast and the night before, kiss the girls, and take the train back to the city with Gil. I call in sick on the way. I can tell from the receptionist's tone that she's heard about Jack and me and knows my pathetic attempts at coughing and sneezing are a sham. I make a mental note to kick William in the ass for being such a bigmouth.

I hesitate at my front door, not sure I can handle the sight of my deserted apartment. As at breakfast, after a couple of deep breaths, I'm able to do it. I walk in and go directly to bed. My bed. Our bed. My bed again now, I guess. I can still smell

Jack on the sheets as I snuggle into his pillow, breathing him in and out, in and out, until I fall asleep.

I sleep for several hours full of fractured dreams about Jack. When I wake up, I'm wrapped around the pillow that smells like him. I lie there for a few minutes, breathing him in until I can't stand it anymore. I don't know who I'm angrier at: Jack or myself for clinging to something that reminds me of him.

My anger fills me with the same feeling I had at Gil and Cathy's, that "I can move past this, this will not take me down" feeling. I'm ready to do something, whatever it takes, to pull myself together. This time, when I sit up and fling off the covers, I'm not stopped by a hangover.

I strip the sheets off the bed and put them in the laundry hamper. Then I take a shower. As I soap and lather, I formulate a plan. I change into my grubbiest clothes and set to work.

I start with the biggest obstacle: Jack's shelf project. It sits half built in my living room, taking up way too much space. I borrow a sledgehammer from the super and smash down the shelves without doing too much damage to the walls. Each time I lift the sledgehammer and smash it through the boards, I feel stronger. When the noise has subsided and it's all rubble, I gather up the debris in several heavy-duty garbage bags and drag them out to the curb. Then I move my own bookshelves over to that wall to cover up the damage, glad after all that we didn't merge our book collections.

Next, I rearrange the rest of the furniture in the living room, putting it back where it was before Jack set up his workspace, the corner he wrote that awful book in. I buy a colorful indoor fruit tree to put in that space. I don't know much about feng shui, but I can feel the energy shift in the room, like it does when you open your windows for the first time after a hard winter.

When it's all done, I look around. I want to make sure all signs of Jack have been erased. But for a few marks on the wall, it's as if he was never even here.

That night I take the card tucked into the frame of the mirror on my bathroom wall, rip it into as many pieces as I can, and dump them in the trash. My good-luck card: that was what I thought.

Maybe now my luck will change.

The next day, over morning coffee, I sort through the mail that accumulated while I was away on my book tour and hiding at Sarah's. Bill, bill, junk, junk. And there it is, in the middle of the pile: an envelope from Blythe & Company. I rip it open. It's an invoice for last month's therapy appointments with Dr. Szwick.

I can't believe their nerve! We didn't even go to our last appointment, and I won't be going to the next. I'm furious with them, with Jack, but mostly with myself, because I gave them so much money, because I was taken in. And even though they don't know any of the Jack part or the book part, this bill is the final straw.

I need to do something, get something from them, get back at them somehow. How, how, how can I get some measure of vengeance?

I consider my options. I can write an article about them, but then I'd be exposing myself. Everyone who knows about my quick marriage will put two and two together and come up with *Anne is a complete freak.* Besides, it might hurt the other couples who used the service, and I don't want to do that.

Then it hits me. I know what to do. If only I have the nerve to do it.


"Ms. Cooper will see you now."

My head pops up from the magazine I've been staring at. As I stand, the magazine drops to the floor with a slippery thud. I put it back on the table and follow the receptionist along the familiar path to Ms. Cooper's office.

"How are you, Ms. Blythe? Or should I say Mrs. Harmer?" she says, smiling her tight smile.

Her use of Jack's last name, particularly in connection with me, sends a shiver down my spine. "Ms. Blythe will do."

I sit down, folding my fists in my lap. She follows suit.

"What can I do for you?"

"I'm here to . . . get a refund."

"Excuse me?"

I say it louder. "I'm here to get a refund."

"As I believe I explained to you, we don't issue refunds."

"The man you found me is no bloody good, and I want a refund."

She looks at me in her bland way. "Is this some kind of joke? Should I be laughing?"

"I assure you, I'm quite serious. I was duped, and I want my money back."

"I have no idea what you're talking about."

"I'm talking about the fact that you were supposed to find me a husband. A *real* husband. You weren't supposed to take my money and match me with a man writing an exposé about your moneymaking so-called service."

I did it. I finally said something Ms. Cooper wasn't expecting. She blinks at me several times and seems at a loss for words. She gives a small cough. "Whatever do you mean?"

"I mean that Jack Harmer wasn't looking for a wife, he was writing a book about having an arranged marriage. An undercover, behind-the-scenes, reality-TV kind of book about this agency and our marriage and me. And so I . . . want . . . a . . . fucking . . . refund."

I slap my hand on her desk with each word. Ms. Cooper flinches at every smack. Then she picks up the phone on her desk, presses a button, and speaks. "Please send security in here immediately."

"Right," I say. "Kick me out, pretend what I said isn't true. But it is true. And I'm going to get my refund."

I reach into my purse and take out a copy of Jack's manuscript. I plunk it down on the desk as two men in black suits and thin ties appear in the doorway.

"Bit dramatic, don't you think?" I say to them. "I only weigh a hundred and twenty-five pounds." I point to the manuscript. "Read that, Ms. Cooper. Read that and think about what it's going to do to this place, what it's going to do to your job, if it gets published. Then let me know whether you want to maintain your no-refund policy. You know where you can reach me."

I stride past the black-suited men, my head held high. They follow me to the reception area, where a pale pretty woman in her mid-forties is waiting nervously. I walk to the front door, open it, then turn back and say loudly to the waiting woman, "Trust your instincts. Don't do it."

She looks startled. "I'm sorry, what?"

"Don't do it. Get up, walk away, leave. They have nothing for you here." The men walk toward me, shoulders set to menace. "All right, all right, don't worry, I'm going."

I stride to the elevator and punch the down button. The elevator pings, and I step in. The doors close behind me and I start shaking. I'm shaking, but I feel better. I feel stronger.

It's in the better, stronger moment that I realize I can survive this. I can.

# Chapter 24
## Kicking It

And I do. I survive that first week without Jack. I survive a second and a third, and then a month goes by, and then two, and I'm not thinking about him all the time or wondering if I'm going to run into him. More time passes, until more time has passed than the time I knew him, than the time I knew about him, than the time I was contemplating finding him. Our time together starts to seem distant, like a memory from childhood, like a tiny star at the edge of the universe.

I work a lot and hang out with Sarah and Mike and sometimes with William. I'm there when Cathy gives birth to her fourth daughter. I hold her when she's a few minutes old. As I cradle her tiny body against mine, her whole chest moves up and down to the rhythm of her beating heart. She smells clean and new, and when her eyes crack open, they're seeing everything for the first time. A world to discover. My tears drop onto her sleeper, onto this child who looks like she could be mine, like she could've been mine and Jack's. But then I push that thought away, and she's just my darling fourth niece. I pass her back to her mother.

I do a few book signings, though my book isn't setting the publishing world on fire. Still, I have a two-book deal and a deadline, so my nights and weekends are spent furiously writing and trying not to hate every word I put down on paper. My second book is about a woman whose life gets turned upside down when she takes a trip to Africa that doesn't turn out as she planned. Halfway in, I'm cursing myself for not taking the easy way out and writing a sequel to *Home*. But one thing's for sure—the heroine of *this* book is not going to be saved by a man.

Another birthday comes and goes. I'm thirty-four, one year away from the dreaded thirty-five. Sarah and Mike throw a dinner party for me, and no one asks me anything about Jack.

Every day I scan the mail for an envelope from Blythe & Company, hoping for a refund, but it never comes. I decide in the end to let it go. The important thing was having the courage to ask.

I go on a couple of dates when someone asks. But though the guys are nice enough and interested in me and cute enough, I don't feel a connection, and there's never a second date.

"What was wrong with him?" Sarah asks over a beer at the bar a few days after my first and last date with Gary, the nice new guy from her office.

"Would you like to see my list?"

Sarah perks up. "You made a list? Really?"

I pull over a napkin and take out my pen. I write a word on it and hand it to her.

"What does this mean?"

The word I wrote is "me."

"It's what was wrong with him. I can't judge if he's good or not. I can't even make a pro-con list. I think I'm done with dating."

"You can't give up on dating at thirty-four."

"Who says?"

"I do."

"You're not the boss of me."

"I am, though, you will remember, the boss of your dating life."

I agreed to this a month ago, after a few too many beers. "I'm not sure that's an enforceable agreement."

"Oh, it's legally binding, I assure you. I've got it in writing."

"All right, then. If you're the boss, what are you going to do to get me out of this predicament?"

"I'm going to use my powers and magically find the perfect man for you." She waves her hand as if she's holding a wand. She swoops it over me one, two, three times.

"If only it were that simple."

"Ah, but it is. I don't know why you continue to doubt my powers."

I finish my drink and change the topic. "So, all ready for the wedding?"

"Yeah. I can't believe it's here already," she says with an anxious gulp.

"You've only been planning it for a year."

"I know. I just want everything to go as planned. And for everyone to have a good time."

"Everything's going to go as planned, and it will be fantastic. You're in charge, after all."

She pulls a face. "Seriously, I'm nervous."

"About Mike?"

"No, just all the stupid things that can go wrong. Which reminds me, did you go for your final fitting?"

"Yes, Sarah."

"Great."

"It *will* be great. You're marrying a great guy, and you'll live happily ever after."

"I thought you didn't believe in that anymore."

"I don't. But I'm making an exception for you."

She smiles. Then she gets a look in her eyes as if she's remembered something she didn't want to remember.

"What is it?" I ask.

"What? Nothing."

I put my hand on her arm. "Come on. What is it? Is your mom sick again?"

"No, she's fine."

"Then what?"

She sighs. "I saw Jack yesterday."

"What? Where? Did you speak to him? What did he say? How come you waited this long to tell me?" My heart is beating so loudly, I can hear it.

Sarah pushes her drink toward me. "Here, drink some of this."

I take a sip of her beer and try to calm down, but I can still feel my heart *boom, boom, boom*ing away.

"Thanks. Now spill."

"I'm sorry I didn't tell you sooner, Anne, but I wanted to do it face-to-face. Then you launched into the story about your date with Gary, and we were having such a normal evening, you know, a pre-Jack, pre-Blythe-and-Company evening. I didn't want to ruin it."

"It's okay, I understand. Now tell me everything."

"I was in the Starbucks in my building, getting coffee. At least that was my excuse for leaving this ridiculous meeting I was in—"

"Sarah! Focus, please."

"God, sorry, Anne, it's been a long day. Anyway, I turned around and basically slammed into Jack. I almost spilled my steaming coffee all over him."

"And?"

"He didn't seem surprised to see me. I had the feeling he knew I'd be there somehow. Anyway, he asked if I'd talk to him for a minute, and I was trying to figure out what you'd want me to do: tell him to go fuck himself and throw my coffee in his face, or hear what he had to say."

"Both, clearly."

"Right, I know, that's what I was thinking. I figured if I listened to him, I could tell him afterward to go to hell."

"Good thinking. So?"

"We sat down, and he told me that he *had* been hoping to run into me. I guess he goes to that Starbucks a lot—it's near his editor's office or something—and he'd seen me there a couple of times before."

I feel a flash of anger. "So he's stalking you now?"

She shakes her head. "No, I don't think so. It didn't come across like that."

"It wouldn't, would it? He's an Oscar-worthy actor when he wants to be, you know."

"Anne, I know."

"Why did he want to run into you? Was it because of the annulment?"

We sent the papers to Jack months ago, and he still hasn't signed them.

"No." She measures her words. "He wants to see you."

"He wants to see me?" My voice is barely above a whisper.

"Yes."

"And he sought you out to what? Get your permission? To get you to convince me?"

"I'm not sure why, exactly."

"What *did* he say?"

"That he felt awful and that he completely understood why you kicked him out . . . Oh, and something about how he tried to respect your wishes and stay away, but he was miserable." She rolls her eyes at this last part.

Miserable. I like the sound of that word in connection with Jack.

"Did he look miserable?"

"Kind of."

"Good. But I don't understand. Why would he talk to you about this?"

"I don't know, Anne. I only gave him about three minutes."

"But what did you say? Did you tell him you thought I'd see him? Are you supposed to be convincing me to see him?"

"No, no. I didn't say anything. Really. I just listened. I didn't even say I'd tell you I'd spoken with him. Anne, are you okay?"

I breathe in and out slowly, trying to stop what feels like the beginning of a panic attack. "I think so."

"So, what do you want to do?"

"About Jack?"

She nods.

"I don't know," I tell her. "I'm not sure I want to see him again. I mean, what could he tell me? That he's sorry? That he loves me? He's already told me these things. And how can I believe anything he has to say?"

She frowns. "I don't know, Anne. I don't have any answers."

"You always have all the answers."

"Not this time."

"What would you do?"

"I never would've married him in the first place."

"Hey!"

"Sorry. What I meant was that you need to figure it out yourself. I'll support you, whatever you do. If you want to see him, I understand. If you don't, I understand that too."

I consider what she's saying. "What if I want to do both?"

"Then why don't you see him and tell him you don't want to see him anymore." She reaches into her purse and takes out a business card. "He gave me this."

She hands it to me. His name stares back at me in bold

black type. I hold it in my hands, feeling its edges like I felt the edges of his file so many months ago in Ms. Cooper's office.

"Thanks, Sarah."

"What for?"

"Too many things to list."

She smiles. "You can *always* make a list."

"Not this time."

I spend the next several days trying to decide what to do. I barely sleep. I can hardly write.

All I can think is: What could he have to say? How would he look saying it?

His business card haunts me, its presence a ghost in my apartment. In the end, my curiosity gets the better of me. I email him and set up a meeting.

I agree to meet him at a bar. Not my bar; I choose a neutral Irish pub downtown that I haven't been to in years and don't care if I ever go to again. I have no memories there, and after tonight it will just be the bar I met Jack in the last time I saw him. I have the same attitude toward what I wear. I pick a pair of jeans and a cream T-shirt out of a pile of clothes I'm giving to charity. Tomorrow they'll belong to someone else.

Jack arrives before me. I find him sitting at a table for two, his face half lit by a small candle in a glass ball covered in a red beaded net. He's made an effort with his appearance, put on a pressed striped shirt and what look like new plain-front chinos. His beard has been trimmed, and his hair looks freshly cut. He stands up as I approach the table. I think he wants to kiss me, but he sits down without making a move when I slip into the seat opposite him and fold my arms across my chest.

"So, what do you want?" I say in the most businesslike tone I can muster.

"I needed to see you," Jack says. He sounds nervous and . . . scared. He's scared.

I look him briefly in the eye, but I can't hold his gaze. I do notice that he's dropped a few pounds. The petty part of me feels happy about this.

"Do you think I give a shit about what you need?" My throat feels tight.

Breathe, Anne. Breathe.

Jack flinches. "I know, Anne. I'm a selfish bastard. And I don't deserve anything from you. I'm really grateful you decided to see me."

My stomach flips and tosses around. "What do you want?"

"Are you all right?"

I was before I decided to see you.

"What do you want to say to me, Jack? Why am I here?"

He looks down at his hands. He's still wearing the wedding band I put on his finger all those months ago in Mexico.

"Did you read my letter?" he asks.

"Yes."

"And?"

"And what?"

"Do you think you can forgive me?"

"Uh, no."

"Uh, no. That's all I get?"

"That's right."

"Is that a definitive answer?"

"What the fuck, Jack? We're not playing *Who Wants to Be a Millionaire*. This is our life you're talking about. My life."

"I know, Anne. I want to be in your life."

He puts his hand on my arm. I let it sit for a second, feeling his skin on mine. Then I realize it's Jack who's touching me, and I shrug it off.

"I can't have you in my life, Jack. I can't."

"But we're married, Anne. Don't you think we should try to work this out?"

"No, we aren't, Jack. I mean, we shouldn't be. You really need to sign those papers Sarah sent you."

"Are you sure you want me to sign them?" he asks in a monotone.

"Yes."

"Oh." He sighs deeply. His breath extinguishes the candle. A trace of smoke wafts between us.

"Can I ask you something?" I say.

"Of course."

"Did you give any thought to the woman in all this before you agreed to do it?"

His face reddens. "Not as much as I should have, but yes, I did."

"And what? You still thought it was okay?"

"I wouldn't say okay, exactly, but . . . I don't know . . . it wasn't going to be a real marriage for either of us, so I kind of told myself it wasn't that big a deal."

"And what did you think was going to happen when your book was published?"

"You mean if you hadn't found out?"

"Yes."

"I tried not to think too much about that."

"C'mon, Jack."

"It's true. I was kind of living two lives. The life I had in real time with you, and this person I became when I wrote the book."

"Did you think you were going to be able to keep me?"

"No. The way the book was written, I knew that wasn't possible. Look, I know you didn't believe me when I told you this before, but I did tell Ted that night that we were going to have to push back publication because I had to rewrite the book."

"Why?"

"While you were away, I read it through from start to finish, and I realized how . . . how *awful* it was. I saw the way I was writing about us, about you, and I knew I couldn't do it anymore. I knew if I left it the way it was, I'd lose you forever." His lips twist in self-mockery. "But I did that anyway, didn't I?"

*Forever.* It sounds so final.

"I think so, yes."

"Is there any way we could start over?"

"No."

His shoulders slump. "I was afraid of that."

I bite my lip and wait for him to say something more, but he doesn't.

"Was that all you wanted to say?"

Jack's eyes find mine. "No . . . I need to tell you something else. Something you should hear from me first."

My heart starts pounding again. "What?"

"My book is coming out in a few weeks."

I can't speak. I can barely breathe.

He puts his hand on my arm again. "Anne, are you okay?"

God, I am so sick of people asking me that. I shake him off and try to find some breath. "How could you?"

He looks grim. "I had to. I received an advance, which I'd already spent. Plus, they paid for Blythe and Company's services. My publisher insisted. If I refused, they were going to sue me."

"So this is just about money?"

"No, Anne. Not in the way you mean. But this is how I make my living. If I don't publish this book, I'll never publish anything again. And what am I supposed to do with myself if I can't write anymore? It's the only thing I know. It's the only thing I'm good at."

I feel a twinge of sympathy. I'm not sure what I would do if I were faced with that possibility. Thankfully, that's not the mistake I made.

"Maybe that'll just have to be the consequence."

"I thought about that. But I also feel like I had to finish writing the book. For me. For you. For us. I changed it, Anne. I changed it."

"You changed it?"

"Yes. I got them to agree to let me change it. It's different, I swear—"

I cut him off. My anger is back, and it's stomping on that twinge of sympathy. "Is this still a book about you having an arranged marriage with me?"

"Yes, but—"

I give him the hand. "And you're still you, and I'm still me, and everything that happened in the book is what happened to us?"

"Yes, but—"

"You don't get it at all, Jack, do you? I asked you to do one thing for me. I asked you not to publish the book. And here you are, looking all sad-eyed and regretful, but you're still publishing it, and you don't have any regrets at all, do you?"

He looks hurt. Really hurt. "How can you say that? Look at me. I'm a mess. Of course I have regrets. I love you, Anne. I love you."

My heart flutters at these words, but I try to ignore it. What good has my heart ever done me?

"But you're not doing anything differently. Take tonight. You didn't tell me you were publishing your book before you asked if we could get back together. You played that card first. You're still keeping things from me."

"It's not like that. The reason I wanted to see you was to tell you my book was coming out. The other stuff just slipped out because, well, because I can't help myself around you. I can't."

"You only came here to tell me about the book?"

"Yes, but—"

"Then I think we're done."

I stand up and nearly trip over my feet. Though Jack reaches out to catch me, I avoid his touch and almost sprint for the door. Outside, I take in big lungfuls of air, trying to catch my breath, trying to keep from throwing up on the sidewalk, trying to keep from going back into the bar and beating Jack to a pulp.

"Anne."

"Please leave me alone, Jack. Please."

I don't want to look at him. I don't want him to see me crying. I don't want to see him anymore.

"Anne." He takes me in his arms and holds me against his chest.

"Please, Jack, no," I mumble into the front of his shirt.

He holds me closer, and I stop struggling. I breathe in the smell of him: soap and woods, that little-boy smell. I feel his hands move up my back and into my hair, his rough hands catching in its smoothness. He starts to kiss the side of my face, the space near my ear, and he's mumbling words I can't hear, although I'm not sure I want to. A shiver runs down my jaw as his lips brush across my cheek. And then his lips touch mine, and we're kissing.

For a moment we are kissing.

I put my hands on his chest and push him away. "Jack, no. I can't."

I turn away. Tears are streaming down my face, and I can't stop them. I see a cab and walk into the street to flag it. I can sense Jack standing behind me; I don't turn toward him. The cab pulls over, and I open the door and slide into the seat.

I hear a tap on the glass. I look up. Jack has his hand, palm open, flat over his heart. There are tears on his face. He speaks, and I can hear the timbre of his voice and read the words on his lips.

"I'm sorry," he says. "I'm sorry."

# Chapter 25
## The Clanging Gong

The meeting with Jack puts me back where I was when I first asked him to leave. I spend my days trying not to think about him, and at night, in the moments when I sleep, I dream about him kissing me outside the bar. I find myself wondering too often whether we could start over, if I could ever bring myself to forgive his betrayal. I don't even get any satisfaction from telling Sarah about our conversation or from her shock that he's publishing his book. Because unfortunately, the cease-and-desist letter was an idle threat: A lawsuit is public, which meant everyone—not just my friends—would know who the female lead was.

After a third nearly sleepless night, I realize I need to talk to someone after all. And though I'm not sure I can face him again, I know that Dr. Szwick is the person I should see. Dr. Szwick, with his odd ways and sharp insights, and his knowledge of both of us, might be the only person who can help me figure out what I want to do.

When I call to make an appointment, the receptionist hesitates and asks me to hold. I smile to myself, imagining the surprise my call is creating, even for the prescient Dr. Szwick. It occurs to me while I wait that he might refuse to see me, particularly after my scene in Ms. Cooper's office, but his receptionist comes back on the line and gives me an appointment in my old Friday time slot.

So in the early afternoon on a late-fall day, with the first snowflakes wisping toward the ground, I settle into the familiar armchair across from Dr. Szwick and his black notebook. The ballad of Jack and Anne.

"Are you surprised I'm here?"

"Somewhat."

"I assume you heard about Jack?"

"I did."

"And my meeting with Ms. Cooper?"

He smiles. "It was the talk of the company."

"Why did you agree to see me?"

"I believed I owed it to you, Anne. If you thought you needed my help, I wanted to give it to you."

"Thank you."

"Not at all. Do you want to tell me why you're here?"

"All right." I fill him in on how I found out about Jack and about our meeting last week. When I'm finished, he lays his pen down and closes the book on me and Jack.

"How have you been coping with all of this?"

"Some days are worse than others, especially these days."

"You sound surprised."

I raise the edge of my turtleneck over my chin. "I guess I thought I was over him."

"And when you saw him, you realized you weren't?"

"Yes."

"What made you realize that?"

I feel a flash of Jack's lips against mine. "Just everything about the meeting. How sad he looked. How easy it was, on some level, to talk to him. The feel of his hand on my skin. I can't point to one thing. It's all bound up together."

"It sounds like you're still in love with him."

"I know. But I'm not sure I want to be."

"Because you can't forgive him?"

"Should I?"

"You'll have to decide that for yourself, Anne."

I try to smile. "I was hoping you'd do that for me."

"You know me better than that."

"I know. But . . . can we do that chair thing? Being off-balance somehow makes things clearer for me."

"We can do that if you like, but the purpose of that exercise is to start you on the path of living consciously. I think you know what you want to do, and you don't need me or an oversize chair to show you what it is."

"You're wrong. I do need help."

He looks firm. "No, you don't. You just need to be honest with yourself about what kind of life you want. And once you do that, you'll know what you want and how to get it."


Early on the morning of Sarah's wedding day, a package arrives at my apartment. It has Jack's handwriting on it, my name spelled out in messy block letters. I put the package on my kitchen table. Huddled in my bathrobe, I look at it while I drink my morning coffee. I have a feeling I know what's in it, and I'm not sure I have the strength to face it.

In the end, I take my kitchen scissors and cut away the wrapping. There are several smaller packages inside: a stack of photographs, a folded set of papers, a small box, and a copy of Jack's book.

I start with the papers. It's the annulment application Sarah prepared, the one Jack hasn't signed. Only he has. The name Jack Harmer is written in triplicate just above mine. And so that's it. We're not married anymore. We never were.

I pick up the photographs and flip through them slowly. They're the pictures Jack took in Mexico. The hotel we stayed at. The ocean at high noon, the ocean at sunset. There's a great night shot of the palm tree on the beach with lights wound around its trunk. There are pictures from our trip off the compound—the shots we took from the top of the pyramid in the jungle. A shot of Jack and me taken by another tourist, standing on the edge of the stairs, his arm around my neck, my hair blowing in the wind. A picture I took of Jack reading by the pool, another of him scribbling in his notebook. His goddamn notebook. He was probably scribbling about me.

The last picture is of us lying in a hammock together. I'm asleep on my back, my face flushed from sleep and the sun. Jack is curled next to me, his body around mine like he's protecting me. I don't know who took the picture. Someone must've thought we looked cute and picked up the camera lying next to us.

I'm staring at this picture when my doorbell rings. I realize I've been crying. I wipe my face hastily and open the door to let William in. He takes one look at me and, without speaking, wraps me in his arms, holds my head to his chest, and lets me cry. He leads me over to the couch and waits until I can speak again.

"What's the matter?" he says gently.

I hand him the picture clasped in my hand. "Jack sent me this."

"Ah."

"He sent me his book too. And something in a box. I'm not sure what."

"The rat bastard," he says flatly.

"He *is* a rat bastard."

"I know, I just said so."

I untangle myself from his arms. "What's with the tone? You sound like you're defending him."

"I'm not defending him, Anne. I just don't think he's a bad guy for sending you this picture, or his book, or trying to get you back."

"You don't?"

"No. Think about it, A.B. If he hadn't tried to do those things, you'd probably be even madder."

"Yeah, okay, smartass. But that doesn't mean that fundamentally, he isn't a rat bastard."

"I hear you. But these are his good parts showing."

"That's not helping. I don't want to think about Jack's good parts."

"Sorry."

"Why did you come over, anyway?"

"We had plans, remember? We were going to go for a run ..." He gestures toward his body, and I notice for the first time that William is in running pants and a long-sleeved Gore-Tex shirt. "You forgot?"

"I got distracted."

He looks resigned. "You want to show me the book?"

I go to the kitchen to get it, grabbing the little box that came with it. The book cover is white with a bouquet of flowers on it. Looking at it, I realize the bouquet looks remarkably like the one Jack gave me on our wedding day, and I don't know whether to scream or cry.

God, I'm sick of crying.

I hand it to William. He starts flipping through it. "You going to read this?"

"Don't think so."

"How can you resist?"

"I already read it, remember?"

"Didn't he say he changed it?"

"So?"

"Aren't you curious?"

Yes. No. Maybe.

"Not really."

He looks skeptical.

"Not enough to read it," I tell him.

"Maybe he'll surprise you."

"There you go, defending him again!"

He puts his hands up in front of him. "Relax, Anne. I swear, I'm not."

"You want to read it?"

"What, and tell you what it says?"

"Yeah, maybe."

"Nuh-uh. No way."

"Why not?"

"I don't want to suffer a messenger's fate."

"Fucker."

He eyes the box in my hand. "You going to open that?"

"I don't know. Do you think it's going to make me happy or sad?"

"I have no idea, A.B."

"Very helpful, as always." I bite my lip. "All right, I'll open it."

I slide the cover off the little silver box. Inside is a pink enamel heart on a threaded gold chain. The ends of my fingers start to tingle.

"What's that all about?" William asks.

"It means he's still trying to manipulate me."

"How do you figure?"

"I thought you said you read my book."

His eyes shift guiltily. "Did I say that?"

"Uh, yeah. And lots of other stuff about how good it was, and how funny . . ."

"Well, I started reading it, but it's really not my thing."

"What page did you get to?"

"Twenty-nine?"

"Jeez. Thanks for giving it a real chance. Anyway, if you *had* read my book, you'd know that Ben sends Lauren a necklace like this when they aren't speaking, and it's what makes her start to realize that maybe they should be together again. I kind of lifted the idea from one of the *Anne* books, actually."

"So you think that's why Jack sent you the necklace? To try to change your mind?"

"Pretty sure."

"What's the matter? Are you afraid it's going to work?"

Yes. No. Maybe.

"No need to be so insightful," I say.

"I'll take that as a compliment."

"So, are we running or what?"

"You running in that?"

"Give me a minute to change."

I set the book and the necklace on my bed and change into my running clothes: old sweats I've had since I was a teenager. I look at the book. Part of me wants to pitch it in the garbage. Part of me wants to read it. I'm not sure which part is going to win. I walk back to the living room. William starts laughing.

"What?"

"That's what you're wearing?"

I look down at myself. I look kind of like Ally Sheedy in *WarGames*.

"What's wrong with this?"

"Oh, it's fine, Anne, if you're running in 1984. Do you have a Walkman too, or is that technology too advanced for you?"

"You'd better run fast, little man."

William and I get back in half an hour from our pathetic attempt at a run. I grab a quick shower and take a cab to the hair salon to meet Sarah.

The salon is one of those old-fashioned ones where women my grandmother's age come to get their weekly permanents. It even has those hairdryers in baby-blue enamel—the kind with the cone that comes down over your head—lined up in a row at the back. The air smells like burned hair and peroxide. I wonder how Sarah ended up in this place.

Sarah is sitting in a chair, looking tense. I give her a kiss on the cheek. "What's up?"

She points to her head. "This is take two."

The hairdresser is wearing a look of extreme concentration as she sweeps up small pieces of Sarah's hair and pins them into place.

"It looks pretty," I say.

"Would you tell me if it didn't?"

"Not sure."

"Anne!"

"Of course I would, silly. It looks amazing."

It really does. It's all soft and flowing curls falling from her head. She looks . . . like a bride.

I get my hair washed and sit in the chair next to hers, a bright pink towel draped over my shoulders.

"You looked wiped," Sarah says.

"I went running with William this morning."

She smiles. "Did you wear that horrible eighties outfit again?"

"Hey, I look cute in that."

"You think you look like Ally Sheedy."

"So?"

"You don't."

"Sarah, if it weren't your wedding day, I'd make you pay for that."

"But it *is* my wedding day."

I smile at her in the mirror. "That it is."

"Freaky."

"I know."

She frowns. "I feel bad, being so happy when—"

"Oh God, don't worry. It's normal to be nervous on your wedding day. I was." I smile at her to show I'm okay.

"It is, right? It's normal to be nervous. It's normal to be nervous, it's normal . . ."

I put my hand on her arm. "It's going to be fine, you'll see."

"I know. I'm doing a good thing today." She looks so happy that I can feel tears forming. I think they're tears of joy. I cry so much these days, it's hard to tell.

"Stop that," Sarah says. "You'll get me going, and I'll have to redo my makeup."

I wipe my tears away. "Sorry. Hey, you want to hear a funny

story?" I'm not sure it is funny, but I want to change the subject. "I got a copy of Jack's book in the mail today."

She gets a look on her face. The same look she had when she told me about her meeting with Jack.

"Sarah?"

"Please don't be mad at me, Anne."

"Mad at you for what?"

"I read it."

"What do you mean?"

"Jack sent me a copy a few days ago, and I read it."

I try to act indifferent. "Was it any good?"

"Why do you want to know? Are you going to read it?"

Yes. No. Maybe.

"Don't think so."

"Why not?"

"I don't know if I can."

"I think you should read it, Anne."

"What's with him sending it to you, anyway? I really don't like this whole pattern you two have going. Will you be going for drinks soon?"

"Don't be silly. He sent it to me for the same reason he sought me out before—to convince you to read it."

"His strategy seems to be working." I sound petulant, I know, but I feel like pouting.

"Anne, I'm your best friend. I wouldn't tell you to do something I didn't think was good for you. I don't care about him. But I think you might feel better after reading it. It might allow you to put this all behind you."

The hairdresser picks up a can of hair spray to polish off Sarah's look.

"Wait. Don't put that stuff on her!" I reach up and bat the can away from Sarah's head.

"Thanks," Sarah says, turning her chair toward me. "So, what do you think?"

"You look beautiful."

And she does. She looks beautiful and happy and ready to get married.


I clink my wineglass to get everyone's attention. I'm in my soft pink bridesmaid's dress, facing a roomful of people in their finest. Large round tables glow with candles and pink and white tulips.

"So, I'm here to talk about Mike . . . I mean Sarah, of course. Sarah." [laughter] "What can I say about Sarah? First of all, I think she deserves a round of applause for pulling off this flawless event today." [clapping] "If you only knew how many lists went into it, how many trees were killed with the endless drafts and redrafts." [small laughs] "Seriously, tonight's been lovely, and I think everyone knows that planning parties is not Mike's strong suit." [a drunken yell from a college buddy whom I can't quite make out]

"Okay, enough jokes, before Sarah never speaks to me again. I do want to say a few words about my best friend. We met in the third grade. I believe the exact occasion of our meeting involved a barrette emergency (guess who needed the barrette and who provided it). All I know is, one minute I was having the worst day of my young life, and the next, everything was all right again. And ever since then I've had someone in my life who's there for me unconditionally. It sounds so trite to say that out loud, but it's rare, so rare, to have that in your life. And if you can have one person like that, you're so lucky.

"Mike has been there for Sarah since they met. He sees how beautiful and smart she is, but I know he loves her most for her little quirks. So I'd like to raise a glass to Mike and Sarah. Sarah, you're the best friend I've ever had. I don't know how I'd get through my life without you. And Mike, you've restored my faith in happy endings. To Mike and Sarah."

I lift my glass, and the room follows suit. I take a drink of the fizzy champagne and walk over to Sarah to the applause of the guests. Her eyes are shining wet. We hug, and she whispers in my ear, "Read the book, Anne."

"Looks like it's just you and me." William extends his hand, inviting me to dance. He's wearing a dark suit and a white rose in his lapel. He'd look serious and handsome if it weren't for his untamable hair. I take his hand, and we walk onto the dance floor among Sarah's cousins and college friends. The band is playing an old U2 song. He waltzes me around the floor in a fast slow dance that feels like high school. We look ridiculous, and are attracting a bit of attention from the crowd. Sarah and Mike, glowing, half drunk, and exhausted, left a few minutes ago.

"I feel like this is the end of *My Best Friend's Wedding*," I say.

"That's because it is."

"No, silly, that Julia Roberts movie. You know, the one where she tries to break up her best friend's wedding and she's left dancing with her gay friend at the end."

William pulls away from me. "Am I the gay friend in this scenario?"

I roll my eyes. "It just has the same feeling."

"I'm not gay, Anne."

"I know, William."

"I had a date last week. With a *woman*. I'm thinking of calling her again."

"That's great. Anyway, she's left dancing with her friend. Is that better?"

He starts waltzing me around again. "So? Sounds like a helluva good time."

"Yeah, but she ends up alone. She doesn't get the guy."

"Did she want the guy?"

"That's not the point. She wanted *a* guy."

"You want me to tell you you're going to get the guy?"

"Yeah, maybe."

He touches the pink enamel heart I'm wearing around my neck. "You can have the guy if you want, Anne."

## Chapter 26
## Let's Try This Again

William drops me at my apartment at one in the morning. I flop down on the couch in exhaustion. I take off my high heels, which have been killing me for hours, and throw them across the room. They hit the wood floor with a satisfying thud.

With no more distractions, I start thinking about Jack's book. It's sitting where I left it in the bedroom, waiting for me there like Jack waited for me one night when I had to work late to meet a deadline. He was reading in bed when I got home, but I knew he was waiting for me. I sat down next to him and kissed him hello, and he brought his hands up to my face in that way he has and kissed me in that way he has. His kisses traveled down my face, my neck, and down and down and everywhere, and we made love without saying another word. The experience was so intense that thinking about it now, months later, brings a blush to my cheeks.

Afterward, we lay in bed talking for hours. Talking about my article, about a weird conversation he'd heard in the park when he took a break from writing, about my favorite park as a child, about other things I don't remember now. Our talking was nearly as intense as the sex. It felt so great to lie in his arms and talk about whatever came to mind. And I knew with the certainty you sometimes have about other people that it was what we both wanted to be doing most of all—talking to each other. We fought off sleep, and even the lingering arousal that might have led to a second round, so that we could talk and talk and talk.

The book in the bedroom calls to me. I want to hear Jack's voice again. I want to hear him talking to me through the night. Jack telling me things I didn't know, or giving me a new perspective on things I know. I want his perspective on things. The book in the bedroom calls to me.

In the end, I give in. I go to the bedroom and pick it up, running my hands over the picture of our wedding bouquet. I snuggle under the covers, open it, and start to read.

### Married Like Me
### Prologue

All my life I've had this idea of what the woman I'd eventually marry would look like, would be like. It sounds silly, it sounds *girlish*, but it's true.

I don't know where this idea came from. Maybe it was the girl whose pigtails I pulled once instead of telling her I liked her. Maybe it was a dream I had. Maybe I invented her. But I knew she was out there, somewhere.

I grew up. I met other women. I even fell in love. But I never stopped waiting for her to show up.

And then one day she did.

I was standing outside her door. I was supposed to knock on it. I was supposed to make this woman my wife. We'd met the day before. I was nervous as hell. We'd met the day before, yet I felt like I'd been waiting for her forever.

I met her in a miniature bullfighting ring at an all-inclusive resort in Cancún, Mexico. I'd gone there on purpose to meet her and marry her. To meet her, marry her, live with her for a while, and then leave her and write a book about it.

She was there because she believed the company that brought us to Mexico had matched us based on our compatibility, and that I was her perfect match. She came there to marry me without knowing me, or anything about me, without even seeing a picture of me.

When we came face-to-face for the first time, we shook hands like the other couples, all there for the same reason.

I led her outside to a bar I'd scoped out the night before as the most romantic spot in the place. We sat at a table facing each other awkwardly, both of us wondering what to say.

I studied her face. She looked like I'd expected she would. White skin with a scattering of freckles across her nose. Green eyes that looked gray in some lighting. Long red, red hair. An intelligent face.

I knew this face. I knew it from years of dreaming, and I knew it from the research I did before I came to Mexico. I wasn't supposed to know it, or her, or anything about her. If I'd been there for the right reasons, this would've been the first time I'd seen her.

As it was, because of the book I was there to write, I already knew too many things about her. I had all kinds of advantages.

We ordered drinks from the waiter and sat and stared at each other, trying to look like we weren't staring, until I broke the silence.

"This is awkward," I said.

"It really is," she agreed.

"I don't even know your last name," I said, extending my hand, though I did know. "I'm Jack Harmer."

She told me her full name. I lied again and asked why her name seemed familiar to me, and she told me she wrote for a magazine. I pretended to recall one of her articles and made some joke about the topic.

She knew I was a writer too. It was one of the few small details they'd told her about me, one of the few small details she was allowed to know, and so we talked about my writing.

Because I often write about outdoor things, I asked if she was an outdoor girl. She said sometimes. She might be.

Then she asked me the question I was waiting for.

"Can I ask you something?" she asked, fluttery and nervous.

"What am I doing here?" I replied.

She blushed, a light pink trail that rose from her neck to the tips of her ears. "Yeah."

"Well . . . the same reason as most people, I expect. I've been in some long-term relationships that didn't work out. I work alone most of the time, and it's hard to meet people. I'm thirty-four, and I always thought I'd be married with kids by now. I heard about this service from someone I know who used it, and he's still married, happy, has kids, so I thought why the hell not?"

This was the answer I'd worked out in advance. It sounded plausible to me, as plausible as I could make it.

She smiled at me. She had a good smile. "So you're totally normal?"

I laughed and raised my hand to my heart. "I swear, I'm totally normal. What about you?"

She told me why she was there: a bunch of failed relationships, the desire to have a family. All the things you might expect.

"So you're totally normal too?" I asked her.

She made an X with a finger over her heart. "Cross my heart and hope to die."

We stared at each other, and I felt something. A connection, a conspiracy between us. A feeling I hadn't felt in a long time. Maybe never.

We went to dinner and told each other our life stories, and the hours flew by. After dinner, she had a moment of doubt, and I convinced her to go through with the wedding. I kissed her for the first time on the beach under a nearly full moon and gave her a silver ring with a turquoise stone set across its flat top. Later, I saw her flirting with another man, and I felt jealous. She told me I had nothing to worry about, and I kissed her again, holding her close.

So there I was the next morning, trying to decide whether to knock. Could I really marry the woman I'd been waiting for all these years? Like this?

And then I did it.

My knuckles raked across her door. She looked very pretty that morning in her cream-colored dress. Her hair was pulled back from her face and trailed down her back. A touch of sunburn emphasized the green in her eyes.

I took a deep breath and said, "Ready, Emma?"

She gave me a nervous smile. "Ready, Jack."

"You look great."

Her smile widened. "You look nice too."

I pulled my hand from behind my back and handed her a bunch of summer flowers. She brought them up to her freshly washed face and drank in their smell.

"I thought you might like to carry these," I said.

"Thank you, Jack, they're beautiful."

She hooked her arm around mine, and we walked through the resort to the room where the marriages were being performed.

We were married by a funny little man with a thick accent. Emma looked like she wanted to laugh throughout the ceremony. I asked her in a whisper what she was laughing about, and she told me shush, she'd tell me later.

"Do you, Emma Ellen Gardner, take this man, John Graham Harmer, to be your lawfully wedded husband, to have and to hold, in sickness and in health, for richer and for poorer, and forsaking all others as long as you both shall live?"

She smiled and said, "I do." She sounded nervous, but she said, "I do." And when the minister repeated the words, I said, "I do" too. We exchanged rings, and he pronounced us man and wife. I kissed her soft lips, and we were married.

But all this is getting ahead of myself. I should start at the beginning. I should tell you why I did this. What it did to her. How I lost her.

I should tell you how I ended up married like me.

# Chapter 27
## A Book of Revelations

A week after Sarah's wedding, I'm sitting in a coffee shop, waiting for William to show up, when I see Stuart come through the door.

I haven't laid eyes on him since the day I walked out of our apartment a year ago, and my first reaction is to duck under the table.

Come on, Anne. This is completely ridiculous. It's just Stuart.

I pick up the newspaper I was reading, nervously wondering if he's going to notice me. Do I even want him to notice me?

I reach for my coffee and end up spilling it all over the table. Perfect.

"Anne?"

I drop the napkin I'm using to contain the mess. "Hi, Stuart."

He's wearing the blue corduroy jacket I gave him for his birthday two years ago and a pair of dark jeans that fit him perfectly. He looks like he's been on holiday somewhere warm. He looks great, as always.

"Wow. Long time no see," he says.

"Right."

"Do you mind if I sit down?"

"I guess not."

Stuart turns an empty chair around and sits on it, his arms resting across the back. "Well, well, well. Anne Blythe. Looking good, Anne."

I'm wearing a light blue cashmere pullover my mother gave me for Christmas, and my hair is pulled back in a ponytail. I can't remember if this is how Stuart liked me to look. Hair up or down?

Who the fuck cares, Anne? This is *Stuart*.

"Thanks."

"How the hell are you?"

"Same old, same old. You?"

"Yeah, you know. Same old, same old."

He glances around, already looking for something else to focus on. He always used to do this. He always needed to be stimulated by something more than me. Hence the cheating, I guess.

His eyes trail back to me. "I hear you published a book."

"True."

"Is it any good?"

Typical. Stuart never read anything I wrote when we were together. Of course not. It wasn't about him, so he wasn't interested.

"Some people seemed to think so, I guess."

He laughs. "Always so serious. I read it."

"You did?"

"Of course. I liked it. And I could totally tell you'd written it."

"Really? How do you mean?"

"It had that destined-to-be feeling to it. I remember you always thought that you'd just know if two people were meant to be together."

Holy shit. Stuart Johnson is showing some kind of insight about me. Hell must be about to freeze over.

"Yeah, I did think that."

"You ever think that about us?"

Sadly, yes.

"Maybe. Sometimes," I tell him.

"Such a sweet kid."

God, he really is an enormous asshole. I was kind of hoping my memory was exaggerating. No such luck.

I give him a tight smile. "So you always said."

"You with someone?"

"I was with someone, yes."

His eyes mock me. "And were you meant to be?"

I thought so. To be honest, I've been thinking so again, ever since I stayed up all night reading Jack's book.

"Oh, I don't really believe in that anymore," I say.

Stuart looks at me intently. "You're still in love with him."

Yup. Hell has just frozen over.

"Why do you say that?"

"C'mon, Anne. I've known you for a long time. I can tell you're still into this guy."

"Well . . . we broke up."

"That's too bad," he says gently. Surprisingly so.

"Thanks, Stuart."

"Whether you believe it or not, I only want the best for you."

I look at him, and it's as if I'm seeing him for the first time. And he's not a monster. He's not a god. He's just a man I once knew.

He glances at his watch. "Hey, sorry about this, but I kind of have to go. Do you mind?"

"No problem. William will be here any minute."

"You know, I always thought he was in love with you."

I laugh. "How much simpler life would be if that were true."

"See you around?"

"Sure."

He stands up and turns to walk away.

"Stuart."

"Yeah?"

"Thank you."

"What for?"

For reminding me what I don't want. For being enough of an asshole that I was forced to change my life. For everything. For nothing.

"It's complicated."

He grins. "You know I hate complicated."

"I know."

• • •

A few days later, I'm on my way to meet Sarah at the bar. She's just gotten back from her honeymoon in Greece. It's a cold night, a reminder that winter's almost here and I really should be wearing a warmer coat. The stores are lit up, waiting for the after-work crowd to get in some early Christmas shopping.

I still love the feel of this neighborhood: the people on the street, the laughter and smells spilling out of the restaurants, the quieter streets behind the strip. No matter what my mood, walking these streets always makes me feel lighter, happier.

I get to a street corner a block away from the bar and hit a red light. The light changes, and something fluttering across the road catches my eye. I think for a moment that it might be the flyer for Jack's book launch, but when I pick it up, it's just a flyer for an exhibit at the art museum.

Jack's book launch is taking place tonight a few blocks away. He sent me an invitation, and I left it lying around my apartment, unable to throw it out, half wanting to go, half not sure I was ready to see him yet. Jack's book cover was on it, and a picture of Jack, a picture I took one day on the beach in Mexico. If you look closely enough (and I did), you can see me holding the camera in the reflection in Jack's eyes.

A horn blares. I'm in the street. I cross to the other side and start walking faster, not paying attention to where I'm going.

I slam into someone. "I'm sorry," I mutter, trying to get past her.

"Anne? Is that you?"

I look more carefully at the person I almost plowed down.

It's Margaret. She's wearing an oversize black puffy coat and a knit hat with a pom-pom on top. Her nose is red from the cold.

"Yes, it's me. Hi, Margaret." I try to smile. "How are you?"

She gives me a big grin. "I'm great!"

I realize after a moment that she's rubbing her belly; she must be six months along.

"That's great, Margaret. I'm so happy for you."

"Thanks. What about you guys? Any kids yet?"

"No."

She smiles sympathetically. "I guess you've been too busy."

She looks so happy, I can't bear to tell her what I know. About Jack. That Brian was probably just randomly chosen and isn't her perfect match.

"Something like that. Listen, I've got to go . . ."

She nods. "Sure. You're going this way, right? I'll walk with you."

Before I can ask how she knows which way I'm going, we're walking in the same direction, and Margaret has hooked her arm into mine.

"I read your book, Anne. It's great. I've recommended it to all my friends, and my book club's going to read it next month."

"Thanks."

"No problem. I tell everyone I know about it, and that I know you. Not where I know you from . . . don't worry." She giggles conspiratorially. "I mean, just because all my friends know where I met my hubby doesn't mean they have to know about you. Right?"

I wonder when I'll be able to escape her. Where's she leading me, anyway?

"And I can't wait to read Jack's book. Have you read it? Of course you have. It's so funny I ran into you, because I saw a poster for his book signing today. Coming here was really a spur-of-the-moment decision, you know me, and then I run into you and everything—"

"Listen, Margaret, I'm meeting my friend, and I think I walked past the bar a block or so ago."

"What are you talking about, Anne? The bookstore's right here. You're going to Jack's book launch, right?" She blinks slowly, her eyes all wide and innocent.

"Um—"

She grabs my arm again. "Come on, silly. What's wrong with you today?"

She pulls open the door and nearly drags me into the bookstore. I let her take me through the lobby and up to the second-floor mezzanine, where there's a short line of people waiting for Jack to sign copies of his book. I can half see his head bent over an open book and his hand scribbling away. I tuck myself behind the person in front of me, hiding.

Is this what a heart attack feels like?

"Why don't you go up to the front, Anne?"

"Um . . . I thought I'd surprise him."

She gives me a look. "You two are so funny."

I peer around the person standing in front of me to sneak a peek at Jack. There's a woman standing behind him. She's tall, blond, and tanned. Very pretty. She leans forward and puts her hand on Jack's shoulder, speaking next to his ear.

"Is that Cameron Diaz?" Margaret asks.

"Of course not."

Jack smiles at whatever it was the beautiful girl said to him.

"It really looks like her."

"It's not Cameron Diaz, Margaret."

But . . . oh, shit. Didn't Jack tell me way back in Mexico that his ex-girlfriend looked like her? Getting back at me for my Pierce Brosnan reference, I thought then. Only this must be Kate. Kate from his adventure-racing book. Or whatever her real name is.

I need air.

My phone rings, and I dig around in my purse trying to find it, wishing it were quieter.

Please don't look up. Please don't look up.

"Hello," I whisper into the phone.

"Where the hell are you, Anne? I've been waiting for twenty minutes."

"Sorry, Sarah. I ran into someone I know, and . . . can you wait a second?"

I duck down and skulk away from the line of people waiting for Jack. I get some funny looks, but I don't stand up again until I'm outside the bookstore.

"Sorry. I ran into someone I knew from Blythe and Company, and she assumed I was coming to Jack's book launch. She kind of dragged me here."

"Have you seen Jack?"

"Not really. Just from a distance."

"Are you going to talk to him?"

"I don't know. I think his ex-girlfriend is here."

"What makes you think that?"

"I saw him talking to a girl that . . . It's too complicated. I'm just pretty sure that's who it is."

"How are you feeling?"

"I think I'm going to be sick."

I sit down on a bench facing the entrance and place my head between my legs.

"Anne? Are you okay?" Sarah asks.

"I don't know."

"What? Speak up, I can barely hear you."

"Anne? Are you all right?" a male voice asks.

I look up at Jack. My heart is pounding, and my throat is dry. He's wearing khakis, a dark blue pullover, and a blazer, all properly pressed. He looks like he did all those months ago when we first met.

"That has yet to be determined," I say.

Shit. Why did I say that? Why am I repeating something he said to me back when everything was good between us?

I can tell by Jack's expression that he realizes I just quoted what he said that morning on the beach in Mexico. He's trying to figure out if that's a good thing.

I snap the phone shut on Sarah. She'll understand.

"What's going on?" he says tentatively.

"I, um, felt sick."

I start shivering. I don't know if it's from the cold or from Jack's presence. Maybe both.

"You want to go inside?"

"Not sure."

I stand up. My legs are wobbly. Jack takes off his blazer and drapes it over my shoulders. For a second he's standing so close, it's like I'm in his arms. Then he steps back, and I'm merely enveloped in a blazer that's too big for me and smells like Jack. I feel dizzy.

"Thanks," I say.

"Did you want to talk to me about something?"

Did I? Why did I let Margaret lead me here? Why am I standing here, lost in his jacket?

"You invited me."

"I know, but . . ."

"But what?"

Jack expels the breath he's been holding. "Did you come here for a reason?"

I look at Jack. This man I married. This man who broke my heart. This man who still makes it beat, beat, beat—and I have a revelation. You know those moments when you look at something obvious and it's finally obvious to you?

I want to forgive Jack. Maybe I already have.

"I read your book," I say.

He looks both pleased and apprehensive. "What did you think?"

"I think . . . it was a better book for me."

"How so?"

"The first book made me furious, and sad, and furious. This time it made me sad for us, Jack. Sad that we seemed to have something and it got so fucked up."

He looks resigned. "Because I fucked it up."

"Yeah, but also because I never should've been there in the first place. I didn't buy in to what they were selling, not really. I was looking for love, not friendship."

"And did you find it?" he asks, his voice catching.

The blond woman from earlier pokes her head out the door. She looks pissed. "What're you doing out here, Jack? There's a bunch of people waiting."

"I'll be there in a minute."

"Jack—"

"I *said* give me a minute."

She looks at me, frowning slightly. And then something occurs to her, and she closes the door without saying another word.

I can barely speak. "Is that Kate?"

"Kate from my book?"

"Kate from your book."

"Yes."

"What's her name?"

"Jessica."

"She's pretty."

Jack takes a step toward me. "It's not what you think."

"It's not?"

"No. We're just friends. She works at the publishing company. It's how we met."

"I thought you met her during the adventure race. Like in the book."

"Not everything in books is true, Anne. Not even in my books."

"So you're not back together?"

"No, Anne. Come on. There never could be anybody else for me but you."

My heart skips a beat. Is he quoting *Anne of Green Gables*?

"There couldn't?"

"No."

I take the first real breath I've been able to take since I saw Jessica talking to Jack in the bookstore.

"I remember a boy who pulled my pigtails when I was little," I say, surprising myself.

He takes a step toward me. "You do?"

"He had brown curly hair, but I don't remember his name."

"Do you think it was me?"

There's still one step between us. I want to take the step. I want to, but I'm not sure I can.

"I don't know. I've wondered. Since I read that . . ."

"Maybe it *was* me. Maybe it's a sign."

"Maybe. But I told you before that I don't believe in signs."

He reaches out and brushes my hair away. "Don't you?"

"Are you going to pull my pigtails again?"

"I might." His thumb strokes the side of my face, and I feel the tingling connection that's always been between us. "Only if you promise not to break a slate over my head."

"Don't you start calling me Carrots."

He laughs. "I wouldn't dare." His eyes turn serious. "Do you know what you want, Anne?"

"You sound like Dr. Szwick."

He grimaces. "Maybe he wasn't always full of crap."

"He told me that if I decided what kind of life I wanted, I'd know what I wanted to do about you."

"What kind of life do you want?" he asks, a tremor in his voice.

"I think . . . I want a life with you."

Jack takes a swift stride toward me, and as his lips meet mine, the world seems to fall away until we're the only two people on the street, in the city, the world, the universe.

When my lungs start screaming for air, Jack pulls away. His hands are shaking. He looks happy. Happier than I've ever seen him. I can't tell what my face looks like, but I think it might be the same.

He leans his forehead on mine. "The last time I kissed you, you ran away from me in tears."

"Can you blame me?"

"I can never blame you for anything." He kisses me again and drops his hands to my waist.

"What about Blythe and Company?"

"Nope. Can't blame them either. Though I heard Ms. Cooper got fired."

I smile. "I asked them for a refund, but they have this no-refund policy."

"I guess I wasn't what you paid for."

"No."

"I'm sorry, Anne."

"I know. Besides, I'll be getting a cut from your book when it hits the best-seller lists."

Jack frowns. "Yes, I got Sarah's letter."

"What? She sent a *letter*? I asked her not to. Shit, why do I always fall for that?"

Jack laughs out loud. "Don't ever change, Anne."

"It's too late for me now."

We smile at each other, our breath frosting in the air.

"Was that Margaret I saw you standing with?"

"Yeah."

"Where did she come from?"

"I ran into her on the street. She's the one who brought me here."

"I'll have to thank her, then."

"I told you she wasn't that bad."

"No, obviously, you're right. You're always right."

"Sometimes yes, sometimes no."

"You look frozen."

"I'm okay."

"I love you, Anne."

"I love you, Jack."

"I know."

"Really, Han Solo?"

"What's not to love?"

"Seriously."

He looks very serious. "Seriously. Those are the best words I've heard in a long time. Maybe ever. There's just one more thing . . ."

"What?"

"I asked you a question a while ago, Anne. If I ask it again today, will you give me a different answer?"

Oh my God, he *is* quoting from *Anne of Green Gables*. More specifically, from Gilbert's second proposal in *Anne of the Island*.

"Been reading up, have we?"

His lips curl into a smile. "You know, those books aren't half bad."

"Blasphemy."

"Will you?"

"How about we take things slowly? Try dating for a while."

"I like the sound of that."

"Where do we go from here?"

"Do you want to come inside? Meet my friends?"

"I'd like that very much."

## Acknowledgments

On the list of great things about getting a second book published is the chance you get to thank the people who helped make your first book a success. So, I'd like to thank:

My friends, for buying a zillion copies and telling everyone they know about my book. Amy, Annie, Candice, Chad, Christie, Dan, Eric, Janet, Katie, Kevin, Lindsay, Marty, Olivier, Patrick, Phil, Presseau, Sara, Stephanie, Tanya, and Thierry, my life is better because you are in it.

My family. Mom, Dad, Cam, Scott, Owen, Liam, Mike, Grandpa Roy, and Grandma Dorothy. And Tasha and Phyllis, for a lifetime of friendship.

All those who read early drafts, especially Amy, who literally read this as I wrote it, and without whom I might never have finished it.

April Eberhardt, for your editorial contribution and for bringing me to HarperCollins Canada.

At HarperCollins Canada, my editors, Alex Schultz and Jennifer Lambert, for making what I write better. Publisher

Iris Tupholme, for, well, publishing *me*. And everyone in sales and production.

At William Morrow, my wonderful editor, Emily Krump, and the sales team, especially Mary Sasso and my publicist, Stephanie Kim.

The gang at IMK for being so understanding.

Diane Saarinen, for her online marketing savvy.

My amazing agent and friend, Abigail Koons, and the whole team at Park Literary.

All the writers I've met along the way who have been an encouraging force, including Cathy Marie Buchanan, Tish Cohen, and Nadia Lakhdari King. And especially Shawn Klomparens, for your friendship and for making this book better.

Lucy Maud Montgomery, for creating Anne and writing wonderful books. My childhood would not have been the same without you.

To all the readers of *Spin*, thank you, thank you.

And David, who is the reason I wrote this book in the first place.

Read on
for an excerpt from

**FORGOTTEN**

Catherine McKenzie

Available now

# Chapter 1
# Out of Africa

*Six months later*

I'm sitting on my suitcase beside the muddy road that leads through the village, waiting for the signs that indicate the arrival of transport—birds taking flight, a tremor along the ground, and since the rains started, the sound of mud slipping through off-track wheels.

Birds wheel overhead, their cries a constant background music. The air is thick and damp, a physical thing that's been getting heavier by the month.

I remember the first time I saw this place, the ragged row of shacks with corrugated iron roofs, the gathering circle made of big round boulders, and the frame of a half-built schoolhouse, its wood a bright, freshly sawn yellow. The rough structure reminded me of the buildings I always imagined Laura Ingalls Wilder living in when I read her books over and over again as a child.

The safari guides left me here, sick, sick, sick, promising to come back as soon as they could with a doctor, but it didn't work out that way. Instead, it was Karen and Peter—the NGO workers building the schoolhouse—who nursed me back to health, using up their small store of medical supplies.

Karen is waiting with me now. Peter is in the village behind us. The confident blows of his hammer ring out, a practiced rhythm. A few children sit watching him, hunched on their heels, eager for him to be finished. When he's done, classes will begin, and they're keen to start learning.

After all these months of working on the building alongside him, I can't imagine not being here when it's finished.

"Maybe I should stay a few more days," I say.

Karen shakes her head, her brown face and matching eyes calm and certain. "We need to get you home, Emma. It's almost Christmas."

I shudder. It's hard to keep track of the days here; I'd almost forgotten. Christmas without my mother. That seems like a pretty good reason to stay exactly where I am. But I've used that excuse for too long now. It's time to get back to my life.

"You'll be home soon, though, right?" I ask, because my home is also Karen and Peter's. I don't know why we had to come all this way to meet. Life works like that sometimes, I guess.

"A few weeks after Christmas, if everything goes to plan."

"I'm glad."

In the distance I hear the low rumble of an engine, and I know it can't be long now. I stand and face Karen. She's ten years older than I am, and a head taller; stronger, broader, more substantial, somehow.

She puts her hand in the pocket of her loose work pants and pulls out a small Mason jar full of dirt. Reddish like the ground. Like the mud slipping through tires under the thrum of the approaching engine.

"I thought you might like this to add to your collection," she says.

I take it from her. Some of the dirt clings to the outside, sticking to my fingers. "Thank you."

A Land Rover is visible, only seconds away. I slip the jar into my pocket and embrace Karen. Her arms are steely around me. She smells like the humid air and the tall bleached grass— like I must too.

"You'll say goodbye to Peter?" I ask.

"You said goodbye to him yourself ten minutes ago."

"I know. But you'll tell him?"

She holds me away from her. "I will."

The Land Rover shudders to a stop, spraying mud in our direction. A large piece lands with a *splat* on my pant leg. I wipe it off as a short, stocky man in a sweat-stained shirt gets out.

"You are ready to go, miss?"

"Yes," I say. "Yes."


I'm mostly happy for the mud on the long drive back to the capital. It clings like a film to the windows, obscuring the worst of the view. But after a while it's impossible not to wipe it away and stare at the changed countryside. The odd jumble of images. A too-white running shoe lying at an odd angle on the side of the road. Things on the ground that shouldn't be: trees and twisted metal. The ground seems rippled, folded, like a mirage over a hot highway. And as we get closer to the epicenter, there's a smell that must have been much worse before the rains came. That might never be washed away.

The level of devastation, even after all these months, is shocking and saddening. And as the Land Rover bumps slowly along, my mind slips back to the long days listening to the one radio in the village—its voice so faint that sometimes it felt like messages from the moon—trying to imagine what was happening. But no amount of listening, no amount of imagination, was enough to conjure the destruction outside my window.

I feel helpless, and now I want to go home very much indeed.

The airport is chaotic. Though it's been a week since a few airlines resumed service, the staff behind the counters in the half-rebuilt building don't have reliable electricity or working phones. When I find the end of the line, I almost weep at the length of it, but there's nothing to be done. It moves at the speed it moves—glacial—and crying or yelling won't change anything, though I observe several people trying both tactics over the next four hours.

When I finally reach the counter, the thin, dark-skinned woman behind it is much politer than I would've been. She takes my open-ended ticket and passport and finds me a place on a plane to London leaving in two hours. Security consists of two impossibly tall men giving passengers the evil eye as they pass through a metal detector that has seen better days. I file through quickly and have time to locate some food at a small kiosk that's selling, of all things, Chicago-style hot dogs. I wolf down two of them gratefully, and when my plane is at last ready to depart, I shuffle onto it feeling like I'm running away.

The plane rattles across the roughly patched runway, full of cracks and tufts of grass, and leaves the ground. The turmoil below is momentarily toy-village small, then invisible below the clouds. I rest my head against the hard molded plastic and am asleep in minutes.

At Heathrow, a rainy sleet almost keeps us from landing. It's midday here—early morning back home—and the sun is nowhere to be seen.

I make my way slowly through the massive structure. The airport bears the markings of the season. Extra lights and Christmas trees try to give the place a festive air. Compared to where I've been, it's so clean and bright that it feels like it was built yesterday, as if the last lick of paint is still drying. The cooled and filtered air scratches the back of my throat, and I feel dusty and dingy as I pass the clean, clean faces around me.

I find the counter for my airline and use my open-ended ticket to book myself a flight home. As I search for my gate, I keep an eye out for somewhere to send a message to Stephanie and Craig, something I haven't had the chance to do in a long time. Too long. I don't want to think about why I let that happen; I don't have any answers, for that matter.

I pass a few public computer kiosks full of people who look like they've settled in for longer than the time I have left before my flight. I queue up behind one anyway, until I notice its user pushing unfamiliar coins into a slot, buying ten more minutes. The only change I have would barely buy me a Coke in a vending machine back home.

I give up and head to my gate with thirty-five minutes to spare. I take a seat next to a man in his mid-thirties typing aggressively on his laptop. A glance at his screen shows an email full of caps and exclamation marks. I feel a flash of sympathy for s.cathay@gmail.com.

He looks at me with an unfriendly expression. "Can I help you?"

"Oh, sorry . . . it's just . . . do you think I could borrow your computer for a minute? I really need to send a couple of emails, and all the kiosks are full, and I don't have any coins, and . . ." I pause to catch a breath that has turned borderline hysterical, a good imitation of those people at the airport whom I was happy to leave behind.

The angry man's eyes widen in dismay, his expression softened by my tone. "Hey, don't freak out on me, okay?" He shoves his laptop into my lap. "Send all the emails you want, all right?"

I thank him and open a new Web browser, leaving the angry email in place. My fingers feel clumsy on the keys, and I have to erase the first few attempts to enter my account information. When I finally get the combination of letters and numbers right, I'm informed in angry, flashing red type that my account has been shut down for sending too much junk mail. I curse silently under my breath at the spammer who hijacked it.

"Is something wrong?" the less angry man asks.

"My account is blocked."

"Why not just open a new one?"

Why not, indeed? I tap on the keys, and in a few moments emma.tupper23@mail.com is up and running.

I hit the "compose" button and pause. What the hell am I going to say after all this time? How do I even begin? Will they even *want* to hear from me?

I can feel the minutes slipping away. I brush aside those thoughts and type in Stephanie's and Craig's email addresses as quickly as I can.

From: Emma Tupper
To: stephanie_granger@oal.com, craig.talbot@tpc.com
Re: Coming home!
Hey guys,
This is such an odd email to write! I'm so, so sorry I haven't written till now. I'll explain everything when I get home, I promise. Anyway, I'm in London, my flight is leaving soon and should be arriving around 4 P.M. I'm on BA flight 3478. I can't wait to see you both. I've missed you so much.

Love, Em

• • •

I read it over quickly. It'll have to do. I hit "send" and hand the computer back to my neighbor, thanking him as a chime sounds. A polite, clipped voice announces that pre-boarding is about to begin. Anyone who has small children or needs assistance should come to the gate. General boarding will begin momentarily. I stand and stretch, taking a last opportunity to look around. So this is London. All I've ever seen of it is the airport. I'll have to remedy that someday.

The polite voice calls the first-class passengers. I line up briefly and walk down the gangway. The plane is brand-spanking-new. Each passenger gets his or her own capsule, a private space to eat, sleep, and watch six months' worth of movies. Maybe it's the flashy technology or the warmed-up, lemon-scented towels that the flight attendant brings, but a beat of hope starts in my heart. Soon I'll be back where I should be, and then, like the song says, everything will be all right.

But everything is not all right, which I should know when there's no one at the airport to meet me. Or when the ATM spits out my card as if it's contaminated, and my car isn't where I left it in the long-term parking lot.

I should've known, but I'm too distracted. Despite everything that's happened, I feel too happy.

I'm home.

Finally, the air smells familiar. I understand the curses hurled at me as I cross the road without looking properly.

Even the cold bite of winter and the annoying loop of jangly carols escaping from the outdoor speakers seem perfect, as they should the week before Christmas.

So when I give up looking for my car and sink into the back of a cab, I don't have a clue. In fact, it's only after I've handed over my last forty dollars to the ungrateful driver and tried to put my key into the lock of my apartment that I begin to panic.

Because the key doesn't fit. The lock doesn't turn.

And it has begun to snow.